Also by Mary Wine

WICKED
HIGHLAND
WAYS

MARY WINE

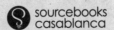

sourcebooks
casablanca

Published by Sourcebooks Casablanca, an imprint of Sourcebooks
P.O. Box 4410, Naperville, Illinois 60567-4410
(630) 961-3900
sourcebooks.com

Printed and bound in Canada.
MBP 10 9 8 7 6 5 4 3 2 1

This book would never have come into being without the belief of my amazing editor, Deb Werksman. I know readers see this sort of dedication a lot; believe me, without this woman believing in my books, there never would have been any titles on the shelves for the readers to discover. Deb is the first person to fall in love with my creations and the one who is fighting to make them into a reality for the readers. Thanks, Deb.

One

1579

IT WOULDN'T BE THE FIRST MARRIAGE CONTRACTED FOR the gain it would bring to the groom's family.

Brenda contemplated the road in front of her and felt almost nothing.

That was by far the saddest part of what would be her second marriage. She felt nothing much about it at all. Not that she expected to be happy about being ordered to leave Scotland and wed a man she'd never met by a king who was only fifteen years old and therefore too naive to understand what he was sending Brenda off to do.

But feeling nothing?

She thought she might at least have felt a sense of injustice over it all.

For it was vastly unfair for her to have to wed at James the Sixth's command simply because the boy was enamored of Esmé Stewart. Of course she would hardly be the first person to suffer from royal lack of concern when a king was intent on smoothing the ruffled feathers of his dearest friend.

Her temper stirred at last as she thought about the Frenchman known as Esmé Stewart who had fought so hard to ensure the land that was now Brenda's dowry was returned to his English cousin. He was the young King's favorite and closest friend. He was also a man with ambition and an eye on his family having more holdings than anyone else. At least the King had settled the land on Brenda. It meant her cousin Symon could keep his new bride, who had arrived in Scotland fleeing from the man Brenda was being sent to wed. Noble families like the Stewarts did stick together.

Well, Brenda could hardly find fault with such actions. Family members should watch out for one another, and land…well, land was the truest form of wealth. It was the thing that kept the nobles in power because they could charge rent for land. She felt her temper rising over being sent to wed because of a dowry. However, the flare of anger didn't last very long; it sputtered out before her mare had crossed even half a mile. The reason was simple enough.

At this point, Brenda expected to be used by men for their personal gain. She simply didn't think any better of the world around her.

Jaded.

It was bound to happen. Honestly, she really didn't know why she lingered over the idea of knowing she'd completely lost her faith in the world around her. Her first marriage had smashed her illusions to little bits, her tears drying when she realized her husband only viewed her as an amusement to bring him notice from his friends. His father had eagerly collected her dowry as the wedding was celebrated in fine style at the Scottish court.

And she'd been bedded in full view of more than a dozen of her husband's friends.

Drunken sods who had leered at her and enjoyed her horror all while calling themselves noble lords.

Now, it seemed impossible she had ever been so tender. Brenda felt her lips rise into a little grin. It was at her own expense, and yet she just couldn't keep herself from marveling at the difference between who she'd been then and the woman she was now.

She had been so naive to think her future might include love or even something as simple as a marriage where husband and wife treated one another with kindness. Clearly she had failed to look around her. As the laird's niece, she'd been born into the role of bargaining chip. The matter of her marriage was one for discussion and planning.

Yet there had been a time…when ye'd listened to songs of love and dreamed…

Brenda stiffened, banishing the memory, because she had decided long ago never to allow her first husband to hurt her ever again. She'd wed at her father's command for the alliance it would give her clan. It had been her duty. She'd gone to him with ideas of her obedience yielding understanding from him. Truthfully, her anger should be directed at the upbringing that had taught her erroneously that dutiful behavior led to happiness.

Or perhaps she might think ill of her Campbell relations, who had so gleefully enjoyed seeing her tender illusions shredded on her wedding night and through-out her first year of marriage, when her husband had seated his mistresses right at the head table alongside her and the laird of the clan Campbell. They'd encouraged him to show off how vigorous he was in keeping a mistress, and he'd discarded each poor woman the moment another one took his fancy. In the end, Brenda had learned to have a measure of understanding for her kin in wedding her to him because a wife could not be tossed out. No, she'd been there to see her husband's women come and go, while all around her people told her to accept her portion with dignity.

Well, he's dead now...

She was her own woman at last.

Or at least she had been until her cousin found Athena Trappes in May. The English girl had been escaping from Galwell Scrope, who wouldn't be expecting Brenda to arrive with orders to wed him. In fact, Galwell had tried to make Athena his mistress. So horrified had she been that she had dressed as a boy and managed to get hired by a traveling merchant, thus escaping from Galwell.

Brenda smiled sincerely now. Her cousin Symon had been smitten with the girl. It had been a dream come true because Symon and Brenda were the last of their line. They'd spent more than one winter evening recognizing the need for them both to wed. And then, in a moment, Symon had met Athena. Oh, she'd made him court her, but not out of a need to twist him around her finger.

Brenda liked Athena even more for her sweet ways.

Brenda felt her expression tighten. Esmé Stewart

had done his best to ruin it all without a care for how deeply in love Symon and Athena were. The nobleman had discovered the dowry left to Athena by her father and used his friendship with the kind young King James to attempt to send Athena back to Galwell so the land would stay in the Stewart family.

At least young James hadn't been willing to take Symon's wife away, so once Symon married Athena, there was nothing to be done. The Scottish king might have been only fifteen, but he had proven himself worthy of his royal blood by settling the land on Brenda and sending her to wed Galwell. The land had been transferred to her because the King had upheld Symon and Athena's marriage. Thus, the land was a Grant holding from thence forward.

Her lips rose into a sarcastic twist. Galwell would soon learn that nobles and royals arranged matters to suit themselves first. If Galwell expected the delicate, sweet, and soft-spoken Athena to return to him, Brenda imagined a fiery Highlander woman would be quite a shock to the English nobleman.

However amusing it might be to contemplate how unhappy Galwell would be, Brenda knew for certain that she, as his wife and chattel, would be the one to suffer for his disgruntlement.

There it was: the way life had always treated her. There was no kindness, only a very determined dictate that she never maintain a happy state of being for too long. As soon as she believed she was safe, fate would reach out and slice her open with its talons.

No, she only managed to get tastes of happiness long enough to allow her to recall with perfect clarity how much she enjoyed those brief respites. However, she was very pleased to know Athena was happy, and Galwell wouldn't find her so easy to intimidate. Brenda had learned how to live as chattel, and she thoroughly enjoyed knowing Athena would never know how the position chafed. And there was the knowledge that her cousin Symon wouldn't face the displeasure of his king. All in all, as far as doing her duty went, Brenda decided her English marriage suited her far more than her first one had. The reason was simple: she wanted Symon to be happy. If it meant she had to obey James of Scotland and wed an English noble, well, Brenda would far rather it be herself heading to England instead of Athena.

Brenda smiled again. Athena wasn't jaded, and Brenda was going to enjoy knowing she'd helped ensure the girl would have only a happy life. The knowledge offered a little glimmer of hope that Brenda was going to clasp tightly to her heart.

Symon wasn't happy with her though. Her cousin had wanted to protect her as well as his young wife.

He was a good man. Which was why she'd spoken up and declared she'd obey the King when Symon had been set to protect Brenda. Symon would have gotten himself thrown into chains for defying the young King. Brenda didn't fault her cousin for his need to shield his family. No, James had neatly twisted the situation so Symon might keep his new bride, Athena, but at the expense of having Brenda promised to the English noble from whom Athena had fled. The man only wanted the land. It was a common enough thing, for certain. So there was no reason for Symon to anger his King. No reason for Brenda not to step up and do as the King demanded. No reason to think about how much she didn't want to wed again.

At least there was the comfort of knowing she was ensuring her cousin was happy and her clan in good standing with the King. Her first marriage had also brought an alliance that prevented bloodshed.

Yes, it was her duty to wed Galwell Scrope.

By royal command.

However, she found less comfort in going off to face Galwell than she had the first time she'd wed. Protecting the Grants? Well, she knew her kin and clansmen. A piece of land? Galwell wanted the rents from the property. Land was the truest form of wealth. Noble families owned it all, keeping the lower classes paying for its use.

Hence she was heading to England. So be it. She'd face whatever came her way, as she always had. As the Highlander she was.

She would do her duty.

❧

Chief Bothan Gunn pulled his horse to a halt. He reached forward to rub its neck as he contemplated the view before him.

Maddox, his captain, came up beside him, tilting his head to one side as he waited to see why Bothan had stopped. Both of them peered at the land in front of them, the place where Scotland ended and England began.

"I never thought to lay eyes on that," Maddox declared when Bothan remained silent. His voice drew out the last word, making it clear Maddox cared little for the place they were heading.

Bothan turned to look at him. "Or cross into it."

Before them were the borderlands. England lay on the other side of them. He didn't belong there, but Bothan set his stallion into motion because Brenda Grant wasn't suited to England any more than he was.

She was wild.

And he was going to ensure she could remain unbridled by those who didn't understand the value of a woman with the spark of life burning in her. Let the English keep their wives in submissive obedience. He craved a wife who would singe him with her heat and give him children with the strength to rise up to the challenge of living in the Highlands.

Brenda was that woman.

She would spit in his eye, though. At least until he proved his worth to her.

He slowly chuckled as he contemplated the battle ahead.

It was a fact; he was going to enjoy it.

And so would Brenda.

He'd see to that…personally.

Of course, first he had to rescue her. His lips curved into a grin. At last there was something pleasing about his journey into England. Snatching a prize from the hands of the English—well, there was something he would enjoy full well. They told tales in England of wild savages such as himself.

Highlanders.

Not that he was planning on changing the way the English thought about him.

No, he was riding onto their land to retrieve the woman he craved. Any who stepped between them was going to discover he was tenfold worse than any story they had ever heard.

❦

The English captain escorting Brenda was happy to be on home land at last. His face bore the marks of his worry, and Brenda watched the way he ran a hand over his face before sitting down at a long table in the common room of the tavern they'd stopped in for the night.

An English tavern. Which, by the look on the captain's face, made a world of difference to the man.

Well, Brenda could hardly think ill of him for being happy to be home. She would have smiled brightly indeed if she were spending the night beneath the roof of Grant Tower.

The captain caught her looking back at him from the top of the stairs.

"You will find your supper abovestairs, Mistress," he called out. The man was well suited to his position; his tone was full of authority, no hint of insecurity. And it was loud enough to fill the common room of the tavern.

But she knew he was just a bit shaken by her appearance or he wouldn't have spoken from where he sat, so that his voice bounced between the walls and made his wishes clear to everyone there. She allowed her eyes to narrow and enjoyed the way his lips thinned in a hard line. He was wise enough to know she might be a great deal of trouble if she decided to be a thorn in his side.

She could see the fear lurking in his eyes.

But she did not bother. It was best only to pick a fight when she needed to win. Tonight she wouldn't be making an attempt at gaining her freedom because her own word bound her to the journey. The captain knew it too, which was why there was no man posted outside her door. At that moment, Brenda could see the man thinking through his choice to trust her at her word. Brenda offered him a serene expression as the men in the common room went silent in response to the rising tension.

"I would like some water," Brenda said as she came smoothly down the steps. A few of his men cast her harassed looks. They were drunk on their own arrogance, thinking her nothing more than a nuisance.

If only they knew just how difficult she might be if she hadn't given her word to see the wedding through. They misjudged her simply because she'd been riding without any comment for so long. They mistook her compliance for docility.

"Drink the ale in your room, woman," one of them groused at her. "Water will poison you. Ye'll get the fever from it."

The captain didn't take his eyes off her. She watched as he gauged her reaction to his man's order, surprise flickering in his eyes as she merely kept moving at the same pace. The captain's jaw was set, but he never denied her, so Brenda turned and moved toward the back of the common room, heading to the door that led to the kitchen.

"Addams, go with her," the captain ordered from behind her.

Brenda heard a bench skid against the wooden floor of the tavern as Addams stood with a grumble and reluctantly fell into step behind her. The kitchen was smoky as the end of the day meant it was time to let the fire burn down to conserve wood.

Peat was often laid on top of the coals to keep them alive until the morning. It made for a slow, smoldering fire that smelled like a barn floor. The back door was open wide to let the smoke escape, but now that they were in the city, the air beyond the doors smelled less pleasant.

Another marriage wasn't the only reason Brenda had to loathe her return to what so many considered civilization. She'd take the Highlands over the congested city any day.

The cook was yawning and sitting by the fire as he nursed a mug of cider. His apron was stained and grubby. He looked up as Brenda came through the doorway, clearly not interested in another request from his patrons.

"She insists on water," Addams spoke up.

The cook started to rise, resigned to his duty. "I will fetch it, sir," Brenda muttered sweetly.

The cook settled back down with a pleased smile on his lips. He pointed toward a barrel sitting near the open back door.

Brenda picked up a pitcher sitting on a table and took it toward the barrel as Addams grunted and crossed his arms over his chest. "No one drinks water."

"We drink it often in Scotland," Brenda answered.

"Best get used to the way we live in England," Addams informed her as he came up to snatch the pitcher from her fingers. He dipped it into the water without a care for what might be on the outside of the vessel.

Brenda offered him a disapproving glare. He shot her a smug grin that froze on his lips as he looked over her shoulder and dropped the pitcher into the barrel.

Someone pulled her back, encircling her waist with a hard arm and lifting her right off her feet. It happened in an instant, and Addams was knocked in the jaw with a hard fist as a man grabbed a handful of his doublet front to keep Addams from flying into the wall. His head jerked and his eyes rolled back in his head before he was lowered to the floor in an unconscious heap.

"He needs a wee nap to think about the tone he was using with ye," Bothan Gunn informed her firmly.

Brenda didn't care for the way her heart accelerated. Perhaps if she could have attributed it to fear, it might not have mattered, but she knew that wasn't the cause. Which only alarmed her more.

She knew the danger of emotions. Aye, she knew it well.

"Chief Bothan Gunn," she muttered as she caught sight of his captain offering a coin to the cook. The man took it in a blink of an eye before settling down and casting his attention toward the hearth. "Ye should not have followed me."

Bothan Gunn was a huge man. He'd ducked to make it beneath the roofline and had to stay away from the edges of the kitchen because the roof sloped, preventing him from standing upright. They were still close enough to the border that his kilt did not cause too great a disturbance with the men he'd walked past in the yard. But she knew him for what he was: a Highlander. The English around them might make the mistake of believing all Scots the same, but Brenda knew better, and anyone who took the time to look at Bothan Gunn would see he was far harder than any Lowlander.

Bolder too because he was standing there. Somehow, she wasn't really surprised. Bothan Gunn had always been a man who wasn't afraid to reach out and grab what he wanted.

"Did ye think I would no' come for ye, Brenda?" Bothan asked softly, his lips twitching up into a mocking grin.

I'd hoped.

Brenda stiffened, chastising herself for the stray thought. She couldn't afford such things as personal ideas.

Especially with regard to Chief Bothan Gunn. It wasn't his clan the King of Scotland would hold accountable if she didn't go through with her wedding.

Duty. So very sharp-edged. She felt like the very word left open wounds as it crossed her soul. She drew in a deep breath, looking at Bothan and the freedom he represented and knowing she had to deny herself.

Deny yerself…what?

Brenda had refused his suit and ignored the stirrings inside herself.

And she would not be acknowledging any of them now.

Not now when she had duty weighing her down like a heavy yoke.

"I didn't realize ye were one to waste yer time," she muttered as she reached into the barrel and retrieved the pitcher. Water drained down from her hand as she fought to maintain her composure. Her tone wasn't as bored as she would have liked. And the way his eyes narrowed suggested he saw through her pose.

Bothan always had affected her oddly. Of course, tonight she was certain her heart was beating faster because she longed to be free of her English escort and her date to be wed. The response was only natural, after all.

Yes, that was why she felt so very breathless.

"Keeping ye from being forced to wed a black-hearted bastard is no' what I'd call a waste of me time," Bothan informed her.

He eased closer to her. She caught a glimpse of his blue eyes in the dim light and realized she was savoring the moment, putting off answering him because he was correct—she had no liking for her circumstances.

Still, duty was duty. Bothan was not just a man. He was chief of the Gunns. It was somewhat more than laird because he'd been elected by his fellow clansmen. He didn't just have their loyalty; he'd earned it beside them. She drew in a deep breath and stood firmly in place.

"Me cousin will be branded a traitor if I do not wed Galwell Scrope." Brenda forced the words past her lips. "I will not shirk from my duty to me family and laird. And ye would not have me if I did. Yer clansmen would vote against ye if ye brought home a woman who turned her back on her kin. Ye should go now, for there is no reason for ye to stay."

Her words gave Bothan a moment of pause. That in itself was remarkable. There was something about him, a sense she gained by being so close to him, that made her shudder as she seemed to recognize his strength on some deep level. It was a strange idea, one that she dwelled on because she'd never encountered it before in a man. She was no maid and not even a young woman, and yet Bothan struck her so very differently than any man she'd ever known.

If only she might indulge herself and discover just why she was drawn to him.

Do nae!

She had no idea why her inner voice warned her away from him so intensely, only that it raised gooseflesh along her arms. His lips thinned, which made her think he knew precisely what she was feeling.

"This wedding is an unjust thing, demanded of ye by a boy who is no' yet man enough to understand he is being manipulated by his friend Esmé Stewart. James may be King of Scotland, but he is still a lad," Bothan insisted. "Come away with me, Brenda. I will no' leave ye here."

She was so very tempted, and still she felt herself stuck in place, bound by the repercussions that would land on her cousin Symon Grant.

"Ye must leave me, for I will not shrink from this wedding. My kin will suffer if I do." And she didn't care for how despondent she sounded. Just because she had no fondness for her predicament didn't mean she should allow her personal feelings to bleed into her tone.

Crying was for the weak. In the end, tears would change naught.

No, she'd learned a very long time ago to keep her personal feelings hidden from others. She suffered less that way. Dignity was poor comfort when she was alone with her plight, but it was the only thing she seemed to have any control over.

Bothan cocked his head to one side. He had dark hair, black as ink, like he'd been carved out of the darkest hours of night sky. He was reaching for her, stretching out to capture her hand with his large one.

Part of her liked the idea of being drawn into the dark hours of the night where she might at last be free...

She drew in a startled breath, recoiling as their flesh met.

Ye couldn't like the feeling...

"I will perform my duty," she hissed at him in a near whisper. "Just as ye would, as me cousin Symon has always done. Do no' insult me by telling me it is acceptable for me to run away like a coward because I am a woman."

She jerked her hand free, but all he did was release her fingers in favor of catching a handful of her skirt. His grip kept her in place as he moved up so that she had to tip her head back to maintain eye contact.

"There are a fair number of things I've contemplated telling ye to do because ye are a woman," he muttered softly.

She caught the flicker of a promise in his eyes. It should have rubbed her temper, for she'd told him she would not have him.

Instead, her insides twisted with anticipation.

"And it's the truth I've thought ye frightened of me more than once," Bothan continued.

She let out a hiss, flattening her hands on his chest to push him back. "I am no' afraid of ye, Chief Gunn."

Bothan didn't budge. He stood steady, while her breath became raspy and she felt like her insides were warming, melting the wall she was trying to maintain between them.

"Perhaps it is more correct to say ye are over-whelmed by the way ye respond to me." He shifted so he was whispering next to her ear. "I understand that, lass. It's the truth I contemplated staying in the north Highlands, far away from ye so I'd no' have to admit how much ye enchant me. Find meself a bride who did no' stir me the way ye do."

A shiver went down her spine. Her flesh responded to him so immediately that there seemed no way to prevent it.

"I will not allow my cousin to be branded a trai-tor." Brenda shifted her head so she could lock gazes with him. "I cannae believe ye'd have a woman so lacking in loyalty to her family. Ye may be very certain yer men will no' thank ye for bringing home a mistress with scandal staining her name."

His expression tightened. For a moment, she was staring at Chief Gunn. A man who would do what needed doing for the sake of the men who had pledged their loyalty to him. An understanding passed between them, one that left her with a sense of achievement. She knew she had earned respect from him.

It also made her hope evaporate like a puddle on a hot summer day. Nothing was left but hard dirt. No life. Just dry dirt.

"It's the truth I would have overlooked it because

of the injustice of asking this duty of ye," he offered. "But ye're right that there would be others who would always consider it a flaw in yer character."

His agreement left a bitterness on her tongue. Bothan was a man of his word. He'd leave her to her fate now, and she would miss him, no matter how much she forbade herself to. At least there was a measure of satisfaction now. One that stemmed from knowing he approved of her.

"Goodbye, Chief Gunn," Brenda stated firmly. Her tone was more for herself than for him.

His lips twitched. "Ye'd send me off without a kiss? Unkind of ye, lass."

She should do exactly that.

But not because she didn't want to discover what his kiss tasted like.

No, she wanted to refuse because she knew without a doubt that she would never forget what it felt like to be kissed by him.

The memory would be a torment. One she willingly visited upon herself.

"It would be unwise," she muttered, pushing at him.

His teeth flashed at her as his lips curled up into a smug grin. "Aye, on that point we agree."

She watched his fingers release her skirt, and disappointment stabbed through her. A lament for the thing she was going to be denied. Could she not even have a memory to savor?

"No' that I'm ever the one to take the wisest course of action." He slid his hand up and around her hip, locking his arm around her waist so he could pull her completely against him. "The truth is I prefer to play with fire. Which is why I've come looking for ye, Brenda. The offers for obedient brides in me study leave me cold."

She gasped, looking up at him in shock as Bothan caught the back of her head in his opposite hand.

"I'll have a kiss from ye, Brenda, for ye've denied me it for more than a year now," he accused her softly.

Bothan wasn't planning on taking the kiss quickly. He took his time, pressing his mouth to hers. Lingering over the first brush of their lips as he turned his head and fitted their lips together.

She shuddered.

He shifted with her, holding her as her body responded almost brutally to the contact. There was an eruption of sensation, one she was helpless to control.

And she wasn't alone.

She felt him quake as well, the tremor running through his limbs as he pressed her mouth open for a deeper kiss.

Reason vanished as they tasted one another. Passion ignited between them, roaring to life in the space of a heartbeat. Brenda reached for him, certain she couldn't survive without the feel of him beneath her palms. Need was a living force inside her, beating against the hold she'd maintained against it for so long.

"Now that you've had your kiss, it's time to leave the lady in my keeping."

Bothan released her in a flash. He'd turned and pushed her behind him before she realized the captain was speaking from the doorway of the kitchen. Her senses were still swimming with intoxication, leaving her blinking in shock as the English captain eyed them.

The captain was wise enough to stand back out of Bothan's reach.

"It's my duty to deliver her to the Queen, and the lady has explained her intentions quite well," the captain continued. "So do not lay my men low again, Chief Gunn."

The two men faced off, taking measure of each other for a long moment. Brenda let out a huff before coming around Bothan.

"He will listen to you, Captain," she muttered as she retrieved the pitcher of water. "Because I have made it clear I intend to honor my word to my king. Chief Gunn is a man of honor."

The captain shifted his attention to her, but only for a moment before he returned his focus to Bothan.

It would seem the English Queen had wise captains in her employ, for Bothan wasn't a man to take lightly. Not when it came to anything, it would seem, for her heart was still beating fast, and moving back across the kitchen took every bit of self-discipline she had.

All she truly longed to do was leave with Bothan.

Well, ye do no' get to do what ye want…and it's no' the first time ye've faced it, either.

Indeed. There was a solid truth, one she'd encountered more than once in life. She kept going, crossing through the door and back into the common room.

She didn't dare look behind her.

No, it might prove too much temptation.

But what weighed the most on her mind as she made it through the tavern toward the stairs was the fact that she had kept Bothan waiting for that kiss for an entire year.

He'd made his desire for her clear.

And she'd denied it.

Back in the room abovestairs, she was free to let her emotions surface. Although it was more a matter of they refused to be contained any longer. She sat down on a stool, feeling the walls closing in on her just as if they were the stone walls of a prison cell.

That was why she'd refused Bothan. Marriage was a prison for women. It was one thing to be wed for duty, another to walk into the bonds of her own free will.

So she'd denied Bothan a kiss or anything else, for it would have led to the desire she still felt pulsing through her flesh.

Duty was something she could perform and still maintain her sanity, for she could tell herself the cruelties of her spouse were insignificant because she didn't care. Marriage was naught more than a chore to be completed.

But with Bothan, she feared she would care.

So she'd denied him.

And meself…

Only now did she wonder if she'd been foolish. It was one thing to make decisions for solid reasons and another to realize she was facing a future without any choices. She would be wed to a man who didn't know she was coming and wouldn't be any more pleased with the arrangement than she was.

All for the gain of the families.

And she would be chattel. Husbands didn't lose their rights when they wed. No, Galwell would go on with his life, enjoying whatever or whomever he pleased. She would be the one maintaining her virtue. Her temper heated as she considered how very unjust men were. The Scriptures didn't say only women should not commit adultery, and yet men never suffered for the transgression. Oh yes, there were plenty of women who took their lovers behind closed doors when they found their marriage bed cold.

She wouldn't be one of them. Once more, dignity seemed her only true possession, and Brenda admitted she didn't want to part with it.

Brenda suddenly allowed the heat from Bothan's kiss to linger on her lips, savoring the memory as she admitted she would have liked to see how much more passion there might have been between them.

Memories she might indulge in. So she closed her eyes and let the moment in the kitchen surface completely. A kiss had never moved her so deeply, nor had she ever recalled one in such vivid detail. Even now, she was certain she remembered the scent of his skin, the way it touched off a need to press herself closer to him while he kissed her. Bothan knew his strength, holding her so firmly yet tempering his hold so he'd never hurt her.

She smiled as she opened her eyes and made herself let the daydream go.

No, he hadn't hurt her, and still she felt like he'd carved the experience into her mind. But as she took in the sounds of the English guards below her, she decided she would savor the encounter.

The King's demand certainly wasn't going to offer her anything better.

༄

Maddox would never be far from his side.

Bothan wasn't surprised when his captain surfaced from a shadow to fall into step beside him once he'd emerged from the back of the tavern.

"So," his captain began, "since she's told ye she will go through with this wedding…are we riding north?"

Bothan shot his man a look. "She has to say such." He crossed the street and moved off toward the tavern where his men were spending the night. "Ye'd no' accept her as yer mistress if she were one to take her own whims over her cousin being branded a traitor. None of me men would. It was never going to be as simple as taking her back to Scotland."

His men had taken over the tavern. The few patrons who had been inside when the Gunn retainers had arrived made quick work of paying and leaving. Bothan lifted his leg up and over a bench before sitting down to enjoy the remains of a supper that had been served by the wife of the tavern owner. She was watching him and Maddox, judging whether there was ample fare for them.

Bothan enjoyed seeing an English woman with a solid backbone. He reached up and tugged on the corner of his bonnet. She nodded before disappearing into the kitchens.

"If Brenda Grant intends to wed, there is little point in following her," Maddox stated. A good number of Bothan's men turned their attention toward them, waiting to hear what Bothan would say.

"Brenda will fulfill her promise to the King," Bothan said clearly. "What I want to know is how does England's queen feel about the Stewarts increasing their wealth and holdings through this union? I've come along to see if this queen is of a mind to allow the wedding."

Maddox stroked his beard in response.

"We're in England now," Bothan explained. "I plan to petition England's queen for Brenda Grant. James will have to be content if the English Queen forbids the wedding. I only showed meself to her so she'd no' despair and think herself abandoned."

"Clever," Maddox conceded. "I do nae see how that will make Brenda Grant any more receptive to yer suit. Even if the lass is happy to have ye take her back to Scotland, it will no' mean she's of the mind to accept ye for her husband. She's unbridled, as most of the Highlands knows because she makes certain to say it plainly."

Bothan slowly grinned. A maid was pouring cider into a mug and caught sight of him. Her eyes widened, and he enjoyed knowing he intimidated her.

Strength was respected.

And being known for his ability to defend his land meant there would be fewer attempts to take what was his.

That translated into less blood spilled.

"Leave the matter of Brenda's opinion for me," he informed his men. "For all that I am yer chief, I hope ye'll agree getting that lass into me bed is more of a private matter between Brenda and meself."

There were chuckles in response. Bothan settled down to finish his supper as he contemplated the task in front of him. He'd left his land to seek out Brenda because he couldn't shake her from his thoughts. The hunt was far longer than he'd anticipated, but even her stubbornness was making him wonder if he should rethink his attempt to win her.

So he'd see it through. Which meant he'd have to outsmart those thinking to keep him from the prize he'd decided to claim.

There was nothing he enjoyed more than a good fight.

Victory was sweeter that way.

✧

Queen Elizabeth Tudor, the first of that name, didn't stay in London during the summer.

The Queen fled the heat and rising stench as she embarked on her progress. It was also a way to visit the northern parts of her realm and allow her close supporters to make certain there were no plots brewing against her.

And then there was the cost of feeding and entertaining her court. When she visited her northern nobles, the court came too. People lined the roads, watching the baggage carts and wagons as they passed. It took a full two days for Progress to pass by a single point on the map. The large country estates where her nobles lived provided fresh game meat and plenty of room for her court to set up pavilions and enjoy the warm days of summer. Merchants would follow, setting up market fairs that generated tax income for the crown.

Elizabeth herself enjoyed riding. She took to the road on a mare with her favorite gentlemen alongside her. Galwell Scrope rode confidently by her side as

Robert Leicester sent him a narrow-eyed look when the Queen wasn't looking.

Galwell needed to be dealt with.

Robert followed the Queen into what had once been the Duke of Norfolk's holding and was now in the hands of a more loyal noble. Lord Berkley was waiting on the steps, his senior household staff at attention, when the Queen of England rode up.

"Welcome, Your Majesty!" he called out as he removed his hat and lowered himself. Of old, noble blood, Lord Berkley had been raised to be the perfect host to his monarch. He smiled as he gave a small gesture of his fingers toward the musicians waiting to begin playing a lively fanfare to complete the moment. He was a slightly rotund man, his cheeks full from his enjoyment of feasting. Toward the back of the large house, the scent of roasting meat was wafting over the rooftops to prove Lord Berkley was going to welcome his monarch in grand style.

After dismounting, Elizabeth smiled and offered Lord Berkley her hand. He took it and placed a kiss on the back of her glove.

"Richard," Elizabeth declared as he recovered and replaced his hat. "It has been too long since I have seen you."

Baron Berkley smiled, his cheeks coloring. "All for good reason, Your Majesty," he informed her jovially. "For I needed to return home and prepare for Your Majesty's visit. No member of my staff could attend to the details as well as I might. It is my supreme hope that Your Majesty shall be impressed by my efforts!"

He extended his arm toward the front door of his

home. Robert followed the Queen inside as behind them servants began to raise pavilions for the bulk of the court to reside in while the Queen was there. Ambassadors and other dignitaries were among the horde of people following Elizabeth on her summer progress. Whether she'd see them was always in question. Elizabeth liked to keep everyone guessing. It kept them all near and attentive to her whims.

He was no exception. Leicester made his way into the rooms provided for him. His servants had ridden ahead to make certain his things were ready to receive him. Two new suits of clothing were hung out and ready for him to inspect, while a groom sat polishing a pair of his boots in preparation for a hunt. There was a tailor working a needle while seated at a small table as he secured pearls to a sleeve for the earl to wear for a banquet while the Lord Berkley entertained the Queen. All of Robert's personal belongings were there, ready for him the moment he arrived. Lord Berkley knew to extend the greatest amount of hospitality toward the earl—only the Queen ranked higher. A small stack of letters was waiting as well.

He broke the seal on the one from the dowager Lady North Hampton and smiled when he finished reading the letter. Galwell's sins were going to ensure the man didn't enjoy being at the Queen's side for much longer. Galwell had made a fatal error in judging the Queen. Elizabeth Tudor had spent her younger years as a pawn of those battling for control of the country. As a girl, she'd often been considered too feeble-minded to grasp the part she played in the struggle for power.

Robert knew better.

Much better.

He'd been there with her through it all. Elizabeth's truest companion in darker times. He would never forget that though Elizabeth was a girl, she was Henry the Eighth's daughter down to her bones. Galwell had missed it as he admired the female form she was encased in. Galwell would discover his error too late, when Elizabeth jerked the ambitious noble back into line like a hunting hound.

Elizabeth had survived countless years when she should have died in the darkest hours of the night at the hands of those seeking to have the throne or been shipped away to a far-off land to wed for the benefit of England. Somehow, between being branded a bastard and daughter of a witch, Elizabeth had survived to sit on the very throne her gender should have denied her. Her mind was Tudor, sharp and calculating. She was playing the marriage game now, keeping every man holding out hope that she would choose him and England would become a vassal state without a single drop of blood spilled. Galwell didn't have even a glimmer of hope of gaining the hand of the woman Elizabeth was behind her smile.

But Robert did.

He was Elizabeth's companion in cheating death. His own brother had lost his head for wedding Lady Jane Gray. It had been carefully plotted out by their families, of course, and they were mostly gone now. It was just Robert and Elizabeth, as it had been in the darker days. There was a bond between them, one no one could break. Galwell had his eye on the Queen of

England, but Robert saw Elizabeth behind the presence of the Queen. It was Elizabeth's heart he wanted to claim.

Robert put the letter down and eagerly began to prepare for the evening.

He had a queen to woo.

～∽

The estate to which the captain delivered Brenda was more like a large city.

There were huge pavilions erected all over what had once been sprawling greens around a manor house. Servants were rushing to deliver food and clothing to their different masters. At the edge of the green, kitchens were set up to keep everyone fed. The amount of meat roasting and bread set out to rise was extraordinary. Brenda had never seen so much being prepared at a single time. Not even when the entire Grant clan assembled.

Beyond the pavilions, there were scores of women doing laundry along the banks of a river. Maids and grooms were hurrying across the expanse in a hundred different directions as they served their masters. It was astounding to see the highest nobles in the land making camp in order to stay close to their queen. The logic of it wasn't lost on Brenda either. England's Queen was sparing herself the expense of feeding her court and keeping everyone busy with traveling so they didn't have as much time to plot against her. It really was quite clever. Just like a mother who made sure her children had plenty to do so they wouldn't get to squabbling.

"It might be a bit before you are summoned by the Queen," the captain informed Brenda once he'd escorted her to a small pavilion. "I'll have to go up and deliver the formal letters from James and see when she's of the mind to grant you an audience. I suggest you settle in."

There was a dryness to his tone that implied he was understating just how long she could expect to wait.

Well, she was in no hurry, and that was a fact.

He swept Brenda up and down.

"I'll send over a tailor," the captain said. "You will want to be seen in a gown that is more English in design. Your husband-to-be can settle the debt."

The captain inclined his head before moving away, leaving her to the care of his men. They were well back from the main house, in a city of pavilions. Behind her was a smaller pavilion the captain had claimed for her. Inside it was rather nice, with a receiving room complete with table and chairs. There was a chest with silver plate for the table and even glass goblets.

Two flaps opened to a bedchamber. The bed was assembled, with sheets and plump pillows awaiting her. Brenda smiled as she recalled summers in the Highlands when she'd been a young girl and run through the fields and slept in the stable loft simply for the adventure of it all. The grass beneath the carpet laid down under the bed was fresh.

Of course the estate would be destroyed by the time Elizabeth packed her court and left. The large expanse of lawn would be covered in brown patches from the pavilions, and there would be numerous tracks worn into it by the coming and going of the servants. The local game would be depleted for the rest of the season, leaving the locals to make do with meager fare. Not that things were so very different in the Highlands. Summer was a time to feast and enjoy the ample resources provided by nature. Once the harvest was in, winter would be a long, bleak season of bowls of porridge and not much else.

"Scots…ye do nae belong here!"

"Savages…"

"Go home to yer own country!"

Brenda heard the slurs, turning around to return to the flaps that made up the front of her pavilion. She looked out, her eyes widening as Bothan Gunn rode up to the front of the house. It was a huge estate, but its size didn't deter him in the least. He sat proudly in the saddle, unconcerned for the way he was looked at by the English around him.

Brenda lifted her hand and stifled a little sound of amusement.

If she were to be completely truthful, she'd say Bothan was proud of the difference between himself and those sneering at him.

Ye do tend to agree…

Really, she should have chided herself for the thought, but what did it truly matter? Still, she schooled her features and felt something shift inside her. An odd little sensation that sent a shiver down her spine.

He came in spite of yer promise to wed at the King's command…

Beyond the boldness of it, Brenda was left feeling something very foreign.

It was almost as if she might depend on him.

Brenda drew in a stiff breath. She must not allow herself to be weak. Thinking of Bothan's arrival as anything such as a rescue was permitting herself to be less than strong when it came to what must be done.

Duty wasn't meant to be enjoyed.

It was a tax one had to pay for the sake of higher morality.

Bothan wouldn't be rescuing her because she would not permit him to.

The royal guards blocking his path didn't impress Bothan. He argued with them, his back straight and the pleats of his kilt declaring him different from those watching.

A crowd was gathering as he stood his ground. There were parties of dignitaries who had not even been granted entrance to the main house. They waited, in full court clothing, for admittance past the royal guards. They had lace ruffs at their throats and handkerchiefs dangling from their hands, while the sunlight twinkled off the precious stones sewn to their capes and sleeves. Servants waited behind them with gleaming silver trays holding sugared grapes and slices of precious oranges from Spain.

The excess made Bothan want to growl. Now, he was not against enjoying a fine meal with treats to delight the palate, but the clothing made him angry because it was ornate and impractical and the expense of it could have fed an entire family for a year if not two.

He didn't have time for games and vanity. The seasons were shorter in the Highlands. He needed to be home, overseeing the planting and building. The

English Queen would simply have to deal with him sooner rather than later.

He dismounted and strode toward the door, intent on getting his business finished. He didn't bother to smooth out his features but let his mouth settle into a scowl. Let the English yeomen fear him; it would make it that much simpler to get past them and before the English Queen.

But Bothan didn't fare any better. He was barred from the main house, and he was fairly certain that wherever Elizabeth Tudor was, she could feel his frustration.

Bothan stood for a long moment, contemplating the yeomen of the Queen's guard. Well, he'd already learned one thing when it came to his quest to have Brenda Grant for his own: there wouldn't be any easy way of achieving his goal. If one path was blocked, he'd simply have to find another way around.

Robert Dudley, the Earl of Leicester, was accustomed to hearing disputes over entry into wherever Elizabeth was staying. He'd been her confidant and friend for so many years. Now that she was the master, she enjoyed making sure everyone knew it. Such was not a matter of vanity or corruption. No, Robert understood how Elizabeth thought. She meant to keep everyone guessing as to what she was about to do. Her enemies would be far less likely to make a move against her if they were unable to predict her behavior.

Many felt she was wielding the power she'd inherited arrogantly, but he knew different. She was making sure everyone who vied for her attention learned the only way to get what they wanted was to mind their place until she summoned them. Only when she was in a pleasant mood would they receive the rewards they were all seeking from her. Failing to be patient with her would result in their suits being dismissed.

Robert had learned to obey her, while other would-be suitors made the error of attempting to use the Queen's favor to bend her to their whims.

Today, though, Robert turned and contemplated the group of Scots arguing with the royal guard. They were not the normal Scots who came to Elizabeth from time to time. These wore kilts, in the Highland fashion. They were huge and rough, and their leader was a great hulking man who made it plain that in the harsh conditions of his northern home only the strongest survived. He wasn't the sort of man who played at dancing or masquerades in an effort to gain an audience with anyone. No, he was there to take care of business and be gone.

Another captain had been admitted, coming up the steps with a look of disgust on his face.

"What does the Scot want?" Robert inquired.

The captain had been minding his steps. He looked up and ripped his hat off as he recognized Robert. "My Lord Leicester." The captain lowered himself instantly.

Robert gestured the captain closer. "Tell me who that Scot is."

"Chief Bothan Gunn," the captain replied. "He's here to convince the Queen to release Brenda Grant from a wedding agreement James of Scotland has decreed will be so."

"I have never heard of Brenda Grant," Robert replied.

"She has just arrived," the captain answered. "I was tasked with escorting her down from Edinburgh. James thinks to settle a dispute concerning the Stewarts over a dowry property with her."

"The Stewarts are always looking to increase their wealth," Robert muttered. "I am glad to see someone willing to stand in their way." He looked back to where Bothan and his men were standing. "I believe I will meet this man. Allow him inside."

The captain was surprised, but he hid it well. He nodded, turning to hurry back down the steps and catch up with the Scot.

❦

Knowing something and cultivating the patience to deal with it were two vastly different things.

Brenda remembered well the time needed for fittings when she had wed her first husband. Of course, she'd been young and impressed with the attention, still dreamy-eyed over silk and lace. The bite of a tightly laced corset for the sake of fashion had only thrilled her instead of making her think it was all such nonsense.

That was before she'd learned all of the dresses and accessories were in reality baubles for a pet meant to delight the owner while she was displayed.

And she was to become the pet.

She had no taste for it now. The tailor was flustered with her lack of interest in his wares.

"You cannot go to see Glorianna, the Queen of

England, looking like some barbarian!" he exclaimed, flustered. "I insist you take off that wool dress."

The man's nose was wrinkled in distaste as he eyed her.

"I thought it was the law in England to wear wool on Sunday," Brenda replied.

The tailor rolled his eyes, his two assistants looking at her as though she'd muttered something unholy.

"No one attending court actually wears wool; they simply pay the sumptuary tax." His tone was rich with judgment. "And you simply must do something about your speech."

Brenda fluttered her eyelashes. "Ye do nae care for me brogue? I learned it from me mother."

"Who was likely a sheep." The tailor expressed his disdain.

Brenda's eyes narrowed. "She was a kind woman who did nae judge others, or teach me to value things such as lace ruffs over more important things like behaving decently. Get out."

"With pleasure," the tailor declared. "Go to see your betrothed looking like that"—he flipped his hand toward her—"and he will break the contract. Mark my words."

I enjoy that idea so very much.

And with the flap of the pavilion that served as the front door falling down into place after the abrupt departure of the tailor, Brenda was at liberty to allow her emotions to show on her face.

It was a relief.

At least for a few moments.

Galwell wouldn't refuse to wed her, not when she came with land. Property was the truest form of wealth. Noble families remained wealthy because they wed within their own class. Yes, many claimed they arranged their marriages for the sake of keeping their blue blood pure.

She didn't believe it. Land meant rent. It was the way nobles maintained their incomes. Since her dowry was land recently separated from the Stewarts, Galwell would be ordered by his fine-blooded family to retrieve it by wedding her. That same family would be delighted if she never presented them with a child of inferior blood. They'd advise her husband to bed her once for the sake of validating the contract between them and then to leave her alone.

At least her cousin Symon was happy.

Brenda indulged in a moment of bliss as she contemplated how Symon had found Athena. Neither had known about the land left to her by her father's family. James the Sixth had first considered separating Symon from Athena because she had been pre-contracted with Galwell. The man had proved himself a black-hearted scoundrel, though, when a greater match had been presented, and he'd tried to force Athena to become his mistress.

She'd fled to Scotland instead. Brenda smiled, enjoying the memory. For all that Athena was an Englishwoman, she had spirit and would be a fine wife for Brenda's cousin Symon. James had decided to make Symon give the land as dowry for Brenda and send Brenda to England to wed Galwell.

Well, it was hardly the first time fate had turned nasty toward her.

She'd given her word, and she'd keep it. She

doubted Symon had returned home easily though. Her cousin hadn't liked the bargain the King had forced down his throat.

Ye have Bothan Gunn to thank for the fact that Symon had gone home at all…

Brenda couldn't deny the validity of the thought. Symon wouldn't have trusted many men with retrieving her. Bothan Gunn was a man Symon called friend. A man who had earned Symon's respect.

Well, Bothan wouldn't be taking her home either. With enough time, Symon would see his duty was to return to Grant land and make certain the clan had a solid leader and future. Athena would give him children to kindle life once again inside the walls of Grant Tower.

It had been far too long since the place had felt alive.

Ye won't be there to enjoy it…

Brenda cursed her inner thoughts for they offered her little hope. It was the single thing that had kept her fighting to live for so many years.

Hope.

Or at least the knowledge that there was a part of herself no one could take away.

But it could be strangled.

She let out a sigh and turned around, gasping when she found herself staring at Bothan Gunn in her bedchamber. She blinked, wondering if it was just the ramblings of her mind.

No, he was still there. Very, very much in the flesh.

"It's only a pavilion, but the truth is, I enjoyed knowing I'd snuck into yer private quarters, lass." He crossed the distance between them, his lips set in a rather smug grin.

But his elation faded as he locked gazes with her. Concern flashed through his eyes.

"Do nae be so troubled, Brenda," Bothan scolded her gently.

Bothan had been many things to her in their short acquaintance. He'd been the rogue teasing her on May Day, the man she'd felt confident enough to taunt in return, and he'd been the one to declare he'd court her in spite of her declaration to remain her own woman.

He had never been her confidant or a man who spoke to her gently.

No, only Symon was that, and he had a new wife. She'd allowed her cousin to see her weakness. She couldn't let Bothan see that part of her. Weakness might be exploited.

"I am quite well," she answered, moving off to one side because Bothan filled the space between them with his presence.

She was so very aware of him. Part of her wanted to linger over that fact and absorb it.

But her wisdom argued against it. For it would be like whisky; once she allowed it inside herself, the effect would undermine her ability to maintain her control.

Bothan crossed his arms over his chest, facing off with her with his feet braced shoulder-width apart. In his kilt and rolled-up shirtsleeves, he appeared far more the northern barbarian the tailor had accused her of being.

"I brought ye good news, lass," he began.

Brenda's eyelashes fluttered. It was a far wiser idea to keep from locking gazes with him for he seemed to see past her confident mask and into her innermost feelings, into that place she reserved for only herself.

Such was her sole private possession.

But she failed, looking up when he didn't continue to talk. No, he was waiting for her to give him her full attention.

Waiting for her to allow him to gaze into her eyes.

"There are those who do nae favor this wedding James has sent ye to." Bothan moved closer, maintaining eye contact. She caught the flicker of victory in his blue eyes and wanted to believe in it.

Ye mustn't waver.

Bothan reached out and lifted her chin when she looked down.

She felt the connection right down to her toes. It drew a soft sound from her because no one had ever affected her in such a dramatic fashion before.

His eyes narrowed when she recoiled.

"I have never put rough hands on ye," he defended himself.

She blinked and lifted her chin. "I made no such accusation."

He tilted his head to one side, contemplating her very much like one of her cousin's hawks might. "Ye shy away from me."

She felt heat teasing her cheeks.

Ye must not blush!

"Would ye have me be the sort of woman who is used to having a man's hands on her?" Brenda asked before thinking her words through.

Heat flickered in his eyes. "I'd enjoy knowing ye are accustomed to having my hands on ye, Brenda."

She should have expected such a response. Brenda offered him a flutter of her eyelashes before she shook her head.

"Perhaps I am only attempting to accept me circumstances." She meant to place distance between them. Instead, Bothan's eyes glowed with another flare of victory as though she'd made some sort of admission. "Why are ye here? I have made it clear I intend to keep me word," Brenda said.

"As do I, Brenda Grant." Bothan spoke in a firm tone. She'd always taken him for a man who had earned his position. Today, she was face-to-face with the side of his nature that had earned him the title of chief. He'd proven himself worthy.

"I gave yer cousin me word," Bothan continued, closing the distance between them one silent step at a time. "And I will bring ye away from this match."

"Maybe it's for the best. This match." She wasn't lashing out at him. No, her words were more of a confession of just how much she realized she would never trust any man enough to allow him into her life.

And Bothan deserved a woman who would welcome him.

"I will not reconsider me position on accepting yer suit. I mean ye no unkindness, Bothan, and tell ye to go because it would no' be correct of me to see ye waste yer time," Brenda finished softly.

She wanted to flinch away from her own words and just how bleak they made her feel.

"Ye are worthy of me time, Brenda." Bothan reached out to cup her chin, raising her face so their eyes met.

For a moment, she felt like there was enough hope in his eyes to blow everything else aside.

"I'm too old for ignoring the way the world is, Bothan, and so are ye." She stepped back to remove her chin from his fingers. "What we want is no' how things are going to be. Not when kings are involved."

Bothan looked past her to where the garments the tailor had been trying to get her to try lay on the table.

"Well now, lass." Bothan slowly grinned. "If ye are intent on staying, ye are going to need some of those skirts that are rigid, making ye walk like ye have yer ankles tied together because ye'd look like a bell being rung if ye took longer strides…"

He reached over and plucked a farthingale up, letting it hang down like a bell, the hoops sewn into it widening until they reached the hem. He swung it back and forth as he chuckled. "And one of these… things…" He plucked a neck ruff off the table and dangled it like a frog he was trying to frighten her with.

Although she did admit she found the garment rather repulsive.

Brenda turned and sent him a narrow-eyed look. "Ye don't need to enjoy this so very much, Chief Gunn. If me husband keeps me at court, I truly will have to wear that thing."

Bothan's expression went serious. He'd been leaning against the wall, his arms crossed over his chest, making him look impossibly large and full of strength. He straightened and unfolded his arms as he came closer to her.

"Be very, very sure of one thing lass." His tone

deepened as his eyes flickered with promise. "I am going to enjoy ye very, very much."

She should have recoiled. But the promise in his eyes was mesmerizing. Brenda discovered herself caught in his gaze, fascinated by the way his eyes burned with an intensity that made her cheeks heat.

Ye didn't blush.

"If this Englishman wants the land, he will take me as I am," she declared as she looked at the clothing.

Bothan's eyes flashed before he caught her upper arm and tugged her back around to face him. "I'll challenge him before he can claim ye."

The breath froze in her chest. "This is England. Challenge a noble and ye could end up being hanged."

His lips twitched into a cocky grin. "Would it matter to ye, sweet Brenda?"

Brenda drew herself up and looked away from him. "I've no desire to see ye dead."

"Ah," he mocked her softly. "I suppose I'm more interested in discovering if ye desire to see me."

Brenda didn't miss the hint. He was teasing her. And there were different sorts of teasing. She'd become quite accomplished in flirting and leaving men with just enough hope that they'd wait to see if she bestowed her favors on them.

It was an effective form of managing the men who thought to add her to their list of conquests.

"Ye will no' challenge him." But even as she repeated, she realized Bothan would never be bound by her decree.

No, he was far too much of a warrior.

Part of her enjoyed it.

And the other part? Well, she knew she was spending a great deal of effort in making sure there was actually a part of her willing to argue the point. Truthfully, she just wanted to let Bothan have his way and take her away from the cold marriage awaiting her.

Bothan moved closer. "Would ye worry over my fate, Brenda?"

"Is this situation not already difficult enough?" she demanded in exasperation.

He was slowly following her, crowding her. Pressing her.

What alarmed Brenda was how aware she was of it. Her belly was twisting, and her skin was far too sensitive. It defied her reasoning for she was no stranger to the advances of men. But today, Bothan's presence didn't annoy her.

It agitated her.

"Aye, it's difficult, all right," Bothan agreed. He reached out and stroked her cheek. "Yet I promised ye I would be dealing with ye this spring, Brenda. Difficult or no', I will be keeping me word to ye."

Brenda let out a little huff.

At least Brenda intended it to be a huff. What actually crossed her lips was a breathless little sound that unmasked the turmoil inside her.

And Bothan noticed.

That sensation in her belly intensified, pinning her in position as Bothan took the last step between them and laid his hand on the side of her face.

The flap of the tent that served as the door was suddenly flipped aside and pulled all the way back so the man wanting to enter didn't have to do any of the work himself. In fact, he was poised in the center of the opening, perfectly positioned to be revealed. Bothan turned and tilted his head to one side, clearly never having seen the lengths some nobles went to when making an entrance.

She enjoyed seeing the disgust in Bothan's eyes. More than once, she'd wondered if she was the only one who didn't place value on such things.

Stop noticing things ye like about him...

The man who stood in the doorway was groomed to perfection. He had two menservants hovering behind him as he looked inside the pavilion. He was actually holding a sprig of fresh rosemary, sniffing it with his eyes closed. One leg was positioned perfectly in front of the other so she would be afforded a look at his inner calf. His doublet fit him like a second skin, and around his neck was a ruff dripping with lace. Matching lace adorned each of his wrists, and the open flaps allowed the scent of his perfume to waft in to where she stood. Bothan turned and crossed his arms over his chest in the time it took the man to finish sniffing and open his eyes to take in what was inside the tent.

The nobleman's eyes narrowed as he took in Bothan. His expression transformed into one of astonishment as his jaw slacked open and she heard him give a very loud sniff.

Brenda decided he appeared as though he'd bitten into a lemon.

"What..." He drew out the word. "What are you doing in here with another man?"

"It would seem yer intended groom has decided to

come and make himself known to ye at last." Bothan refused to hide the grin curving his lips. He had his head tucked down as he gripped his forearms while trying not to laugh outright.

"I am," the man declared loudly, "Galwell Scrope."

He raked Brenda up and down with his gaze, clearly waiting for her to acknowledge him.

More like be impressed with him…

The servants behind him encouraged her with frantic motions of their hands. Brenda moved one foot behind her and offered him a small courtesy. He was less than pleased, his expression looking somewhat pinched. He drew off another sniff from the rosemary before appearing to resign himself to dealing with her. The ruff around his neck meant he held his chin high.

Looks like a rooster…

Brenda pressed her lips tightly together and looked toward the ground to avoid the English nobleman from seeing the amusement in her eyes. She looked up again when she'd grasped her composure. Galwell Scrope was inside the pavilion now and looking past her to where Bothan stood. Galwell's eyes bulged as he came to an abrupt stop when Bothan didn't budge but stood watching him with an expression that made it clear Bothan would welcome any challenge the man cared to issue.

"She is my bride," Galwell declared. "You do not belong in here with her."

Bothan didn't even blink in response to the outrage in Galwell's tone.

"Ye have never set eyes on her before and did no' even know ye were set to wed her until she arrived."

Bothan didn't waste any time making it clear he thought Galwell had no grounds for his outrage.

"And you...*know* her? Well enough to seek her out in private?" Galwell's implication was clear.

Bothan opened his arms, sending Galwell back a step. "If I had no care for her reputation, I'd let ye think so, for I'd hope ye'd dissolve the contract between ye."

Galwell snorted. He raised his chin and stuck his nose up. "I am not so easy to manipulate," he informed Bothan, sweeping him up and down with his gaze. "You are here for the same reason my father insists I wed her. The land."

"I am no' surprised ye think so," Bothan said. He contemplated Galwell, his lips curling with disgust over the elaborate court clothing. Galwell was wearing short little puffed pants known as pansy slops. Sections of them were decorated with silver trim and pearls, and whoever had outfitted him hadn't forgotten to include a codpiece complete with jewels twinkling in the sun.

Bothan looked Galwell up and down with an expression on his face that made it plain the highland chief was having difficulty believing what was before him. Galwell took Bothan's silence for acceptance of his superiority.

The nobleman couldn't have been more incorrect.

Galwell sniffed disdainfully. "Don't pretend you are not interested in a good dowry. Why else would you be in here, trying to seduce her so her name is linked with yours and the Queen decides to make her marry you in disgrace?"

Bothan's expression tightened.

"I won't have it," Galwell declared loudly before directing his attention to Brenda. "You might be a Scottish slut, but I will not be made a fool of."

There was a flash of wool kilt and a hard connection of flesh on flesh as Galwell went flying into the tent flap. Bothan was right behind him.

"Brenda is a lady of grace and dignity, qualities ye don't know the meaning of," Bothan said. "Use that word again in me hearing to describe her, and ye'll answer for it."

Galwell was helped to his feet by his hovering attendants. One of them wiped the blood from the noble's split lip.

"You will pay for this...barbaric assault!" He pointed at Bothan. "And once you are wearing chains for daring to strike me, I will have this slut whipped before your eyes."

Past the front flap of the pavilion, Brenda's escort was quick to notice the altercation. The men surged in and pushed Bothan back when he lunged at Galwell once more.

"We cannot allow you to strike a noble," the captain informed Bothan.

"He already did!" Galwell declared. "Put him in chains, Captain."

Brenda felt her blood chill. "Just escort him from the grounds. Please." The last word stuck. It took effort to force it across her tongue, but her knowledge of the strained relations between England and Scotland was enough to give her the strength to accomplish the goal.

Her pride wasn't worth seeing Bothan shackled.

She was certain a part of her would die if she witnessed such a sight.

He was too powerful to be chained.

"The Queen will hear of this!" Galwell declared before he turned, his jeweled cape flipping around him as he strode off toward the house.

"I sincerely hope so," Bothan growled. "The sooner the better."

"Ye shouldn't," Brenda argued. "We're in England. Elizabeth could have ye thrown into chains or worse. Her father was not known for his even temperament."

Bothan shifted his attention to Brenda, contemplating her for a long moment. His lips twitched, one side of his mouth rising into a grin. "I'm pleased to know ye care, Brenda."

The captain and his men pushed Bothan away from the pavilion before she might debate the issue. She caught a hint of approval in Bothan's blue eyes before he turned and complied. The men who'd been holding him were relieved to only need to fall into position around him.

Cared?

Yes, she did.

Not that she would ever voice such a thing to him.

It wasn't really a matter of wanting to or not. She backed up as more of the captain's men crowded her further back into the pavilion.

Her husband to be was going to make very sure she never got a chance to speak to Bothan again.

And it hurt to know it.

❧

"Stay here, Lord Gunn," the captain informed Bothan. "Until you are summoned. Galwell has been a favorite of the Queen of late. I don't believe you will wait long."

"That suits me well," Bothan replied. "And it's Chief. No' Lord. Where I live, a man is more concerned with the respect of being elected by his men than some hereditary title passed down."

The captain nodded, a gleam of approval in his eyes. "Makes me think about following you back up to your home. Elizabeth is a fine monarch to serve, but there are nobles who follow her who I have no care for. Still, it's my duty, and I will not shirk from it. Stay here. I have no wish to place you under guard."

"I will be here when ye come for me." Bothan spoke loud and clear. "There is naught I wish for more than to be finished with this matter and on me way north. With Brenda Grant."

The captain started to turn around, stopping to lock gazes with Bothan.

"She's a good woman. I see why you are intent on claiming her," the captain began.

"Save yer breath, man." Bothan stopped so he could temper his tone. He'd never thought much about the way he'd been raised to dislike the English. For certain there was a great deal of blood spilled between their kind, but the man standing before him wasn't a man lacking in morality.

"It would be a great deal simpler for me to not involve myself," the captain replied. "Yet Mistress Grant has surprised me with her self-discipline. It's plain to see she has no desire for this match—"

"Yet she'll carry through with it for the sake of her cousin," Bothan finished with disgust.

"And for you."

Bothan had paced away from the English captain. Bothan turned and fixed the man with a hard look.

The captain stood up to it. "Mistress Grant has enough of a burden. You might think about how it will end for her if you persist in provoking her intended groom."

The captain nodded before turning and moving off toward the house. Plenty of people looked toward Bothan and his men.

Going inside was the last thing Bothan wanted to do. Returning to the pavilion where Brenda was, that he wanted to do. But the captain was correct. Brenda would be the one to reap the anger Bothan stirred up in Galwell Scrope.

His men lifted the flaps and moved inside to sit at the table and benches. Bothan ground his teeth together with frustration. He preferred a man-on-man fight. Not the way the King was soothing tempers with negotiations and dowry gifts. But he wasn't a fool either. Sometimes, negotiation was better than seeing blood spilled. As a chief, he had to do what was best for his people. Just as Brenda was making sure her clan didn't end up branded as traitors. It was a damned mess, but he ducked under the entrance of the pavilion and went to join his men because he wasn't going to give up. He was a chief. Galwell Scrope wouldn't be enjoying the spoils of ill-gotten gains if Bothan had any say in the matter.

But it was only a few moments before someone was striding up to stand in the open doorway.

"I seek Bothan Gunn."

Bothan dressed like his men, ate with them—in short, was one of them in all things because it made certain there was no cause for anyone to say he took luxuries while those serving him made do with less.

The man standing in the tent door opening wasn't able to distinguish Bothan from his men because he didn't understand that the three feathers on the side of his bonnet signified his rank. Bothan wasn't planning on enlightening the man, either. He'd learned more than one thing by leaving himself unnamed. Things messengers such as this one might say if they thought they were only in the company of their peers.

"Who are ye?" Maddox asked.

"Henry Trappes," the man said clearly. He reached into his doublet and withdrew a letter. "Laird Symon Grant wrote to me, informing me I should seek you out when you arrived."

"I am Bothan Gunn," Bothan said, declaring himself. "And ye are Athena's uncle."

The man nodded. "I've been following Her Majesty for weeks in an effort to clear my niece's name. Elizabeth has yet to receive me. I've no doubt Galwell Scrope has played a hand in ensuring my suit doesn't come to her attention."

Bothan scoffed. "Considering the man would be proven a black-hearted liar if ye did gain the chance to speak, I find myself in agreement with ye."

"It seems you may have found the means to ensure we are heard," Henry said. "I could not help but overhear Galwell sputtering like a newly baptized cat."

Maddox chuckled. "He squealed, sure enough."

Henry shook his head. "He's accomplished at the art of deception. Elizabeth has been keeping him close to her side. There are rumors she is even pondering wedding him to punish the Earl of Leicester for his secret wedding to Lettice."

"In that case, it sounds like a fine thing to know Athena is staying in Scotland," Maddox answered.

"Yes," Henry replied. "For all that I was forced to send her north in a moment of desperation, it seems the Lord has ensured she did not come to an unkind end." Relief washed over his face.

"Symon Grant will enjoy knowing he was doing the Lord's work." Bothan chuckled.

Henry Trappes didn't join him in the moment of amusement. There was worry in the man's eyes. A concern Bothan wasn't immune to. Elizabeth Tudor enjoyed keeping her realm under her control. Anyone who doubted she would be the mistress in England tended to learn firsthand how much like Henry the Eighth she was.

Bothan didn't dwell on the matter. He'd go through the famed lion's daughter if needed to gain Brenda.

"Seems ye're right about Galwell being able to get to the Queen whenever he chooses," Bothan said. Past Henry's shoulder the captain was heading back, a dozen of his men following. Henry turned and looked toward the house where the Queen was being entertained.

"At last," Henry muttered.

Henry might be an older man, but there was heat in his tone. Bothan nodded approvingly. Unlike half the men following the English court, Henry wore good wool britches and doublet. His clothing was fine and yet functional. The man wasn't a fop. And his tone told Bothan Henry wasn't going to allow the slight to his family name to go unchallenged.

Maddox straightened his doublet. "Never thought I'd meet an English queen."

"I did," Bothan informed his man as he moved past Maddox and out into the open where the captain was approaching them. "It's what I came here to do."

And God help Elizabeth Tudor if she didn't have more sense than James of Scotland did.

Brenda had no love of monarchs.

Or, more precisely, Brenda decided she didn't care for the way her insides tightened as she was led toward a large drawing room where the Queen of England was currently sitting on a throne-like chair.

There was no dismissing the tension, though. The woman sitting with her fingers resting on carved lion's head that was on the end of the armrest of the chair was very much a monarch. Elizabeth Tudor had red hair and blue eyes, but there was a sternness to her features that made it clear she had every intention of passing judgment and didn't need anyone to help her do it. Nor did she doubt for a moment that it was her right to rule those in front of her.

"Are you Brenda Grant?" Elizabeth demanded.

Brenda lowered herself properly before answering. "I am."

Elizabeth stood and went over to a table. There

were dozens of parchments on it, and a man sat at the end with a quill and inkwell. He inclined his head as his mistress came near.

"James the Sixth of Scotland has sent you to wed," Elizabeth said as she tapped a slim finger on the top of an open parchment. She looked toward Brenda. "You agreed to this?"

"The alternative was to see me cousin lose his new wife," Brenda said.

Galwell grunted. "That is not what the Queen asked you."

"It's the truth of the matter," Bothan added as he came through the doorway. He paused to tug on his cap and incline his head, but that was as polished as his manners went. There was an older Englishman with him who lowered himself before the Queen. Bothan sent Galwell a hard look. "Brenda is loyal to her family and did no' care to see her cousin labeled a traitor because he'd not allow his wife to be taken from him over a dowry she never knew about," Bothan said firmly.

"Yet you know about it," Galwell snapped. "And you're here trying your hand at making it yours." He sniffed disdainfully. "Nothing but a thieving Scot!" Galwell declared loudly with his nose in the air.

Bothan let out a snarl. What made Galwell turn toward him was the very controlled way the sound came from Bothan's lips. The Queen's guards took notice, moving forward.

"My Lord Galwell." Elizabeth stood her ground, her voice firm and just as controlled. "As it would seem you think you know so very much about

Scotland and its people, perhaps we should appoint you as our ambassador to Scotland."

Galwell paled. "Glorianna…you cannot mean to put me so far from your side."

"I mean to have one mistress in England, sir." Elizabeth sent them all a hard look before she slowly sat again in her chair. She settled herself, grasping the carved lion's head at the end of the armrest before she spoke again.

"Henry Trappes," Elizabeth began. "Did Galwell present contracts for your niece?"

The goldsmith inclined his head before he answered. "Indeed he did, madam." There was a crinkle of parchment as he withdrew the documents. "Your Majesty will see that the seals are all here, from the Baron Scrope. I would never have allowed my niece to be courted if the matter were not correctly in hand."

Elizabeth fixed her blue eyes on the parchment. "So I see." She shifted her attention to Galwell. "And the land." Elizabeth snapped her attention back to Henry. "Is it listed?"

Henry shook his head. "I never knew of the land. Not until I received this letter from Laird Symon Grant."

Elizabeth slowly returned her gaze to Galwell. "And now, My Lord, you suddenly find yourself more agreeable to the union?" She made a scoffing sound beneath her breath. "And men claim women are fickle creatures."

Galwell lowered himself. "It is my father who has changed his thinking. I am but a dutiful son."

"I see," Elizabeth remarked slowly. "Henry Trappes,

how did your niece come to be in the presence of James of Scotland?"

Henry looked his queen straight in the eye. "Galwell lured her to his townhome, using these contracts to gain her trust, and tried to force her to become his mistress. When she refused, he had the constables called to arrest her. I sent her north so I could gain support against his allegations. I am a humble man, Your Majesty. My own sister was abandoned by her noble husband when she presented him with a daughter. This noble family has not once asked after my niece, not given a single penny toward her care. Lord Scrope swore to have me thrown into prison as well. I needed time to contact men who would speak on behalf of my character. I have followed you for months in an effort to present my case."

Elizabeth's blue eyes shifted over to Galwell, her displeasure clear.

Henry withdrew another packet of paper, but Robert Leicester stepped forward. "I will speak as to his nature, Your Majesty." Robert offered her a courtly reverence that showed off his inner leg. "The very necklace around Your Majesty's throat is one I had made by this man's hand. I have dealt with him on many occasions and always found him to be of the highest noble character."

The Queen's gaze met Robert's, her features softening. Brenda felt her breath catch for there was no denying the affection displayed. True love couldn't be hidden.

"I spoke in haste." Galwell hadn't missed the exchange between Robert and the Queen either.

Panic flickered in his eyes as he tried to regain her approval. "When I realized I was going to lose Athena, I was mad to keep her."

"As your mistress?" Elizabeth asked, her tone making her distaste clear.

Galwell ducked his chin. "I do not regret it, Your Majesty, for it brought me to your side. Where I have learned a greater meaning of the word *love*."

Elizabeth's face was a perfectly controlled mask. A closer look had Brenda realizing the monarch's mind was as sharp as it was rumored to be. Elizabeth was sorting through everything she'd heard and seen. She was wise enough to realize she might learn a great deal if she did nothing more than hold her tongue and allow the men in front of her to argue.

"Your love is so great, yet you are fighting with another man over marrying Brenda Grant?" Robert demanded slyly of Galwell.

"You have a new wife, do you not, My Lord Leicester?" Galwell parried.

A little sound came from the Queen, a small "harrumph" that spoke volumes about her understanding of the realities of life. She lifted a hand, silencing Galwell as she looked at him sternly.

"From what I understand, Galwell, you were just threatening Chief Gunn with imprisonment for merely being in the same pavilion with your intended bride," Elisabeth said slowly before her eyes narrowed with her temper. "How dare you reproach Robert for the same sin you clearly planned to commit yourself?"

Galwell opened his mouth but shut it as he tried to think his way out of the situation. Brenda fought the urge to say exactly what she thought of him. Elizabeth didn't miss it though. The Queen of England turned to look at her.

"You appear less than enamored with the man my cousin James has sent you to wed," Elizabeth remarked while tapping her finger against the lion's head.

"I am here out of loyalty to my family." Brenda spoke her mind. Perhaps it wasn't the wisest thing to say, for a husband had a great many rights over his wife. "My first marriage was for their sake as well. Were it left to me, I would end my days as I am now."

Many would have told her how rash her words were. Nobles and royals didn't tend to appreciate opinions that conflicted with their own. Still, Brenda decided she would rather be beaten for honesty than duck her chin like a coward.

"You have courage," Elizabeth observed.

Brenda slowly smiled. "I'm often told more than a healthy amount of it for my gender."

"Something I know about myself," the Queen answered before she cast her attention to Bothan.

He was standing his ground, his feet braced shoulder-width apart, his arms crossed over his chest. He was imposing, and Brenda drank in the sight of him, knowing it was very likely her last opportunity to indulge in seeing him. Bothan didn't shrink. He stood firmly in front of the Queen of England, no fear on his face.

No, his expression was one of determination.

Brenda would have sworn she felt the heat from it.

"Indeed, I know a thing or two about being coveted for what I have," Elizabeth said in a tone edged with loathing, "while being told to mind my place as a woman. Yet God has seen fit to make me a Prince."

For a moment, the Queen was lost in thought. Brenda didn't make the mistake of thinking Elizabeth's mind was soft. No, this woman was taking the time to think long and hard on a matter before she spoke. Something life had taught her through bitter experience.

Elizabeth looked at Robert Dudley, the Earl of Leicester, her eyes glistening. "I forgive you the need of a son, Robin."

Robert reached out for her hand, raising it from his lips to his forehead. Brenda caught her breath because the moment was so very touching.

And it made her more than a little envious of the fact that fate had never been kind enough to her to bestow such affection upon her.

"As I expect you to forgive me for not being able to wed you, Robert, because a Prince does not marry for her personal desires but for the interests of her people," Elizabeth continued.

Brenda felt her heart clench. Marriage was a business. She'd encountered that hard reality before. Elizabeth loved Robert Dudley—it was clear in both their eyes—and yet she'd not wed him even though she was the Queen of England and no one could tell her no.

Elizabeth understood that her actions would have repercussions and that a queen must wed for an alliance. To do otherwise was to put her people at risk of civil war or attack from abroad.

Yer father told ye the same when ye wed the first time.

Brenda drew a deep breath, sealing herself against

the tide of regret rising up inside her. It would be a poor marriage at best. She looked at Galwell and saw how very lacking he was. It was a sad truth that she couldn't find a single thing to compliment.

And Bothan was his opposite.

Brenda was looking at him without realizing her gaze had wandered. Bothan shifted his attention, locking gazes with her. For a moment, there was nothing except him. She felt the breath freeze in her chest and heat flicker in her cheeks. Her reaction would be seen, and yet no amount of scolding herself seemed to matter.

"My Lord Galwell." Elizabeth raised her voice slightly. "I find your lack of character disturbing. To offer contracts to a man for his niece and then to attempt to make her turn mistress—"

"It was my father's doing." Galwell defended himself.

"Perhaps it was your father's choice not to finish the contracts, but it was *yours*"—she stressed the last word—"to lure the girl to your home while you knew it was improper and she thought you an honorable man."

Elizabeth slapped the arm of her chair. "I will not have it, sir! Men think to demand virtue in a bride, and yet you believe you might insist on a girl discarding hers because you want her in your bed. Tell me, what would have become of the girl when you decided you craved another?"

Galwell's eyes bulged, but the Queen looked toward Bothan.

"You are amused, Chief Gunn?" Elizabeth demanded. Bothan inclined his head. "I'm pleasantly surprised to see the fire in ye, ma'am. It's the truth there are a few in the Highlands who say ye are weak-willed and merely a puppet upon the throne."

Elizabeth let out a soft little grunt of approval. "I am my father's daughter, Chief Gunn."

"As I see," Bothan replied. "What I want to know now is if ye see James is too much of a lad to understand just how unjust this contract is between Brenda and Galwell." Bothan looked at Galwell. "A scheming man such as he does nae deserve to increase his holdings."

Elizabeth didn't answer immediately. The English Queen sat still for a long moment as she tapped one finger against the head of the lion.

"James is anointed King," Elizabeth stated formally. "As such, we shall give him due respect."

Brenda felt her body tensing, every muscle she had drawing tight as the Queen prepared to announce her judgment.

"However." Elizabeth shifted her attention to Galwell. "Chief Gunn is the leader of his clan, and you have accused him of being a thief, My Lord, while he was here to see our royal person."

Bothan tilted his head to one side as he tried to determine where Elizabeth was going.

"If Chief Gunn challenges you over the slight, I will have to allow him the right to defend his honor, and the victor will claim the right to wed Brenda Grant. James will have to accept the outcome."

Two

BRENDA WAS IN SHOCK.

So was Galwell, but his was more of a mixture of horror and surprise. He looked between the Queen and Bothan, his eyes wide in his face as he paled.

"With pleasure," Bothan growled softly.

Galwell gasped and reached for the pommel of the sword hanging from his hip.

He pulled the rapier free, earning a response from the royal guards. They surged forward, but the Queen held up her hand. "Do not interfere. I have said Chief Gunn has the right to demand satisfaction."

The royal guards obeyed their queen, but several of them took a knee in front of her, making it clear they would defend their monarch should the fight come too near her.

Bothan didn't have a sword. His larger broadsword had been left outside the home, taken by the captain of the guard. That fact didn't give him a moment's hesitation, though. He pulled a long dagger from his belt, his lips curving up as he faced off with Galwell.

"Come here, My Lord, and discover how a Scotsman deals with slurs to his name."

"No," Brenda announced. She really wasn't certain when she decided to interrupt, only that she was in motion, on her way to keep the razor-sharp point of Galwell's rapier away from Bothan.

Maddox slipped behind Brenda, pulling her back as the men circled one another. Galwell recovered his poise as he looked at the dagger with a clear gleam of disdain in his eyes.

Brenda shuffled back at Maddox's urging, setting her teeth against her lower lip to remain silent. The rapier was thin but deadly sharp. She'd seen the Italian weapons at court and knew they could kill with only a small wound to the chest or through an eye or the throat. Galwell handled it expertly, proving why the rapier was becoming well known in England. The rapier meant brute strength was no longer the deciding factor in a fight.

It was a weapon that could equalize a man such as Galwell against a larger one like Bothan.

"Come, Scot," Galwell mocked Bothan. "Let's get this finished so I can get on with my wedding."

Bothan was moving slowly, skillfully, as he gauged Galwell's reactions to his movements. Time became Brenda's greatest tormentor as seconds passed by like hours. Everyone in the room knew how grave the consequences would be. They were deathly still, so much so that the first swish of Galwell's rapier through the air made Brenda flinch.

Bothan turned his body sideways so the sharpened end of the weapon sliced through the air where his neck had been. Galwell had extended his arm with the strike, and Bothan made good use of the opening, lifting his leg and kicking out at his opponent. Galwell stumbled back with a grunt, but he twisted, angling the rapier up so the point neatly cut across Bothan's bare thigh when he brought his leg down.

"First blood is mine," Galwell announced.

Declaring his victory was a mistake. In that moment when Galwell was staring at the bright-red blood dripping onto the floor from Bothan's leg, Bothan lunged forward. The rapier wasn't any good in close-quarter fighting. Galwell learned that fact as Bothan smashed him in the face with his elbow. Galwell stumbled back, colliding with the wall. A second later, Bothan had the edge of his dagger against the Englishman's throat.

"Trust a man such as ye," Bothan growled, "to think a little prick is all he needs to claim victory."

Bothan had his arm wedged across Galwell's neck as he pressed the tip of his dagger against the soft spot in his throat. Galwell's court shoes were slipping on the floor as he tried to gain footing and fight, but the effort was laughable when measured against the pure brawn Bothan represented. They couldn't have been more opposite from one another.

"I suggest you yield, Galwell Scrope," Elizabeth advised him after watching the struggle. "Else there will be a large mess for Lord Berkley's staff to clean up."

Galwell's eyes were bulging. His face was red, and he'd pressed his lips together as he fought to deny the truth.

"He's no' worth the stain on me soul," Bothan said in disgust.

Bothan released Galwell and turned to look at the Queen. Elizabeth Tudor's lips lifted into a very small smile of praise.

"You have proven yourself to be more than the savage Lord Scrope claims you are," Elizabeth said. "The matter is settled. Brenda Grant will wed you."

"I will no'," Brenda exclaimed. "You are a queen in yer own right. Ye of all people should understand why I have no wish to wed again."

Bothan's body tensed. Brenda watched the way the muscles in his neck corded. But Elizabeth chuckled softly.

"It seems you have another challenge to face, Chief Gunn," Elizabeth said. The English Queen shifted her attention to Brenda.

"One I am eager for," Bothan declared gruffly. "I mean no insult, ma'am, but there is nothing else in this life that could have enticed me to cross into England except Brenda Grant."

Elizabeth returned her gaze to Bothan. One of her eyebrows rose. Bothan inclined his head, but that was as far as any manner of apology went.

"Your Majesty," Galwell began. The Englishman had taken time to regain his poise. He was standing in perfect courtly stance, his inner leg on display for Elizabeth's enjoyment. "I really must beg you—"

"Indeed, you should beg," Elizabeth interrupted, her tone sharpening, "for you have played me for a fool." The Queen was gripping the armrests of her chair. "Have you not heard me say I am a Prince? Do you dare to judge me so lacking in sense as to have my head turned by pretty words? That I do not require sincerity?"

Galwell tried to speak. "Glorianna—"

"Seal your lips!" Elizabeth snapped. "I would banish you if I did not worry you would only find another innocent to beguile. You and your family have far too much ambition to suit my taste. So you shall remain with my court, sir, in silence until I bid you speak."

Galwell's eyes had bulged again. His complexion was crimson and his forehead bright with perspiration. But he lowered himself in a long reverence before straightening and doing as he was told.

Elizabeth Tudor turned her attention toward Brenda. The English Queen was no longer in the first blush of youth. Brenda realized Elizabeth's face powder hid a great many fine lines. But Elizabeth's blue eyes were still sharp, proving her mind was not feeble.

"I do understand why you do not wish to wed, Mistress Grant," Elizabeth said. "And yet I also understand what it is like to wait long to wed and have fate make such impossible. That is when regret shows its face." The Queen's gaze fluttered momentarily toward the Earl of Leicester.

Brenda started to argue, but the Queen raised her hand once more. Brenda set her teeth into her lower lip.

"Yet you are here because you understand duty," Elizabeth continued. "I have a duty as a Prince to understand why our royal cousin James has decided it is best for you to wed. Good will between our nations benefits us all. I could not tell James I dissolved his wedding contracts."

Galwell perked up, opening his mouth. The Queen proved how observant she was by snapping her fingers at him. "I am your master, sir!"

Galwell inclined his head instantly.

"As I said," Elizabeth spoke once more, "I shall not dissolve the contracts out of respect for our royal cousin. However, I will have to send word to James on the matter of the challenge issued by Lord Scrope toward Chief Gunn and the outcome." Elizabeth aimed her gaze directly at Galwell. "You, sir, have lost the dowry, and I am the witness."

Galwell was shaking. His hands clenched into tight fists, but he lowered himself in obedience.

"I shall also witness your wedding, Brenda Grant." Elizabeth looked at Brenda. "For to do otherwise would be to insult James. As you have proven how much you understand the necessity of performing one's duty, I expect you to argue no further."

Oh, ye understand.

And still Brenda wanted to scream with fury. For the briefest of moments, she'd felt the noose lifted away from her throat with Galwell's defeat. A short-lived relief. Now she was facing Bothan and the certainty of wedding him.

Better than Galwell but still another man, set to do with her as he pleased. One she would wed for the sake of politics. She lowered herself before Elizabeth Tudor, Queen of England, and watched the way the monarch's lips curled into a soft smile.

It was nice to know someone was pleased.

❧

Elizabeth Tudor wasn't planning on drawing matters out. Brenda barely made it back to her pavilion before the Berkleys' Head of House came hurrying after her.

The woman was flushed from running, the front of her apron wrinkled from where she'd grabbed handfuls of it so she might lift it high.

"You must come with me back to the house, Mistress Grant," the woman said. She stopped to drag in a deep breath. "Her Majesty has decreed the wedding shall be tonight. We must get you bathed and dressed, and there is your hair, and…" The woman stopped stammering long enough to draw in another breath. She was flustered, lifting her apron up to dab at her forehead before she lowered the fabric and sent Brenda a look designed to get her moving.

Brenda didn't argue. Doing so would have been pointless. However, the real reason she went with the Head of House was because she desperately needed escape from her thoughts. The only way to do so was to fill her time with enough tasks to blind her to what she would be facing that night.

And there was much to do.

Brenda enjoyed the bath, taking the time to scrub herself from head to toe. She'd likely not gain another opportunity to indulge in a hot bath before she made it to the Highlands.

She had no idea what sort of home Bothan would be taking her to. Not that it mattered. Her first husband had lived in a finer castle than her father had, and she would have traded it for a croft in a moment if such a bargain would have freed her from the abuse of her husband.

Bothan will not abuse ye…

Brenda went still for a moment, closing her eyes and willing herself to believe those words. He'd never given her a reason to suspect he'd raise his hand to her. But men often changed after the wedding and bedding were over.

"Come now…out with you." The Head of House had returned to the room in the back of the kitchen where Brenda was bathing.

The Head of House was carrying a fresh smock and stockings. She smiled as Brenda stood and a maid brought her a length of linen to dry herself with.

"The mistress has opened her own closets for you." The Head of House beamed as she fingered the fine fabric of the smock. "This will feel like heaven against your skin."

Brenda sat on a bench in front of the fire first so her hair would dry. She recalled well how it felt to have servants in the room without a care for her modesty. It was something else she didn't miss. Living at Grant Tower as a widow had been some of the happiest years in her life. Even better than her childhood, for there had been no one telling her about her duty to wed. She had been her own woman.

Yes, but taking a lover didn't satisfy ye…

It was a truth that still puzzled her. Bhaic MacPherson had shown her there was pleasure in bed sport. She'd truthfully though it nothing but a rumor made up to help men seduce women. She had certainly been disappointed after her first wedding night.

Pain she'd expected on that first night. But the reality had been so much more than what her young mind could have grasped.

There had been the physical pain. And then there had been the emotional torment.

It had been a grand match between her and the Campbells. Her father had settled a fine dowry on her, and the Campbells had been eager to ensure they claimed it before her father changed his mind. So she'd wed before turning sixteen.

She shuddered, struggling to shut the doors on the memories. But with the maids in the room and the Head of House so very content being there while Brenda was completely bare, well, Brenda discovered there was no way to ignore the similarities between her last wedding and her next one.

"Here now," the Head of House announced when yet another maid arrived with a tray of food. "Come and eat, for you'll likely get naught else until tomorrow."

It was sage advice, but Brenda only managed a few spoonfuls. The Head of House propped her hands on her hips and contemplated Brenda for a long moment.

"It's not your first marriage," the woman stated.

"I assure ye," Brenda answered, "I was less nervous before my first wedding, for I did not know what was to come."

She locked gazes with the Head of House. They shared a moment of knowledge only women might truly understand.

"Yes, well, best to get on with it," the Head of House offered.

Yes, best to get on with it indeed.

❦

Maddox was fingering his beard, which meant he was deep in thought.

Aye, it was also likely his friend was trying not to

laugh outright and give Bothan a reason to smash him across the jaw.

Bothan gave his captain a warning look, but true to Maddox's nature, the burly Highlander grinned in spite of the warning. Bothan tightened his fingers into a fist and heard his knuckles pop.

"I cannae refuse to wear it," Bothan defended himself. "The English Queen will be insulted if I turn me nose up at her fine wedding clothing."

Maddox swept Bothan from head to toe. "Oh nae, we could no' have her feelings injured."

Bothan growled, but he turned and looked at his reflection. The room he was in had a full-length mirror. Somewhere, there might be one in the twin towers that made up the stronghold of the Gunn chiefdom, but he'd never gone looking for it. Not that he'd been chief very long. Moving into the upper floors of the towers had been enough of an elevation. He still slept in the hall more often than in the master chamber that was his now. If there were luxuries abovestairs with no purpose beyond feeding one's vanities, he'd not taken time to notice. But he admitted he would favor something more than the rough life he'd been living.

Brenda will make yer towers into a home.

He contemplated his reflection with a little more enthusiasm. Aye, she was strong enough to not turn her nose up at his lack of a castle. The first time he'd seen her, she'd nearly singed his eyebrows off with her spirit.

She's wild enough to draw ye upstairs too…

Perhaps he didn't care all too much about the

clothing. What mattered was the wedding. He'd intended to court Brenda, but the truth was he didn't know much about courting either. Now, chasing a lass, that was an altogether different sort of matter. One he knew a bit more about. Brenda had ignited in his embrace. Having the right to touch her meant he'd be able to explore their reaction to one another.

And she'd take his towers and infuse them with the life inside her.

Was he besotted?

Perhaps.

Maddox was toying with his beard again, enjoying the sight of Bothan shrugging his shoulders as he attempted to get the doublet to feel better.

"You'd better get dressed too. You're the one telling me no' to offend the English Queen." Bothan watched Maddox through the mirror. His captain lost his amused look when Bothan pointed at another suit of clothing lying on the bed.

Bothan chuckled at the stream of Gaelic profanity Maddox let out. His burly captain approached the velvet clothing much as he would a snake, reaching for it with two fingers to pluck it off the bed and hold it up while he scowled.

Maddox shook his head.

Bothan grunted at him.

Maddox rolled his eyes. "Only in bloody England would I be reduced to wearing something such as this!"

❧

Brenda had come to England to wed. So there was no reason to continue to allow it to upset her.

But not at court…

Brenda tried to chastise herself over her fear. And there was no way to avoid realizing what the sensation prickling along her limbs was.

Icy…cold…dread.

Brenda struggled to stand still as she was dressed. But the source of her fear was deep inside her mind where the memories of her first wedding were impossible to avoid.

She'd been so very young. Perhaps that was why the memories seemed so sharp. As they rose up from the dark corner where she'd banished them, she felt like she was being sliced anew by the images. Even at sixteen years old she'd known there would be an inspection of her body. But no one had warned her about the bedding.

Ye must not think upon it…

Her strict instructions worked for a bit. Brenda had never been very interested in clothing, but contemplating her reflection allowed her to dwell on something besides the coming night. In an effort to please their queen, the members of the noble family who were hosting her were truly giving the wedding preparations every effort. The dress Brenda wore was of silk and velvet. A stiff slip beneath it known as a farthingale held the skirts out like a bell. The underskirt was revealed by an opening in the front of the overskirt. Pearls were sewn onto the sleeves, and the corset laced tight beneath the bodice ensured her waist was small.

The last time she'd worn something so fine she'd been a maiden.

Brenda snorted. The sound earned her a curious look from one of the maids. But the lady of the house had arrived.

"Enough now," Lady Berkley instructed her staff. "She appears quite ready."

The maids lowered themselves before heading for the door. Lady Berkley looked at the supper tray Brenda had barely touched.

"This is not your first marriage," Lady Berkley remarked. "Maidenly nerves should not affect your appetite."

The lady of the house came forward, sweeping Brenda from head to toe. But it wasn't done coldly. No, Brenda detected a hint of maternal affection.

"Thank ye for the dress," Brenda replied sincerely. "And for the attention of yer staff."

The maids had done Brenda's hair, weaving ribbons as well as pushing pins with pearls attached to them into it. The finished effect was quite pleasing. If Brenda were in the mood to enjoy it. Even if marrying wasn't to her taste, she admitted to enjoying the way the staff worked toward making sure she was presented well.

"I would think wedding one of your own countrymen would put your mind at ease," Lady Berkley continued.

"It does," Brenda said. "It is wedding at court I have no stomach for."

Lady Berkley drew in a stiff breath. Brenda watched the flash of memory in the other woman's eyes.

"I understand," Lady Berkley said. "Best to hope your husband concludes matters swiftly."

Lady Berkley was doing her best, but there really wasn't anything to be done for the matter. Court weddings meant beddings witnessed by any and all who wanted to follow the bride and groom back to their chambers.

It was a revolting custom.

Oh yes, Brenda understood it had begun as a way of ensuring men did not accuse their brides of being impure. More than one wedding had been arranged to end a bloody conflict between rival families or clans. And more than one of those unions had seen the groom attempt to discard his unwanted bride by claiming she had not been a maiden or that they had not consummated the union. So a witness from each family at the consummation was the best insurance against such allegations.

At court, though, the custom had evolved into something far worse than two unknown witnesses sitting behind screens. Now, the bedding was often a gathering of the groom's drunken friends who leered and shouted vulgarities. Brenda recalled it well.

In spite of how hard she had tried to bury the memories.

It was strange the power the recollections had over her. She hadn't feared anything in a very long time. Once being widowed, she had become her own woman, and yet now she felt perspiration on her forehead as the bells from the chapel started to toll.

She would not have it.

Brenda stood up and turned to face Lady Berkley. The noblewoman sent her a look of approval.

"That's the way of it," Lady Berkley said. "Refuse

to be broken by the idea. Do what you must, and do it quickly. All in the interest of being able to banish it to the past and know it is finished. "

Well said…

Brenda left the chamber with Lady Berkley's words ringing in her ears. Outside the doors to the chamber, several younger girls waited. Their eyes sparkled with anticipation. They reverenced Brenda before one handed her a bunch of wildflowers tied with a ribbon. The girl giggled shyly before she and her companions took up their positions around Brenda.

They were young and innocent. To them, marriage was a time of wearing pretty gowns and sitting at a banquet table filled with delights. They would be kept busy with discussing details of the ceremony and entertainment to be presented at the banquet. The wine would flow, and the music would make it simple for the hours to fly past. Their mothers would have them all safely abovestairs in their beds by the time it came to the bedding ceremony.

Brenda had once been just like them.

Born to a good family, one that kept her closeted. She pressed her lips tightly together against a new wave of bitterness. Oh aye, she'd been a proper lamb on the way to the slaughter at her first wedding. Tonight, during the banquet, the younger girls would all be sent away under the guise of protecting them from men who had indulged in too much wine. Those younger girls wouldn't be there to see the way the celebration turned ugly as the guests began to taunt the groom with vulgar suggestions. Nannies and maids wouldn't dare breathe a word of the matter to their young charges for fear they'd lose their well-paying positions.

Well, ye aren't a lamb now...

No, she'd grown into a she-wolf. Brenda had heard it whispered as she moved through the passageways of her home. It was meant as a slur, yet she embraced it. Allowed it to ring in her ears, drowning out the tolling of the bell. Somehow, she made it to the entrance of the chapel. The girls all hushed as they spied the Queen of England. Brenda sank down into a deep reverence along with them before Elizabeth raised them up.

She-wolf...

Brenda lifted her chin and strode forward. Let Bothan see her as she was, for she would not be transforming into a meek and obedient wife.

❧

The English court had a reputation of enjoying revelry.

Brenda watched as Elizabeth Tudor's nobles danced and feasted. And drained their goblets over and over. She wondered if any of them even tasted the fine wine the Berkleys had provided for the occasion. Lord Berkley himself was the very image of the jovial host. His cheeks were red from how much he'd smiled, and his hat came off his head every few minutes as he proudly oversaw the entire affair, greeting everyone who ventured near him.

"I doubt most of them even know who married," Bothan spoke beside her. "Or care. It seems more important that they have a reason to feast and celebrate."

Her new groom wasn't any more pleased with the

festivities than she was. He'd ripped open the top few buttons on his doublet and sat with one elbow braced on the tabletop as the musicians played and the nobles of Elizabeth's court danced. His wine goblet was left untouched after only a disgusted look toward the fine glassware.

Bothan didn't know the songs, and Brenda had only a dim memory of some of them. However, it seemed not to matter to anyone that the bride and groom sat at the table instead of enjoying the festivities. Brenda picked up her own wine glass and drank deeply to still the tremors shaking her as the candles began to burn lower and she watched the nannies begin to remove their young charges from the hall. She could feel the mood changing, like the very air was becoming soiled. A servant filled her wine glass again, and she brought it back to her lips.

Bothan reached between them and plucked the wine goblet from her fingers. "Are ye truly so displeased with yer circumstances, Brenda?"

Brenda turned her attention toward him. Somehow, she'd forgotten the way the man affected her. Consumed by her own thoughts, she'd not really given him much of her focus. Now, though, he was so very close to her, and his blue gaze was just as piercing as before. There was a flutter in her belly as her breath caught.

"Would ye truly prefer Galwell Scrope sitting here beside ye?" Bothan demanded.

His jaw was drawn tight, irritation clearly evident on his face.

"I do not care for court weddings." Brenda didn't care for how much of an admission her words were.

Bothan's eyes narrowed as he heard the emotion edging her tone. "I am not a child, Bothan." Brenda had lowered her voice.

He tilted his head to one side and leveled a stern look at her.

"Ye declared to one and all that ye would have me, and I am past the age of thinking such a declaration is something I might trust as a future filled with happiness."

She was being blunt. Most people didn't deal well with straight talk. It might have been wiser to keep her thoughts to herself, yet some impulse had sent them past her lips.

She looked away, reaching for a piece of fruit sitting on her plate. Bothan captured her hand, closing his own around it.

He is so much larger than ye...

Brenda shuddered. It was another of those responses she held no power against when it came to Bothan. When he touched her, she felt the connection more deeply than she'd ever considered possible.

"Ye can be certain I will have us on the road north at first light, Brenda," he assured her.

She looked back at him, drawn by the tone of his voice. She'd heard him tease her. Recalled the way he'd boasted to her. Yet this was something different. A familiarity she had no idea what to do with.

Except shy away from.

Brenda tugged on her hand. Being in contact with him unsettled her, to say the least, and she needed her composure to survive the coming night. Bothan's eyes narrowed.

"Ye deny me, Brenda?" he asked softly. "Ye are me wife."

The certainty in his voice made her stomach clench.

"Oh yes," she snapped back. "Yer chattel. Well then, since the courtship has ended, let us get to the matter ye are truly interested in."

She flattened her hands on the tabletop and pushed the heavy chair she was sitting in back. The pages behind her were caught by surprise, but they recovered quickly. They pulled her chair well away from the table, making Bothan release her hand or risk being seen fighting with her. She knew anger was an unwise thing to let rage in her for it would make her foolish, but the flare of her temper gave her the strength to charge into what was eating away at her soul.

Best done quickly…

Truer words had never been spoken.

The English nobles sent up a cheer as she stood and turned for the side of the high ground on which the head table was positioned. Bothan tried to follow her, but several of the men caught him at the bottom of the steps. They were soaked in wine, hooting and shouting as they dragged him away.

Brenda caught only a glimpse of Bothan growling at them before a flurry of women in silk skirts and starched neck ruffs surrounded her. They chuckled softly as they escorted her toward the bridal chamber. The musicians followed, along with servants with trays of food and pitchers of cider.

Her temper failed to keep the dread from her as her clothing was stripped away by the women amid their laughter and enjoyment.

"Your groom is a beast."

"I wonder if his member measures up to the rest of him?"

"Is it true that Scots prefer to mount their wives from behind?"

"I wager he'll not last past twenty thrusts."

"I take your bet!"

Brenda wanted to scream, but she doubted any of them would have noticed. Instead they tugged on the laces, keeping her corset closed. Once the garment was unlaced completely, they tugged it down her arms and pulled her smock up and over her head.

"You're pretty as can be."

"Best we get you into bed before the men arrive with the groom."

But Brenda wasn't ready just yet. Someone pushed her down onto a stool as some of the ladies plucked the pins from her hair and brushed it out.

"Drink up," a woman in a huge neck ruff said as she tried to press a goblet into Brenda's hands. "Better to be merry while you might be."

Brenda was certain her throat was so tight not even a drop of the cider might pass. The women had no mercy in them, or perhaps it might be better to say they simply didn't think she minded that she was bare and they clothed. Once her hair was lying across her back in a simmering curtain, they all circled around her to inspect her. One even reached out to pinch her nipples into sharp points.

Brenda recoiled. "Do not."

The lady lifted her hands in surrender. "As you like, dear. But men like taut nipples. Mark my words. Pinch them up, and your husband will finish in half the time!"

There was a round of laughter as the others nodded in agreement. Brenda ducked between two of them, heading for the large bed and something to help her recover her modesty. The bed ropes groaned as Brenda landed on the bed hard. She grabbed the bedding and pulled it up to her chin.

She made it none too soon, either. The men were heard coming down the passageway. The door was kicked in to the delight of the waiting women. They let out excited cheers as the musicians played and the servants poured more cider.

Brenda was certain she was near to going mad.

"Enough!" Bothan roared.

"He's eager to get to his bride!" one of the men shouted.

"She's ready for you!" someone else yelled.

A moment later, two of the women grabbed the bedding and yanked it from Brenda's grasp. There was a swish and the bedding was tossed aside, leaving Brenda grabbing one of the pillows and hugging it.

"Go and get her!" a man urged Bothan.

Bothan was clad in only his shirt. He looked at the horde of English nobles waiting eagerly for him to join her in the bed. Brenda gasped as one of the women near the bed grabbed the pillow and tried to pull it from Brenda's grasp.

"Get out!" Bothan roared. He wasn't planning on being ignored this time. "Or so help me Christ, I'll break every right arm in sight!"

There was a fight to get through the doorway first.

Bothan's men, who had managed to keep up with their chief, began to toss velvet-clad men toward the exit. It turned into a brawl that the musicians tried to play through until one of Bothan's men grabbed an instrument and broke it across his thigh. A woman smirked and another one fell over as the courtiers fled from Bothan.

Brenda stared at the panic, blinking as she tried to believe her own eyes. As her brain processed the sight of her new husband kicking the last man in the rump because he was moving too slowly, her chest loosened up, allowing breath to flow freely.

"How do these bastards think themselves more civilized than us in the Highlands?" Bothan demanded on his way back into the bedchamber. He grunted in disgust as he reached down and yanked the bedding off the floor. There was a snap as he raised it high and shook it so it unfolded in the air above her. He let it settle down over her before he snorted and went to one of the tables where a servant had left a pitcher behind in his haste to escape the threat. Bothan lifted it up and took a huge swallow from the side of it. Once he lowered the pitcher, he looked at the trays of food sitting on the tables.

"They truly meant to make an evening's entertainment out of our consummation?" Bothan muttered, revolted. "I will never understand the English."

"The Scottish court did the same at my first wedding," Brenda said. There really was no purpose in saying it aloud. But relief swept through her as she said it. The bedding was cold from having been on the floor, but she clutched it close to hide how badly she was shaking.

Bothan turned an incredulous look toward her. "And yer husband permitted such?"

Brenda felt the bitterness rising up inside her again. "He enjoyed it very much."

Brenda refused to cry. She'd made an oath that night to never shed tears over the matter again. Tonight, though, she had to fight to blink away the water flooding her eyes. Success gave her a much-needed boost to her confidence. She steadied her nerves and looked at Bothan, locking gazes with him.

"Thank you for sending them out."

❧

Bothan wasn't normally given to moments when he felt like his mind couldn't process what he heard. But he was struggling with what his new bride had said. There was a pinched look on her face and a glint in her eyes that told him she'd spoken true. Never once had he witnessed her trembling, at least until that very moment.

It sickened him.

God, he hoped her first husband was in hell or at least purgatory. The man had some sins to atone for.

"Ye were young when ye wed the first time," Bothan said. Brenda had represented something he wanted to claim, and he'd made certain to learn about her before setting out to win her. "Too young, as I recall."

Brenda didn't look at him. Instead she was looking past him as she pressed her lips into a hard line. She was fighting to maintain her composure. And he didn't care to know it was his touch she was mustering her courage against.

"Sixteen is considered old enough by many," she replied stiffly.

Brenda shuddered. Bothan watched the way memory gripped her. But she steeled her resolve and looked straight at him. "It does not matter now. I am not a child any longer."

She lay back, making his temper flare. He moved closer to the bed. Brenda had looked away as she waited, but when he didn't join her, she rolled her head toward him.

She had courage. But the look of resignation in her eyes chilled him to the bone.

"Ye're right, we do nae know one another," Bothan said, reminding her of what she'd said at the high table as their vows were being celebrated.

For all that he'd followed her to England to free her, Bothan realized he had not ever felt truly protective of her until that moment.

Now it was a powerful need washing through him, leaving him with a new, deeper understanding of the idea of winning her.

But where to start?

He sat on the edge of the bed, watching the way she eyed him.

"This is no' the way I want to claim ye, Brenda." As far as a beginning, Bothan wasn't sure it was correct. She contemplated him, clearly as uncertain as he was about how to proceed.

"Ye have the rights ye followed me to get," she informed him.

He let out a little sound of frustration. "I wanted to court ye. Ye may be very sure I've never written a letter to a woman before."

She looked away, a delicate blush appearing on her cheeks.

His lips twitched in response. She was not unmoved by him.

But they were strangers. He tightened his grip on his discipline, vowing not to ruin his chance with her by acting impulsively. If he treated her like chattel, the word would be forever between them.

"As for having rights to ye," he continued, "the English Queen provided me a way to end the royal order given by James, so I will no' quibble too much over the details. It's the truth I can no' think of a better solution. She's clever, Elizabeth Tudor."

Brenda returned her attention to him. Bothan enjoyed the way their gazes locked. Perhaps he was seeing what he wanted, but it seemed a small step in the correct direction to have her looking at him instead of looking away and sealing herself against his advances.

Aye, it was a way to begin, at least.

"It seems we need to become less strange to one another," he whispered.

He reached out and fingered a lock of her unbound hair. Something stirred inside him. The strength of it set him back for a moment because it was deeper than lust or longing. The same need to have more from her than he'd ever had from any other woman, leaving him uncertain as he tried to decide how to proceed. She was just like the wine glass someone had placed in front of him at the banquet, delicate and full of something he was certain would intoxicate him.

But he had to be careful to handle the glass stem with care, or it would snap and spill the contents, leaving him with naught but the scent of what he craved and no way to retrieve it.

Bothan stood before he went any further. "We're leaving at first light. Sleep while ye can."

Her eyes narrowed.

"I came to court ye, Brenda, no' have ye bound by duty to surrender yer body to me." He realized he'd never meant anything more in his life.

She sat up, hugging the bedding tightly to her chest. "And if this is the only way I will give myself to ye?"

A spark entered her eyes as she spoke. It was a damned fucking relief to see it too. Bothan felt his lips rising into a grin. He leaned over, threading his fingers into her flowing hair so he could cup her head. He captured the little gasp she let out with his lips, pressing his own down onto hers in a kiss. Bothan felt her shift in uncertainty. He held her firmly as he moved his lips over hers, coaxing her passion to life.

Brenda didn't disappoint him. She let out a little sound that was a mixture of frustration and delight before she was reaching for him. He sat on the bed so she could flatten her palms on his chest. She was kissing him back, softly at first and then with a spark of passion that stirred his member. He indulged in the moment, savoring the feeling of passion.

He wanted more…

But he pulled away, enjoying the look of bewilderment on her face.

"I will win yer trust, or ye can have an annulment," Bothan promised her.

Perhaps he was three times a fool for leaving her. For certain, there would be plenty of men who'd advise him to have the matter of their union settled then and there so the dowry was his without dispute.

Somehow, he realized it wouldn't be enough. Brenda had drawn him to her for more than the gain it would bring his clan, and he wasn't going to settle for less. Even if he wasn't completely sure what it was he craved from her.

"Good night to ye, Brenda."

She blinked, her eyes wide with frustration. But she clutched at the bedding, her knuckles turning white as her reason returned and the passion ebbed.

"I will nae have ye blinded," he informed her gruffly. "Ye will come to me and know full well ye choose me."

⁓

Maddox looked up as Bothan came through the doors into the receiving chamber. The rooms themselves were all one large area with doors between the bedchamber and the receiving chamber, which was nearest to the passageway.

Maddox had pulled a trundle bed from where it was stored beneath a cupboard. His captain lifted his head and fixed him with a curious look.

"What are ye doing out here?" Maddox inquired.

Bothan grabbed his kilt from where one of the noblemen who had stripped him on his way into the chamber had left it. He shook it out before lying down and pulling some of the wool over his head. Maddox didn't take the hint. His man kept eyeing him, as his lips curled up into a grin that begged Bothan to bury his fist in it.

"Proving my worth," Bothan growled when he realized Maddox wasn't going to give him any peace.

Maddox scoffed at him. "I did no' think ye needed to be told how to go about proving yerself to yer bride, but I could give ye a few bits of advice on the matter of pleasing her—" His captain stopped talking because he was choking on his mirth. Bothan raised his head and glared at Maddox.

"What Brenda needs is to trust me," Bothan insisted. "Something that will no' happen if I overwhelm her. As soon as passion is satisfied, she'll see me as naught more than another man who looks to twist her into submission. Taking what I want with no regard for what she might have chosen for herself."

Maddox abandoned his smirking amusement. A serious look took over the man's features. "Aye, well, ye knew when ye followed her here that her past is no' a happy one when it comes to men. The Earl of Morton treated her as a whore."

"He's lucky he's dead," Bothan responded.

"No' to her he is nae," Maddox replied as he lay back down. "It would be a lot simpler if the man might be killed. For now, ye are battling a ghost locked inside Brenda's mind."

More like a demon. Bothan had been labeled one himself, but the Earl of Morton had been far more deserving of the insult.

The man had done truly evil deeds and allowed

them to be committed to those who had the misfortune to fall under his power. Young James might be a lad in need of life experience, but he was far better than the regent who had ruled Scotland in his name. Once the Earl of Morton had been removed from power, it hadn't taken long for Morton's enemies to catch up with him.

Bothan grunted and rolled onto his side. He'd had his fill of royalty, even if Elizabeth Tudor had given him what he wanted. Or at least part of what he wanted.

He craved more, though.

The sight of Brenda lying so submissively in bed turned his stomach. That wasn't the woman who had snared his attention at a May Day festival with her brazenness.

Well, he had her now. It was something to set his attention on as he lay back down to sleep.

Aye, she was his. So long as he could find a way to win her.

Bothan grinned at last. Winning what he set his mind on was something he knew a fair amount about. Brenda had best get sleep while she might because he was going to give her only until daybreak before renewing his suit.

❧

Bothan was true to his word.

It was barely first light when Brenda woke to the sound of Bothan and his captain moving beyond the curtain that separated the bedchamber from the receiving room. Even with the window shutters still closed, she could see the light changing with the rising of the sun.

She smiled.

Joy filled her to the point of bursting as she flipped the bedding back and rolled out of the bed. She looked back at the wide expanse of the bed, realizing her host had given her such a large bed because the idea had been for her to share it with Bothan.

The man was very large.

Brenda reached for her stockings and sat down to pull them on.

Ye should not think about him…

And yet, as she tied a garter in place around the top of one of her stockings, Brenda discovered herself feeling very kindly toward Bothan.

Her husband.

She pulled the second stocking into place as she contemplated that idea.

Well, he wasn't truly her husband, for the union was unconsummated. Advice she'd once given to Jane Stanley came to mind as she reached for her boots.

"Ye may try him and see if he is to yer liking…with no one the wiser because ye are no' a maiden…"

Her clit decided to heat in response to the idea.

She stood and began to dress faster in an effort to banish her thoughts with work. Her quick motions made more noise though.

"Come out when ye are ready, Brenda, me men will have the horses saddled," Bothan called through the curtain. "I have had me fill of England."

"As have I," she answered.

Bothan made a sound of agreement in the back of

his throat. Brenda finished dressing, slowing down only long enough to ensure she tied everything in place with a good knot because Bothan's voice promised her he intended to ride hard and long toward their home.

Something that pleased her well.

He pleased ye last night too…

Her cheeks heated as the memory of Bothan's kiss fill her thoughts. She seemed to have no control when it came to her responses to him. Which only reminded her of her suggestion to Jane. It was true that she wasn't a maiden. Which afforded her time to decide what to do.

Are ye really thinking to try him?

Brenda didn't care for the surge of heat the idea sent through her. It would be like embracing madness if she gave in to her impulses. And foolish, for if any of his men took note of it, she'd be stuck wed to him, her days of being her own woman finished.

So she would simply not allow him to kiss her again.

With her choice firmly in mind, she turned her back on the fine bedchamber. She went happily, eagerly toward the road where there would be few comforts. Yet the sun was rising with the promise of a fine warm day. Winter was well behind them now, and the snow would be melting in the Highlands.

No, there would be no further kissing. No one had everything. Her cousin Symon had pledged to never make her a match. Now that Symon was wed, Brenda didn't need to shoulder the responsibility of ensuring the clan had a clear line of succession.

No. She might be her own woman at long last.

Bothan would simply have to accept her choice in the matter.

❧

"Your Majesty." Robert Dudley lowered himself before the Queen of England.

Elizabeth was up early, as was her practice. She was sitting at a table set up in the garden of the estate, the morning sun shining in her hair and making it look like rubies.

"Join me, Robin." Elizabeth indicated the chair across from her. "It seems too long since we have broken our fast together."

Robert slid into the chair, feeling like a weight was being lifted off his shoulders. Beyond them, the nobles of her court were beginning to stir. The servants were up, attending to the task of getting their masters ready to see their monarch.

Somewhere, musicians began to play from where Lord Berkley had set them up behind some greenery. The meal was simple, fresh summer fruit and cheese along with the first bread of the day. Elizabeth reached for her small beer as horses cried out from farther down on the estate.

"I do believe our Scottish guests are intent on departing immediately," Robert informed her.

Elizabeth smiled over the rim of her goblet, not a fancy glass one but a sturdy silver one. "Chief Gunn struck me as a wise man."

Robert contemplated her for a moment. Elizabeth abandoned her tight control and smiled at him as freely as she had done when they were much, much younger.

"I know there were no witnesses to the consummation, Robin," Elizabeth said softly. "Allow me to see Brenda Grant indulged in her desire to be her own woman without the shackles of duty attached to her."

Elizabeth's smile faded. For a moment, she looked every single one of her years, fatigue wrinkling her brow and darkening her eyes. Robert enjoyed the moment, reaching out to place his hand over hers since they were in private. Or at least as private as the Queen of England might ever be. Cat Ashley was busy working a needle through a piece of fine linen off to his right, her eyes on her needlework. Two yeomen of the guard were stationed six feet away with pole axes, their gazes straight ahead of them.

"Young James will have to be content," Elizabeth muttered as she lifted her gaze and looked into Robert's eyes.

Her eyes brightened as he felt his heart fill with happiness. Aye, Robert understood her well enough. There were many things they had both done because they had to. And then there was the love between them which had to be guarded carefully lest it be strangled by their positions. Elizabeth had seen her opportunity to allow Brenda Grant to return to a life where she had more choices than a queen was afforded.

Elizabeth Tudor, Queen of England, would never be his wife, but Elizabeth was now and forever his truest love.

❧

Bothan pushed hard for the border. Sleeping on English soil was something he wanted to avoid. His horses had been bred for strength and took to the journey without hesitation. His men were eager for their homeland as well.

It wasn't that he forgot Brenda.

No, it was more a matter of thinking she had more reason than any of them to wish to be gone from England that made him press on. His bride didn't disappoint him, either. She kept pace with them, even as they rode into the fading light and continued when a full moon rose to illuminate the road.

In the end, they slept only because the horses required the rest, rolling up in their kilts and lying on the ground.

By first light, Bothan discovered himself wondering if he'd pushed Brenda too far. But his bride was heading toward the river they'd camped near to wash without any indication she had been abused by the demands he'd placed on her.

Not that he had addressed the demands he truly wanted her to satisfy.

"How is that leg?" Maddox suddenly asked.

Bothan tilted his head to one side, giving his captain a hard look. Maddox surprised him with a wide smile. One that showed off the two missing teeth in his mouth. "Just seems, well, seeing the way Mistress Grant is intent on ignoring ye, perhaps ye might need a wee bit of tending for that wound ye suffered in getting her released from her contract with Galwell Scrope."

Bothan narrowed his eyes. "Ye want me to whimper...like a pup?"

Maddox shrugged. "Lassies like puppies. Put them in their laps and cuddle them, they do." His captain winked at him. "Rub them from head to tail and straight across the belly."

Maddox was grinning at him, tempting Bothan to bury his fist in the man's face.

"I'd no' be able to live with meself if I—did something—so befitting a lad—" Bothan lost concentration as Brenda stopped by one of the horses. She reached up and stroked the mare's neck.

A long, sure motion of her hand against the animal's skin.

Christ.

Maddox was choking on his amusement, rocking on his heels as he looked up to the sky in an effort to ignore the sharp glare Bothan tried to cut him with.

"Just seems like all the pair of ye need is a little less distance between ye." Maddox nodded with a gleam in his eyes. "Once ye're together…well…nature can take its course."

"Go and check the horses," Bothan growled. "I'll handle the courting of me own wife, thank you kindly."

"Better to let her handle ye…" Maddox got in a parting jab before he ambled away toward the horses.

There was naught Bothan wanted more.

And yet he realized he did indeed want something more than a victory won through overwhelming her.

But Maddox was correct in one matter. Bothan and Brenda had something they needed to discuss.

And Bothan had never been a man to avoid a challenge.

❧

They rode hard again but stopped before the sun set. Brenda slid from her saddle with a little sigh of relief. She knew how to ride, but so many hours in the saddle had her backside aching. Her skin felt like leather, dry and caked with dirt. One of Bothan's retainers took her horse, offering her the opportunity to venture to the river's edge and wash.

The water was cold.

Very cold.

Brenda didn't let the chill stop her from cupping handfuls of it and splashing it onto her face. During the day, she'd bound her hair up in a length of fabric to keep the dust out of it. Now, she unwound the linen and used it to scrub her face and neck. Her skin was chilled, but it tingled too, leaving her delighted by the clean feeling.

Reaching into her pocket, she withdrew a comb. The sun was still on the horizon, promising her enough light to finish cleaning up. Reaching into her hair, she dug out the pins. After two days, her braids were fuzzy. Working the comb through the stands took patience, but her hair eventually rose into a fluffy cloud because of how long it had been braided.

"Ye're a stunning woman," Bothan said from behind her.

Brenda jumped. The sound of the water had filled her ears, making it possible for Bothan to approach without her realizing it.

"I'd no' allow ye to be at risk," he informed her as he stood. He'd clearly been watching her for some time, crouched low near the tree line, the muted colors of his plaid helping him to blend in with the foliage.

"Ye know ye are fetching though," he continued, his gaze on her unbound hair.

"A fact that has brought me naught but grief," she replied as she stood and came up the riverbank. Sensation was prickling along her spine, some sort of awareness of him and the fact that they were very much alone.

Bothan met her before she'd come very far, standing in her path with his feet braced shoulder-width apart. She was no stranger to men, and yet he struck her as harder and larger than any others.

Stop being childish…he is but a man…

Fine advice, only she couldn't seem to make herself heed it. With Bothan, she responded, her composure slipping from her grip like grains of sand. The harder she tried to maintain her hold, the more it escaped through her fingers.

He reached out for her hair. Brenda felt her breath catch as a jolt of need went through her belly. She stepped back, earning a scowl from Bothan.

"Why do ye act as though me touch is something that revolts ye?" Bothan asked gruffly. "Ye enjoyed me kiss full well."

"Only after ye insisted," Brenda said, defending herself.

Bothan's eyes narrowed. "Ye have no' even tried to like me, woman."

She hadn't, but Brenda refused to ponder her reasoning. Instead she raised her chin and leveled a firm gaze at him. "I have no reason to long to be chattel again. Me uncle granted me freedom to be my own woman."

She'd meant her words to be a hard refusal of

anything further. It was the truth that she was trying to anger him enough to be disgusted with her stubbornness. Instead, he tilted his head to one side, his expression softening. After a moment of contemplation, he extended his hand, offering it to her.

"What are ye thinking, Bothan Gunn?" she demanded. At least Brenda had intended her words to be sharp and cutting. Instead her tone had turned husky and breathless as anticipation of being in contact with his flesh had undermined her efforts to push him away.

"I'm thinking what I found worthy of leaving me home in order to court ye was yer nature," he replied. "If it was a fair face I'd wanted in a bride, ye can be certain I might have found one among the offers I have from men who would have an alliance with the Gunns."

Brenda felt her breath catch again. This time emotion was surging through her, one she really couldn't name, and yet she knew without a doubt that she liked it.

Liked it a lot.

Bothan knew it too. He read her indecision in her face as though they had some connection between them that went far beyond the normal understanding between a man and a woman.

An intimacy…

Brenda stepped back, unwilling to allow him so close to her thoughts. They were the only thing she might never be forced to share.

"A contracted bride does nae have the right to refuse me touch once I have fulfilled me duty in wedding her," Bothan continued.

"I told ye firmly I had no wish to wed ye," Brenda countered.

His face darkened. "Aye, ye did. Plenty of others heard it too."

She'd been harsh. Brenda felt her cheeks heat in shame. She knew well how deeply unkindness cut. Declaring to one and all at the English court that she did not want to wed Bothan had been overly harsh.

Bothan's gaze touched on her cheeks, his lips twitching up in approval over the color staining her face. He beckoned her with his fingers.

"Choose me, Brenda," Bothan encouraged her. His tone was dark with promise. "Ye went to Bhaic MacPherson because ye were no' content with the way yer husband had left ye unsatisfied. It was no' affection that sent ye into his bed but passion and a need to discover whether women might feel pleasure during bed sport."

"Ye would have me, knowing I willingly bedded one of yer fellow lairds?" she asked.

He lowered his hand. The motion sent a shaft of fear through her. Had she said the one thing he could not accept?

"A timid, submissive bride I might have contracted with easily enough," he replied. "I came back for ye...for the passion I saw in yer eyes. The passion that would no' allow ye to live yer life without tasting it. I want that passion in our union."

Brenda was captivated by his response. So much so she didn't realize Bothan was closing the distance between them. She tipped her head back to maintain eye contact with him. There was a flicker of intent in his eyes that enthralled her.

"And I will have ye choose to give it to me," he rasped out as he closed his arms around her.

He didn't kiss her though.

Brenda gasped as Bothan slipped around her. Oh, he had her sure enough, his larger arms wrapping behind her, securing her to his body as she shuddered. The contact between their bodies was a hard blow to her weakening composure, like the sun hitting the ice on a roof. At some point, it would crack, and all the water would flow out from beneath it.

"I will no' take ye, Brenda," Bothan whispered against her ear.

She tried to break his hold, earning a chuckle from him. Behind her, his chest rumbled with the sound while she felt his heat warming her as though she'd been freezing without the contact.

"But I promise," Bothan continued, "I will tempt ye."

He buried his face in the cloud of her hair. She heard him inhale deeply as his hands rubbed her from shoulder to elbow in sure strokes. Delight spread out over her skin. Beneath her bodice, her nipples drew into tight little points that begged to be released from the hard confines of the garment.

Somehow she'd forgotten how nice it was to be touched. Or maybe she hadn't ever known and was learning it now.

With him.

"I do nae want a girl for me wife, Brenda," he continued softly. "Ye are a woman, hardened by life's circumstances." Bothan lifted his head for a moment. "I am sorry for yer past, but I admire the fact that ye've chosen to live in spite of the harshness ye have suffered."

"I will no' let them break me." Perhaps she should have kept her words to herself. But they were across her lips before she'd really thought about them. The truth was she didn't want to waste time on contemplation.

No, she wanted to sink into the wave of sensation Bothan was stirring in her with his touch. Brenda tilted her head to the side, and Bothan needed no further encouragement. He pressed his lips to the tender skin of her neck, sending a ripple of pleasure down her body. Buried between the folds of her slit, her little pearl was awakening. Brenda knew what it craved, and she knew full well Bothan could give it to her.

Did she dare?

It wasn't truly a matter of what she thought she wanted. Her body was hungry for passion. For all that Bhaic had shown her the pleasure there might be in bed sport, Bothan touched something deeper inside her. A wildness that craved only one thing, and that was to be taken so very completely that there was nothing except the moment.

"But I will tame ye, Brenda," Bothan declared softly. He seemed to know her thoughts.

"Ye will...nae..." Her denial didn't leave her mouth with the hard tone she'd intended.

No, instead she sounded breathless as Bothan slipped his hand into her bodice and boldly cupped her breast. Brenda arched, unable to stop herself from reacting. His hand felt perfect there holding her breast. Pleasure surged through her, drowning her thoughts. What was left was the churning need flicking in her insides.

"I will," he promised as he gripped her breast and kissed her neck again.

This time he bit her. Bared his teeth and nipped her

skin. The little touch of pain broke through another barrier she hadn't realized she had. Now, her instincts were rising up, shoving aside everything she'd decided she wanted from life in favor of what she craved.

Wildness…

It was a living force inside her. Bothan felt it, sensed it. What filled her with anticipation was the way he acted upon it. He'd pulled them around so his back was to a large section of rock. Reaching down, he grasped her skirt and raised it up as he lifted one foot and placed it on a smaller rock in front of them. The evening air touched her bare thighs a moment before he was hooking her knee, lifting her foot off the ground, and opening her thighs as he dropped her leg over his.

"And ye will enjoy me showing ye the merit of being me wife," Bothan declared boldly.

She lifted her eyelids, wondering just when she'd allowed them to slide close. The action afforded her a view of Bothan pulling her skirts up once more. This time, he flattened his right hand on the inside of her bare thigh while holding her against him with his left arm.

"I smell yer heat, lass…" he muttered gruffly as he stroked the inside of her leg.

It should have been impossible to enjoy a touch so much.

The level of intensity made no sense, and yet Brenda couldn't deny it. She was arching once more, leaning back against Bothan as he cupped her slit.

"So…wet…" he told her darkly. "But I will nae claim ye…no' yet…"

He stroked her slit. Brenda felt her breath catch.

Her clit was throbbing so hard she felt like climax would take only a slight touch.

Bothan denied her that.

Instead he teased her, drawing his fingers along the outside edge of her slit.

"Did ye think I would give ye release quickly?" he asked as he rimmed the opening of her body with one fingertip.

"Stop toying with me," she begged.

He offered her a soft sound of amusement before pressing his fingertip inside her. She jerked, her hips flexing toward him, attempting to push more of his length into her.

"Ye can be sure I plan to play with ye, lass." Bothan drew his finger up her slit until it was poised over her clit.

Brenda let out a little moan.

"And there is the reason why," Bothan muttered darkly against her ear. He flicked his fingertip across her clit. "I want to hear the sounds ye make when my touch pleasures ye."

He renewed the motion on her clit, and there was no way she could have contained the sound of her pleasure. The level of it was simply too high, too intense. Bothan held her secure to his body as he rubbed her clit, pressing down on the little bundle of nerve endings while she was being driven closer and closer to the edge of madness.

There was no hesitating on her part. She went gladly into the storm of need. Bothan was the only solid thing in her world as he pressed her toward the final moment of rapture. It burst inside her, burning her with an intensity that left her mouth open, but no sound came from her because every muscle she had was clenching tight in that instant of pleasure. She was twisting and turning as it surged through her, racing up her body from the point at the top of her slit where his hand rested.

Brenda ended up lax and spent in his embrace. Without his support, she would have collapsed into a heap at his feet. Instead, he held her tight to his body as he sent her skirts down to cover her.

"Ye enjoy me touch well," Bothan said a few moments later. "The ride home will give ye time to accept our union."

Brenda blinked. Her mind didn't want to do anything more than curl up and sleep. He'd reduced her to a boneless heap, and her temper stirred.

"I do nae want a husband." She lifted her leg off his and moved away from him.

Bothan let her go, but gaining her freedom only allowed her to notice just how weak her knees were.

Brenda turned to send him a glare, only to fear his keen gaze saw far too much of the weakness she was trying so hard to keep hidden from him. The tops of her thighs were wet, and his lips were curved into a smug, male grin.

"Ye want me," he informed her gruffly. "As yer lover."

Bothan lifted his fingers to his nose. She watched the way he inhaled the scent of her body from the fluid lingering on his fingers. His eyes closed to slits as hunger drew his features tight.

"Ye wanted far more than I just gave ye," Bothan

declared. He reached out and grabbed a handful of her skirt. He was looming over her a moment later, the scent of his skin filling her senses and stirring hunger inside her once more.

She did want more…

It was a harsh truth that couldn't be denied. At least to herself.

"I'm going to give it to ye, lass," Bothan promised her as he held her in front of him. "But no' until ye demand it of me."

He smothered her reply beneath his mouth, claiming her lips in a kiss. The grip on her skirt ensured she stayed in place, but the demand of his kiss stole her breath. She wanted to resist him, but the reality was that inside her that wildness was impossible to ignore. Denying him was fighting her own nature.

There was no possible way.

So she kissed him back. Reached up and gripped his shirt to hold him in place as she rose onto her toes so she could take from him as much as he did from her. She heard him groan. Felt the way he wrapped his arms around her body, binding her to him as he cupped her nape to contain her even further.

Brenda slid her hand up and into his hair in response. She wasn't going to be taken.

Bothan pulled away though, putting her from him when she refused to release him. Brenda glared at him, listening to her own breath as it rasped through her teeth.

His lips rose once again. There was a glitter of male victory in his eyes that drew a snarl from her. Bothan chuckled in response. The rogue reached up and tugged on the corner of his bonnet before he winked at her.

He was gone a moment later, climbing away from the river's edge on steps she was forced to admit she didn't hear. Bothan was hardened and very adapted to his environment. Even among Highlanders, he was considered dangerous. A man any wise person thought twice about crossing or disagreeing with.

She let out a little huff and adjusted her bodice so her breasts were in the correct position.

Well, she would be defying him.

And he deserved nothing less.

He knew she was unbridled. The very first time they'd spoken he'd confirmed he knew the gossips had plenty to say about her. And none of it was good.

Aye, unbridled…and she would be staying that way.

✎

Bothan was watching her.

Brenda found his gaze on her more than once during the next few days.

Ye must not allow his intentions to sway ye…

She had difficulty listening to her own words of advice. Worse still was the twinge of foreboding that refused to be banished.

"Ye have no' even tried to like me, woman…"

His words rang in her ears like the church bell did when she was trying to be lazy and sleep through morning mass, the sound attempting to draw her back to good choices instead of lingering in laziness.

"Ye enjoyed me kiss full well…"

She had, and Bothan didn't know the full extent of the truth either. Bhaic MacPherson had been her lover, and she'd learned that a woman might in truth find enjoyment in bed sport. But she'd never been so consumed by Bhaic's kiss.

Not in the way Bothan's lingered in her thoughts. As though she was making a grave miscalculation in not exploring her reaction to his touch.

Bothan was pressing hard. He didn't call a halt to their day until the sun was sinking. When he did, there was a flurry of activity as they all worked to build a camp before night fell.

The labor kept her mind occupied, and once that was done, there was darkness to take shelter in. The men were clustered around the fire. They laughed as they told stories, jesting with one another. They wouldn't have forbidden her to sit with them, but the truth was she was avoiding Bothan.

"I see ye're thinking on it."

Brenda gasped, shooting up off the rock where she'd settled to enjoy her supper. Bothan caught a handful of her skirt to steady her. She'd been facing away from the fire; with his greater height, the fire behind her illuminated his features, giving her a look at the smug grin on his lips.

"It pleases me to see ye torn on the matter, Brenda," Bothan informed her.

"Why?" she questioned him honestly. "The first time we met ye knew full well there is gossip aplenty concerning me."

He crossed his arms over his chest, and his grin widened. "That's the solid truth."

"Why would ye want a wife with so much gossip attached to her name?" Brenda asked, perplexed.

Bothan studied her for a long moment. The silence left her questioning her own opinion on the matter. He was contrary to everything she'd been taught men valued.

"People talk," Bothan began. "A wise man learns to hear what they are truly saying, which is no' found in just the words coming across their lips."

Brenda nodded. It wasn't so much that she'd intended to agree with him as she just found his words striking a spot inside her where she'd never thought to ever find a like-minded soul.

"See," Bothan explained, "those good wives are wagging their tongues over yer behavior, and the truth is they wish they had the courage to do the same."

Brenda scoffed at him.

He offered her a shrug. "Ye are no' the only one who was wed to a man too lazy to share the pleasure of bedding ye."

Brenda shifted, moving a few steps away from him so she could break eye contact. Bothan grabbed the back of her skirt, moving up behind her and keeping her in front of him.

"Ye are also no' the only woman with passion, Brenda." He spoke close to her ear, sending a shudder down her spine as she felt his body heat wrapping around her. "Yet the truth is no' every woman has fire in her. That is what drew me back to ye, and I will have it."

She grunted and twisted, gaining enough space between them so she forced him to either release her or tear the pleats of her skirt off the waistband.

"It is no' yer choice alone," Brenda informed him. "I will not be claimed."

She'd designed her words to be sharp, but Bothan merely smiled at her. His lips parted as he crossed his arms over his chest, making the man appear larger and stronger than he already was.

"Agreed."

Surprise flashed through her. Any retort she might have made died as she attempted to understand his thinking.

"Since we're wed," Bothan explained, "it will be me pleasure to seduce ye."

She'd stopped too close to him. The strange reaction she had to him had her forgetting just how quickly the man moved. As she caught his words and started to recoil, Bothan stepped forward, easily closing the distance between them with his larger stride. He captured her, closing his arms around her and sliding his hand up her back to grasp her nape.

Brenda stiffened. The urge to struggle was strong, but it conflicted with the knowledge that she'd only make herself more aware of his hard body if she moved too much. It wasn't his touch she feared so much as her reaction to it.

He was poised to take a kiss, but all Bothan did was lower his head so she felt the brush of his breath on the delicate surface of her lips.

"Ye've been taken, Brenda," he whispered. "And I've pressed ye for a response…"

A shiver went down her back. Her mind offered a perfect recollection of the way he'd sent pleasure twisting through her. And her clit throbbed softly in response to it.

"Perhaps I should have given ye more time," he said, "before pressing ye."

"Ye should forget the idea of having me for yer wife," Brenda insisted, but her tone wasn't resolved or even stern. No, it was husky and needy, and there was something else, something she didn't want to name because she feared it might be lament.

She couldn't change her mind. No, to be a wife was to be chattel, and for all her brave words, she feared wearing those bonds again. No one could deny her an annulment either. At least not if she was careful.

"Men often tire of their playthings once they have had them." She sent a determined look toward him. "Ye'll be no different."

Her words struck him hard. She watched the way anger flared in his eyes. It wasn't wise of her to stand her ground. Bothan was a hardened man. She knew the difference, could see it in the firm flesh exposed by the way he had his shirtsleeves rolled up. The air was still too crisp for her to bare her arms, but Bothan was used to thriving in far harsher conditions.

"Ye're angry with me now," Brenda stated boldly.

Bothan tilted his head to one side. "Ye're being a shrew, sure enough."

It was a harsh judgment, made doubly so because Brenda agreed wholeheartedly.

"What concerns me most, Brenda," Bothan continued, "is the fact that ye behave so because ye fear what happens when we get close to each other."

She froze, feeling her eyes widen.

"Ye've struck me as many things, lass, but no' a coward." He reached out and caught her up against his body.

She shuddered, feeling the connection as if she'd sat down in a warm bath after standing in the frigid chill of winter. Bothan captured her nape, securing her in place as she battled the urge to melt against him.

He felt so very good against her.

Like...she was touching life...

Bothan's lips were poised over her ear, his breath brushing her skin as she felt the thump of his heart beneath where her hands had flattened against his hard chest.

"Ye've been hiding in yer cousin's tower," Bothan whispered. "Shutting yerself away. Life was unkind to ye, but are ye truly broken, Brenda?"

He shifted so their gazes met and locked. "For if ye go back to yer cousin, it's no' to be yer own woman, it's to lick yer wounds and pity yerself."

"No, that's not what—"

Bothan smothered her retort beneath his lips. She gasped, and he took advantage of her open mouth, kissing her deeply while he controlled the way she tried to shift away from him.

And then she just didn't want to fight anymore. No, her body warmed, awakening like she'd been deeply asleep for a long time. She smoothed her hands on his chest, needing to feel his flesh. The hold he had on her became one she enjoyed because it proved his strength to her.

She craved strength.

Craved him.

Brenda rose onto her toes so she might kiss him back. She caught the little male sound of approval he made as he met her kiss measure for measure. Pleasure spread through her, from where their mouths were fused together to her toes. It was all-encompassing and growing hotter by the second.

But Bothan pulled away, setting her back with his greater strength.

"Think on that," Bothan insisted. "I do nae judge yer situation to be an easy one, but life is a battle. Facing it makes ye strong."

He waited for just a moment to see his words' impact on her before he turned and headed back toward his men.

She shivered. But it wasn't the chill in the air that caused the action. No, it was the knowledge that he was very correct. Living with her cousin was being a coward. Symon had never labeled her such, and she doubted he ever would.

Yet she knew.

And in her heart, Brenda realized her freedom might in truth be the greatest challenge she'd ever been handed. There would be no way to blame others for her plight, for she was in charge of her circumstances.

Well, she was now that Bothan had freed her from the King's demand that she marry.

Brenda drew in a deep breath and sat down. Her mind was full, and she realized she needed to think matters through before she behaved foolishly. It was strange how Bothan unmasked her, taking what she thought she wanted and showing it to be the worst action she might choose. He was correct, though; she wasn't afraid of him.

But of herself.

⁓

Bothan raised his hand in the afternoon the next day. His fingers were closed in a hard fist. His men recognized the gesture instantly, pulling their horses to a stop and reaching down to sooth the necks of the animals to keep them quiet. Tension was tightening all around them as Brenda watched their expressions harden.

It was just after midday; the sun had passed overhead. With the horses still, she caught the sound of the wind. It was moving the tree branches, causing the leaves to brush together. But there wasn't anything else. Brenda gripped the saddle of her mare tighter. No birdsong meant there was someone else near.

The sound of approaching horses came with the next gust of wind. Bothan and his men were out in the open, making it impossible to avoid being seen. Still Bothan turned his stallion to the high ground and moved toward it before the approaching column of men got any closer.

"Campbells." Maddox identified the approaching riders by their tartan.

"They're a fair way from home," Bothan answered.

Maddox shrugged. "It is summer."

Bothan's captain might have been making the argument, but his tone made it clear he wasn't in the mood to welcome the Campbells. Yes, it was true, summer was a season for travel and the only time to get out to market, but Maddox didn't trust the situation.

Not that Brenda blamed him; it was a harsh world.

Brenda had experienced such before, so she couldn't really blame Bothan or his men for being cautious. Alone on the road, well, they had to defend themselves if the approaching riders decided to attack.

It was sad to have to think in such a way, but life had forced her to look on her fellow man with suspicion through lessons she didn't think on very often because of how much pain was associated with them.

"Chief Gunn." The riders had arrived. "I am Hamell Campbell."

Brenda felt her blood chill. Hamell looked at her. She knew him. One of a dozen cousins who had so often been around when she was wed. Hamell was just as hardened as Bothan. His right arm was crisscrossed with raised scars from sword cuts. He liked to fight and not only with the sword. Hamell had made a sport of female conquests, a list he'd invested a fair amount of effort in adding her to in spite of the fact that she'd been his cousin's wife. In fact, she suspected Hamell had pressured her partially because she was wed to his cousin. She had watched more than one naive girl fall under his spell only to realize too late that she would end up beneath his boot when he'd finished with her body.

"Brenda." Hamell greeted her by reaching up to tug on his cap. "The very person I was sent to find."

Bothan's men shifted closer to her. The horses didn't care for the closeness. Her mare let out a shrill sound of distress with so many stallions in such proximity. She tried to control the animal, but the horse wasn't having it. Brenda lost her seat, lifting her leg up and over the neck of the mare so she could at least land on her feet instead of being thrown. Bothan slid from the back of his stallion and caught the mare by the bridle, smoothing a hand down her neck as he spoke soothing words into her ear.

Two of Bothan's retainers joined her on the ground. They pulled her away from the horses as other retainers gained control of the animals. In the end, Brenda ended up on the high ground, farther away from the Campbells and the horses. Behind her, there was the sound of rushing water.

Hamell Campbell grinned and slid from his stallion's back. Bothan stepped into his path.

"If ye're looking for me wife," Bothan stated clearly, "ye can state yer business to me."

Hamell stopped and looked at Bothan. "Word reached us about the English Queen releasing Brenda to ye. Laird Campbell is grateful for the service of bringing our kinswoman back to the Highlands."

Hamell was speaking loudly, making sure every man with him and Bothan heard his words. Brenda felt her shoulders tighten with suspicion.

"Brenda was living with her cousin on Grant land," Bothan answered. "I was doing Symon Grant a favor in making sure she was freed of the contract made by the king. No need for yer laird to think it had anything to do with him."

Hamell frowned. He didn't care for the carefully worded warning from Bothan. And it was a veiled threat, for certain. Brenda watched the way the Campbells shifted their hands closer to their weapons.

"Brenda is our kinswoman by marriage. Laird

Campbell has made another match for her since she is young enough to wed once more. Her widow's portion will stay with the Campbells," Hamell declared firmly.

Brenda sent Hamell a hard look. "That match wouldn't happen to be with ye, now would it?"

Hamell looked past Bothan at her. His lips curved into a grin full of arrogance. "No' that it matters, but aye, with me."

"Oh it matters," Brenda informed him. "What happened to yer wife? Did ye no' wed only last spring?"

Hamell Campbell shrugged. "Died."

"When?" Brenda pressed the matter.

There were a few scoffs from the Campbells. It sickened Brenda to hear them, and she wasn't going to hold her tongue either. "Wasn't she yer fourth wife? How is it yer spouses continue to die so young and often?"

"Yer husband died young as well," Hamell insisted. "No one spoke against ye for the misfortune."

"Brenda is now me wife." Bothan stepped to the side, putting his body between her and Hamell. "So ye can return to Laird Campbell and tell him there will be no match."

"As to that matter," Hamell continued with far too much confidence for Brenda's taste. She felt a shiver touch her nape, like a sense of foreboding. "The match was approved by the Earl of Sutherland," Hamell informed them firmly.

Brenda felt her belly tighten. Scotland had few nobles and even fewer of them in the Highlands. The Earl of Sutherland was Bothan's overlord. He was also her cousin Symon's overlord. The Campbells were being crafty by making sure they gained the earl's approval.

Bothan snorted. "So...yer laird went sniveling to Sutherland...in order to regain Brenda's widow's thirds by matching her up with another Campbell."

"Marriage is business," Hamell replied nonchalantly. "Ye would no' be turning down the land the King settled on her or forgetting to ask for the money due her from the Campbells if ye were able to keep her yerself."

"I will be keeping her, be very sure of that," Bothan informed Hamell firmly.

"Ye should have consummated yer union instead of kicking the English court out of yer bedchamber," Hamell said frankly and with far too much glee. "Oh aye, we've already heard. Laird Campbell keeps some of the best hawks in the land, just so he has news faster than anyone else."

Brenda was torn between the need to retch and the desire to shout at Hamell. But she looked at his men and realized they outnumbered Bothan's retainers two to one. Bothan hadn't left his land with the intent to travel all the way into England. Hamell, on the other hand, had departed from Campbell land with enough men to take Brenda by force. The look on his men's faces confirmed they'd been told to anticipate a fight.

Bothan would make it the hardest one they'd ever faced.

But the odds were not in his favor. She felt dread filling her, rising up to drown her in just how dire the situation was. Not a single member of the Gunn party was showing fear, but she knew the odds, could see the numbers and just how experienced the men Hamell had brought with him were.

The bright-green grass she stood on was about to be watered with spilled blood.

Time was suddenly so very precious, and she was woefully aware of how much of it she'd squandered. She looked over at Bothan, soaking up the details of his form. His hair was as black as midnight, but his eyes were a deep blue. He was handsome for certain, but what she found most attractive was the way he thrived in the northernmost part of the Highlands.

She would not become his Achilles' heel.

Hamell was grinning. She watched the bloodlust rising in his eyes as he began to reach behind his shoulder to where his sword pommel was. But the water was behind her, the sound of it telling her the river was a large one, swollen with snow melt. It was churning and crashing against the rocks that formed its bed. Bothan's men had formed in front of her, pressing her back to where the earth had been eaten away by the water.

"I deny you!" she shouted loudly enough for the Campbells to hear her.

Brenda grasped the front of her skirts, raising the fabric up so she might run. Bothan turned his head, his eyes widening as he realized her intent. He was lifting his hand, reaching for her as she turned and bolted for the edge of the earth. The river below was just as powerful as she'd suspected. The water was frothy and white from how much strength the current had.

But she didn't lament her choice. No, she was her own woman after all. The Campbells would never profit from her again.

❧

The water had no mercy.

So Brenda decided she would expect none.

The current grabbed her skirts, yanking her downstream as it tried to tumble her like a leaf. She struggled to lift her head above the frothy water, fighting for every breath. She struck rocks, clawing at them in an effort to gain a handhold.

But the river was too strong.

It tore her away, tumbling her again, so she fought its grip until she was suddenly weightless. The ground gave out beneath her as she sailed over the edge of a waterfall. For a moment, she was flying, suspended in the air with the water all around her. She caught a glimpse of the green hillsides before plunging into a pool. The speed she was traveling at made her sink deeply beneath the surface of the water. She could see the sunlight above her as her lungs began to burn. Raising her arms, she pulled against the water, swimming up toward the light. Every muscle she had ached, and yet it seemed like she was never going to reach the surface.

But her fingers broke through, giving her a feeling of the air against her wet skin. She pulled her arms down again, and this time her head broke through to the air where she gasped and sputtered.

She laughed.

And coughed.

But laughed more as she looked around the edge of the pool she'd landed in. Fate had delivered some kindness to her at last in the form of dumping her out of the center of the current. There was only a gentle pull on her skirts now, and most of it was from the weight of the water.

There was a large splash, one that sent a huge wave of water up into the air. It hit her in the face as she was swimming toward the shore. Brenda blinked the water from her eyes as her feet touched the ground at last. Looking back, she watched as Bothan broke the surface of the water with a snarl.

He'd jumped in after her.

She blinked, but he was still there, his large arms fighting against the water as he turned and looked around. He froze when their gazes meet.

"What sort of fool are ye to jump in after me?" she demanded.

A chill went down her back, and Brenda realized it had nothing to do with the temperature of the water.

He might have been killed.

"Ye jumped…first, woman," Bothan replied as he swam toward her. "Ye cannae berate me for doing something ye did yerself without branding yerself a fool."

Brenda realized there was no denying the truth of his words. Climbing out of the water took her full attention though, granting her a distraction. The rocks lining the pool were large and covered with slimy green algae. Her skirts were trailing too, the water making them impossibly heavy. She fought to make it to the shore as Bothan came out of the water with far more ease. He caught up to her and stepped past her to the shore, turning around to grasp her wrists and pull her the rest of the way.

"I did jump," Brenda informed him. "And I'd do

it again. Anything to keep Hamell Campbell from making a prize of me."

The fact that she was drawing breath, when she'd fully expected not to be, was speeding through her veins like fire. Brenda should have been freezing, but she wasn't.

In fact, she had never felt so alive.

Bothan was pulling his sword belt up and over his shoulder. He realized she hadn't moved away from him, was in fact standing only a single pace from him as she propped her hands onto her hips and declared her opinion.

Their gazes locked, and the world shifted between them. She'd never felt such a connection or the need for it with another living soul. Moving away was impossible. His lips twitched up, flashing his teeth at her in the same arrogant grin he'd shown her the first time they'd met.

"Ye are just as brazen as the day I met ye." Bothan dropped his sword belt. "'Tis the quality I like best about ye."

She enjoyed his words.

They filled her head, burning though restraints she hadn't realized were holding her back. What was unleashed was a desire so strong she didn't even bother to question it. The reason was simple; she wasn't thinking.

And Brenda decided she liked it a great deal.

She reached for Bothan, fighting to get the buckle on his belt open. The wet leather was slippery, but she grasped the end of the belt and pulled, feeling the buckle loosen as he cupped the sides of her face.

He raised her head up so their gazes met again while his kilt sagged to the ground in a wet heap.

"I want ye," she muttered, delighted by how husky her voice was.

"Ye want to touch life," he replied.

"Yes!" she insisted as she rose up on her toes to kiss him.

He met her halfway. It wasn't a soft kiss now. Bothan took her mouth, and she did her best to claim him. Everything inside her was boiling. Containing it was impossible, and she didn't want to, either. No, Brenda wanted him.

She'd never craved another man this way. She tore at his clothing, fighting to bare his skin. Having her skirts tossed wasn't going to be enough. But she wasn't willing to break off their kiss. So she kissed him as she tugged the lace free from where it was tucked into the front of her bodice. Popping the knot open, she drew the length of the cord from the eyelets.

Bothan pulled away from her so he could rip his shirt up and over his head. It landed with a wet sound somewhere behind him as he reached for her breasts.

"Christ, I've dreamed of seeing these…" Bothan cupped her breasts with only the thin layer of her smock between them.

She arched back, a little sound of delight coming from her lips. Bothan kneaded the soft mounds, sending another jolt of need through her. She fought with her waistband, opening it and tugging on the tie that held her hip roll in place. With a shove, Brenda sent the whole wet mess of her skirts down while Bothan pushed her open bodice over her shoulders and down her arms.

It left her in her smock. The fabric was soaked and sticking to her like a second skin. She stepped out of her puddled clothing, facing Bothan with a boldness many men wouldn't approve of.

Let him see that she wanted him.

"Ye're far more fetching than any dream, Brenda." He moved toward her, catching the edge of her smock in his fingertips and drawing it up her body. For a moment, she couldn't see him, but once she lifted her arms and he pulled her last garment free, she was staring up into his blue eyes.

The desire there stole her breath.

"And ye're mine," he rasped out before cupping the sides of her face in his large hands.

Bothan really was huge. Somehow, she forgot how much larger he was than herself when she was arguing with him. Now, as he kissed her, she felt the way he had to lean down to press his mouth against her. His shoulders were so wide and packed with hard muscle.

Brenda let out a little moan as she flattened her hands on his upper arms and stroked those ridges. He was hard, so much harder than herself. But his skin was smooth and warm.

And she craved it.

There was a burning hunger inside her that wanted more. More contact with his skin, more kisses, just *more*. She was twisting against him, trying to touch all of him as he did the same. His hands were in her hair and then sliding down her back to grip her bottom. A crazy jolt of need went through her as her clit seemed to awaken. The little pearl at the front of her slit began throbbing as she reached down and boldly grasped his member.

"Sweet Christ," Bothan exclaimed as he arched his back. His neck was corded, and he grasped her hips as she drew her fingers along his length. Men liked to boast about the size of their members, but Bothan's was thick and long.

And hard.

Her clit throbbed harder, the hunger gnawing at her insides rising to a fevered pitch. Waiting was impossible. She closed her hand tight around his girth and pumped it hard and quick. He jerked, growling as he returned his gaze to hers. There was a connection when their gazes met, one that shook her to her core. Brenda saw the flare in his eyes as his expression tightened and he drew his lips back from his teeth.

"Aye," he growled as he gripped her hips once again. "Right now."

Her heart was racing, but it accelerated as she heard him. She nodded as his eyes narrowed. "Right… now!" she insisted.

Bothan lifted her up and turned her so that her back was pressed hard against the flat face of a huge granite rock. Brenda locked her legs around him as the head of his cock slipped between the wet folds of her slit.

The first thrust was hard. Brenda felt her body being stretched, but there was something about the hard edge of the sensation that pleased her. She still felt like everything inside her was boiling, and she didn't want to slow it down one bit.

No, she wanted to go faster.

Harder.

Deeper.

"Yes!" She wrapped her arms around his shoulders to anchor herself.

Bothan shuddered. Inside her, his cock twitched. But he was holding back, leaning his head away from her so he might see her face.

"I would…no'…hurt ye…Brenda…" He fought to speak through the hunger that had his nostrils flaring.

Brenda bared her teeth at him. "More!"

Bothan didn't hesitate to act upon her command. He pressed her against the stone, gripping her bottom as he thrust into her body with hard, deep motions. She was completely at his mercy, and yet the hard ride was precisely what she craved. Every thrust connected with her clit, pushing her closer and closer to the edge of insanity.

She went eagerly into the vortex, crying out with the burst of pleasure. It was so bright, so hard, she dug her fingernails into Bothan's shoulders without realizing. There was nothing but the pleasure. It was wringing her, twisting her into a tight, throbbing knot as Bothan hammered a few final thrusts into her and spilled his seed. She felt it coating her insides, shooting out of his member in hot spurts as the walls of her passage milked him for every last bit. Her heart was thumping so hard it was near to bursting, and she simply didn't care.

Nothing mattered beyond the moment and the feeling of her lover against her.

❧

"I see something!"

Brenda opened her eyes as she heard horses coming closer. Bothan cursed but stepped back enough so her legs could lower to the ground. Her wits were slow, but Bothan seemed more awake. He hesitated for only a moment to ensure she was steady on her feet before he was striding over to retrieve her smock.

The sun bathed every inch of his skin. Her cheeks heated as he turned, showing off his member.

"Do nae look like that, Brenda." Bothan had made it back with her smock. "We're married."

She wanted to argue, but the horses were coming closer. Clothing herself had to take priority. She grasped her smock and went around the rock they'd been up against to find some privacy.

Bothan's men arrived a moment later.

"Christ," Maddox declared loudly. "I swear ye tested me faith, Chief."

"Aye," Bothan replied. "I am no' sure why I'm alive, but I'm properly grateful. Keep the men away; me wife requires a moment of privacy."

Maddox made a sound that sent Brenda's temper flaring. Oh, she knew she was taking offense over something she'd gotten herself into, but that didn't seem to stop her from snarling when Bothan appeared.

Her thick cloak was over his arm. He stopped before handing it to her as he heard her snarl.

"Ye are determined to be stubborn about our union," he said in a tone that betrayed how irritating he found her attitude.

Brenda lifted her chin and shot him a hard look. "Oh…I see. Ye think because I am a woman, one encounter means I'm settled in."

One side of his mouth twitched. A look glittered in his eyes, one that sent a warning through her.

"Don't look at me like that, Bothan," she warned as she grabbed her cloak and swung it around her shoulders. "I am no' going to be yer plaything."

The wool settled around her. In the next moment, she was pulled against Bothan's hard body. He clamped her arms against her sides as she tried to escape, one of his large hands clasping the back of her head so she was completely his captive.

She gasped, stunned by just how easily he managed to subdue her. Her temper flickered, and then there was something else stirring deeper inside her belly. A response she detested because it was the opposite of what she'd decided she wanted to feel for him.

But the ache in her passage was confirmation of how conflicted she was.

"Be very sure of one matter," he warned her in a husky tone. His eyes glittered with promise as his breath teased the sensitive surface of her lips. "I intend to enjoy ye and make very certain ye find pleasure in being had."

He kissed her. A hard and demanding press of his mouth onto hers. There was no teasing motion from his lips, just the determination to press her to yield. She wanted to resist, but he held her head in position as he took her mouth. Whatever she might have decided she wanted died in a sizzle of rekindled passion. His kiss sent her insides twisting. An insane

shaft of pleasure went through her, numbing her to
logical reasoning and anything that didn't include
kissing him in return.

He lifted his head from hers a moment later, staring
down into her eyes as she blinked and tried to decide
why he'd stopped.

"Ye will be mine, Brenda."

He left her with his words ringing in her ears. Her
lips still tingled from his kiss, and her skin yearned to
make contact with his. The world around her was cold
without his embrace.

And all of it scared her nearly to death.

❦

"Seems the pair of ye have settled matters between
ye." Maddox waited until after moonrise to voice
what was on his mind.

Bothan tossed down a twig he'd been snapping
into pieces. The fire they'd built and cooked over
was out now, even the embers covered up to avoid
any of the Campbells seeing the light if they still had
a mind to fight.

"Naught is settled," Bothan answered while scan-
ning the area in front of him. Maddox was beside him,
looking the opposite direction as they took the first
round of watch. "However, I did nae expect a woman
such as Brenda to accept me easily."

"Glad to hear ye knew that little bit afore ye had
us ride all the way to England for her," Maddox
responded. "That female is unbridled, and I do no'
mean it as an insult."

Bothan didn't answer. He was too easily angered

when it came to the topic of his new wife. Trust took time to grow though, more time than he seemed to have the patience for.

But he felt the rise of heat in his loins as the memory of their encounter filled his mind. She craved him as much as he was drawn to her. Whatever was between them, it was stronger than either of their wills.

Caught between the intensity of the pull toward her and the frustration she left him with when she pushed him back, Bothan discovered himself contemplating the form of his wife where she was sleeping. She took to the road as well as he'd expected, pulling her arisaid up and over her head and settling down to sleep like any of his men.

Aye, she was well suited to him.

His life was a challenge. One many of the brides offered to him wouldn't have faced with such ease. Hamell Campbell had best hope he never crossed Bothan's path again because Bothan wasn't giving Brenda up.

Ever.

"Ye are ignoring me," Bothan accused the next night.

They'd stopped and built two fires. Several of the Gunn retainers had split off from their party early in the day, rejoining just before they stopped with a dozen rabbits. The game was cleaned and spitted by the entire group while they talked.

But the Gunn retainers kept their voices low.

Bothan had broken off, silently sneaking closer to Brenda. She jumped and looked up only to catch the look of approval in his eyes.

"I do nae think yer men would enjoy the presence of a female," she replied.

Bothan lifted one shoulder in a shrug before he came closer. She shifted, responding to his nearness. It simply happened, and it earned her a narrowing of Bothan's eyes.

"Ye crave me too," Bothan told her bluntly. "And ye enjoyed being taken by me."

Her cheeks heated in response. Their encounter was something she'd spent a great deal of time attempting to banish from her thoughts.

"Ye should have realized I am no' adverse to passion," she began, "after hearing I was Bhaic MacPherson's mistress. There was no point in being in the man's bed if I didn't enjoy it."

Bothan's expression tightened. Guilt tried to stir in her, but she ignored it. Better to end his fascination with her now before she lost control again.

"A match between ye would have been something both yer fathers found acceptable," Bothan said. "But then again, ye made certain to blacken yer name by openly being the man's mistress instead of having yer father attempt to negotiate a contract between ye."

Brenda knew it.

"In fact," Bothan continued as he came closer and his voice dropped, "as I understand the matter, ye made sure the MacPhersons saw ye. Bhaic would no' have darkened yer name by parading ye about."

Their gazes met. For a moment, she caught a look at the raw determination in Bothan's gaze.

"I did," Brenda replied. "Because I was not going to have me father make another match for me."

"Not even with a man you found pleasing in bed?" Bothan asked.

"I will not be owned," Brenda insisted. "Never again will I be chattel."

She'd never meant anything more in her life. Part of her lamented just what she'd done to ensure her father couldn't make her a match, because a man like Bothan had pride.

"I am not the right woman for you, Bothan." She forced the words out. "When we pass Grant land, ye should leave me and annul the marriage."

"Ye appear to not understand me at all," Bothan whispered. There was a note in his tone that sent a shudder down her back. She searched his eyes, seeking to understand just what it was that caused her hairs to feel as though they were standing on end.

"I would no' have come for ye if I was the sort of man who gave up," Bothan warned her. "Ye will be mine."

His tone rung with a promise that made her recoil.

"So…ye simply plan to claim me?" Brenda demanded. "With no regard for what yer people will say?"

Bothan sent her a look that made it plain he was thinking her question through. She felt her insides tighten in response. Perhaps she should have kept her mouth shut, held her tongue instead of giving him any ideas.

Perhaps ye want him to take the matter out of yer hands…

"My people will say ye have passion in ye," Bothan answered her after a moment. "A passion to match me own."

"I do nae wish to hear of yer conquests." The

words were past her lips before she realized she was exposing herself.

Bothan flashed her a smile. "Ye sound jealous, Brenda. Do ye no' care for the feeling ye were so intent on filling me with?"

"I am no' foolish enough to think ye have no' had yer share of mistresses," Brenda replied.

"Gunn land is no place for things such as mistresses," Bothan informed her. "Me tower is no' like the Grant stronghold. Ye will find few luxuries inside it. For certain there is no' enough room for any woman who makes her place through her position in me bed alone."

Brenda liked what he said. Oh, she had no right to enjoy knowing he didn't have a mistress, and yet she couldn't deny that she did. At least to herself. She bit her lip to keep her mouth closed. Bothan grunted after a moment of silence between them. He reached out and caught her wrist. He pressed a stick with a generous portion of roasted meat on it into her fingers.

"Get some rest," Bothan told her firmly. "It's full moon now, and I will no' be taking a chance on the Campbells finding us again. As soon as the horses are ready, we'll take to the road."

He left her with the roasted rabbit. It wasn't really hunger that made her lift the stick to her mouth. No, it was more of a sense of respect for Bothan and his men to ride longer hours than she had ever done before. They were hardened, and she wasn't going to be the weakest member of their group.

So she ate and lay back, pulling the cloak around herself and over her eyes so she might lock out the last of the sun and rest while she could.

❧

It was later in the week when they heard riders again. Bothan had them traveling at night to make use of the full moon and the cover of darkness. Brenda heard the sound of the hooves approaching and felt her shoulders tense.

Only men with a purpose traveled at night, ones who didn't want anyone knowing what they were about. Sometimes it was as simple as lifting a few head of cattle from a neighboring clan. Rivalry between clans was common, but it often turned into feuds.

Brenda listened intently, gauging the number of horses—more than ten, she was sure of it—and in the next few minutes, she knew there were at least twenty.

But they were in a bad spot. On one side of the road the earth rose up above their heads, and on the other it dropped away steeply. The road had been cut through the slope. There was nothing to do but go forward and right into whoever was on the road.

The Gunn retainers drew their swords.

Bothan made for the place where the slope gave way to open land. It wasn't forestland where they might hide easily, but at least it was better than where they were.

Brenda clamped her thighs tight around the saddle, leaning forward to make certain she stayed on the back of the mare. Bothan dug his heels in, and they surged forward. In the distance, Brenda caught a glimpse of their company. Whoever it was, they had been taken by surprise. She heard their horses recoiling from the sight of other horses coming toward them.

The turmoil gave Brenda and the Gunns the time

to make it off the slope. Bothan's men galloped up onto the open space, forming a hard line against the other men while Brenda found herself firmly pressed behind them.

Bothan didn't intend to run, though. He faced his unknown adversary, sword in hand. The moon was full, but the clouds were thick. They shifted slowly, moving out from in front of the moon so silver light illuminated them all.

"Bothan Gunn?"

Brenda gasped. She knew her cousin's voice. Symon Grant lowered his sword and nudged his horse forward. It was enough for the moonlight to show his features clearly.

"Symon," Brenda declared. Relief surged through her as the Gunns replaced their swords.

"Riding in the dead of night is dangerous, Laird Grant," Bothan said as he dropped off his horse to give the animal a rest. He slid his hand along the animal's neck before walking forward to offer Symon his hand.

Her cousin Symon clasped Bothan's hand, the two men closing their fingers around each other's wrists.

"I had news ye were riding north with Brenda," Symon said, "so I wasn't about to waste time sleeping when there was a full moon to ride by."

Her cousin looked past Bothan to where Brenda was. Maddox and two other men had planted themselves in front of her.

"Christ in heaven," Symon declared as he looked back at Bothan. "I'm grateful to ye, man."

Brenda pushed on Maddox's shoulder. "Allow me to greet me cousin."

Maddox didn't budge until Bothan turned and nodded toward his captain. It was a blunt reminder of who held the authority over her. But Brenda didn't dwell on it because Maddox turned to the side, allowing her to slip past him. She grabbed the front of her skirts so she could run and barreled toward Symon.

Her cousin caught her, clasping her so tightly her ribs ached.

Brenda didn't care. Tears eased from the corners of her eyes as she held on just as tightly to him.

When Symon released her, Brenda discovered her knees were weak, but her shoulders felt so much lighter.

It was finally over.

The last few months of turmoil were finished at last. She turned and smiled at Bothan.

"I wouldn't be here if it wasn't for Chief Gunn," she said after she managed to drag a deep breath into her lungs.

"Aye," Symon Grant agreed. "I know I argued with ye, man. When the King decreed Brenda must go to England."

"As I said at the time, Laird Grant," Bothan replied, "it had to be me, and I would no' fail to retrieve her."

Brenda felt lament shifting inside her. Bothan had faced a challenge he wasn't required to in riding after her. Life was often hard and unfair. When royals became involved, more than one of their fellow lairds had discovered personal choices had to give way to the decrees of the monarch. Many would have told Brenda to do her duty and make the best of it.

She'd intended to do so.

Yet she was so relieved to discover she didn't have to.

"We have much to be grateful to Chief Gunn for, indeed," Brenda added.

Something inside of her was threatening to break loose. A need that would undermine her choice to be her own woman. She found herself torn and completely baffled by the realization of not being content in what she'd decided she wanted for the rest of her life.

Yet she had made her choice back when she went to Bhaic MacPherson's bed. There were a dozen others she might have taken as a lover. The truth was she'd used a fellow laird in order to make her name notorious.

There was no going back.

Bothan locked gazes with her for a long moment. In the darkness, she wasn't certain what she saw, but there was something shifting between them.

Bothan looked at Symon. "Ye say ye're grateful."

Symon turned to contemplate Bothan. They were both hardened men, but Bothan was larger. Not that Brenda expected her cousin to back down simply over a few inches. Still, she discovered herself noticing the difference between them.

"Aye," Symon said. "Ye've done me a service I can no' repay."

"Ye can," Bothan replied. "Get back on yer horse, and ride for home. Leave Brenda with me."

Silence hung between all three of them for a long moment. Brenda felt her heart accelerating as her cousin Symon remained silent, clearly weighing the idea.

Brenda shook her head. "I would return to Grant land with ye, Symon."

Bothan didn't look away from Symon. "I kicked yer arse once when ye needed it."

Symon stiffened. He reached down and curled his fingers around his wide belt.

"Brenda is me wife," Bothan declared firmly. His tone dared anyone to argue with him.

Once more, Brenda discovered herself shocked by the way Symon appeared to be contemplating Bothan's idea. It was as if the earth beneath her feet was crumbling and falling away. She stiffened, her temper coming to her aid in a flare. She wasn't going to let anyone dictate her future. Symon had given her his word.

Brenda stepped back and looked at Bothan. "I will nae go north with ye."

Symon's men were watching their laird, shifting in their saddles as they witnessed the confrontation. But Symon hadn't moved. He was still staring at Bothan, taking his measure. Both of them were ignoring her, thrusting her into the role she'd so often been forced to endure because of her gender. Brenda struggled to breathe. Helplessness was something she couldn't bear, and having it thrust upon her by Symon was the worst form of betrayal.

"Ye claimed yer own wife, Symon," Bothan reminded her cousin. "And I feel as strongly about Brenda. Go home. Brenda and I need time together."

Symon looked toward her. Brenda felt her eyes widening as she realized her cousin was being persuaded. Her cheeks were on fire, as every man riding with Bothan and her cousin was privy to the conversation. She wanted to keep the matter private, but there was no way to do so unless she simply bit her lip and let Symon believe she was amenable to the idea of going home with Bothan.

"Ye gave me yer word, Symon," she reminded her cousin.

"And ye agreed with me last year when we both admitted to needing to start living again," Symon responded gravely.

Symon drew in a deep breath. Brenda watched his features settling into a hard mask. She knew the look, had seen it take over Symon's face when he was facing a decision and felt he was correct even if the circumstances weren't to his liking.

She shook her head. "I will…nae…go north."

Bothan reached across the space between them and captured her wrist. Brenda turned her attention to him. But the look in his eyes stopped her for a moment. Determination was glittering in his eyes. She recoiled from it.

Bothan made a sound under his breath. A moment later, he'd bent over and lifted her up and onto his shoulder.

"Put me…down!" she hissed.

His hand landed on her bottom instead.

"Go home, Symon." Bothan turned back to address Symon Grant. "Ye've seen that I've brought yer cousin home safely."

Brenda tried to straighten up, pushing her hands against Bothan's hard back. He turned and headed toward his horse. She caught a glimpse of Symon watching her being carried off like a sack of grain before her cousin muttered something under his breath and turned his back on her.

Leaving her completely alone with her fate.

Betrayal cut through her heart as surely as a sword thrust through her chest. The only rights she had came from the men around her. She might have been promised her freedom, but without Symon ensuring it, Bothan would have his way.

Over her dead body…

Brenda renewed her effort to be free. Bothan grunted and dropped her onto her feet. She recoiled as he withdrew his dagger, the blade sharp and polished.

"Christ, woman," Bothan declared harshly. "Do nae look as though ye suspect me of doing murder to ye."

He grabbed the front of his kilt where the fabric was overlapped. A quick motion from his wrist and he'd neatly sliced into the wool fabric. He shoved the dagger back into the sheath tucked into his belt and yanked on the piece of wool. It tore down his front, leaving him a wide strip.

Brenda gasped, realization coming too late. She should have run while he was cutting; now he reached out and caught her wrist, turning his body to pull her toward him while he wrapped the wool around her wrist.

"Ye're coming north," he said as he tied a firm knot and reached for her other wrist.

Brenda held her arm away from him. It was a doomed motion, but she couldn't resign herself to surrender.

Bothan's eyes narrowed. He cupped the back of her neck instead, bringing her up against his body and sealing her protest beneath a hard kiss. It stole her breath, smashing into her resolve to deny him. The collision sent a shudder through her, one that felt bone-deep. The shock of it had her rebelling, shoving at his shoulder with her free hand.

A moment later Bothan broke off the kiss, transferring his attention to her free wrist. She realized her error too late. He'd wrapped the wool around her free wrist and knotted her hands together before she'd finished hissing at him.

"Yer choice is this." Bothan cupped her chin and locked gazes with her. "Stay on yer mare or I will take ye up behind me."

Resistance was still boiling inside her. Betrayal fueled her temper, but Bothan's eyes were full of determination. He pulled her closer so he could lower his tone.

"Do us both a favor, lass, get on yer mare," he warned her softly. "If I have ye too close, I fear we'll be stopping so I can take the challenge blazing in yer eyes. Yer spirit is what drew me to ye. I've followed ye all the way to England, so do nae test me here. I promise ye I will have ye here on the trail as me men wait if ye do nae see the wisdom in granting me a wee bit of space right now."

Brenda grunted, trying to push away from him. Bothan held her fast, doing precisely what he'd just promised her he would.

Take her challenge.

But she was still trembling from his kiss.

"I'll ride the mare."

The words were past her lips without her ever realizing she'd decided to bend. Well, perhaps *bend* wasn't precisely the correct word.

Compromise.

She needed to choose her battles, and with Bothan, it appeared selecting the time was going to be her only freedom. It wouldn't be the first time she faced bad odds, though. It was a long way yet to the upper Highlands. Bothan would discover how much trouble she was before they arrived.

The burly Highland chief could bet on it.

"She's planning how to murder ye."

Bothan turned his head and eyed Maddox. His captain was twisting the ends of his beard as he stretched out on the ground.

"Well," Maddox started up again, "she might"—he lifted a finger into the air—"be contemplating how to castrate ye because ye'd have to live with the pain of no' having yer—"

Bothan growled at his captain, cutting off his last word.

Maddox waggled his eyebrows.

Bothan was weary but wide awake. He opened his eyes a few moments later, frustrated by the way sleep eluded him.

Having her wasn't enough.

His mind was turning that fact over and over, trying to decipher it. One more fact to join the odd ones that accounted for his fascination with Brenda. Knowing he'd been choosing her because she was unlike any other woman he'd ever met hadn't prepared him for the strange way she affected him.

Tonight he wanted to discover more about what it was he was seeking in her.

She had beauty.

Red hair and a pleasing form most men would have praised her for. His member stirred at the sight of her, and yet what he was recalling about her most right then was her scent and how much he wanted to have it filling his senses.

Longing…

There was another idea Brenda stirred in him.

Wanting to bed a woman, well, he'd encountered the need before. With Brenda it was stronger because she was brazen enough to face off with him and had been from the moment he met her. It was more than a show to entice him. With Brenda, he'd seen in her eyes the spark of determination to push him away. Just as she had on their wedding night.

Only she'd sealed her mind against him once he'd become her husband.

Bothan sat up, the idea of her shutting him out too much to bear. It was like lying back on the point of a dagger. He felt it pricking at his skin, making relaxing impossible. The only solution was to stand and move closer to the thing occupying his mind so completely.

Brenda was lying on the ground near a large rock face. It would be the warmest spot for the night because the wind would be cut by the stone. But that wasn't to say it wouldn't be cold. The weather might be fine by day, but at night, it was still chilly.

❦

Brenda should have been asleep.

She wasn't, though, and she couldn't even claim fear was keeping her from getting some much-needed rest. She opened her eyes and caught sight of her bound wrists.

Ye should be afraid…

Well, she wasn't. That fact in itself was a puzzle her mind seemed far more interested in solving than gaining some rest to help her make it through the next long day of riding.

Ye're a fool when it comes to Bothan Gunn.

Aye, she was certainly that!

Bothan had used a strip of wool from his plaid to secure her wrists. The wide length of fabric didn't cut into her skin. The result left her somewhat limited in what she might accomplish with her hands but not helpless.

Thank Christ…

Brenda felt a wave of true despair wash through her. She couldn't be helpless again. Too many memories already crowded her mind from times when she had been bent and unable to help herself. For all that she claimed to be able to stand up against those memories, the truth was when she was alone and in the dark, she wondered if insanity wouldn't take her away if she was forced to face one more moment of pain.

"Ye're awake."

Brenda stiffened. Her eyes opened out of instinct, affording her a view of Bothan on his haunches beside her. There wasn't much light, making him appear to be carved out of the fabric of midnight itself.

He nodded slowly before reaching out to brush some hair back from her face.

"I can do that meself," she told him.

"Aye." He looked down at her wrists. "I made sure to bind ye so ye can see to yerself."

"Are ye expecting me to thank ye for it?" she asked.

Bothan appeared to contemplate her question for a long moment. She watched the way his eyes narrowed before he came to a decision.

"Ye're correct, Brenda, we're strangers," he said.

He reached for the section of his plaid that went across his shoulder and raised it up and over his head. She realized he would not take his kilt off, not here on the trail where he might have to roll onto his feet and face an impending threat. Bothan wouldn't place his comfort over his ability to defend his men.

And her.

"So 'tis time for us to get to know each other," Bothan said as he settled down beside her.

Brenda wiggled away from him. He was just so large.

That isn't the reason…

She didn't care for her thoughts. They were dangerously undermining to her determination to remain unaffected by Bothan.

He followed her, stopping only when she ended up against the rock face.

"Go to sleep, Brenda," he advised her softly.

She blinked at him, so fully awake there was no possible way she was going to relax enough to sleep. All of her senses were heightened now, telling her he was close to her and just how little control she had over noticing all the details of his body.

Bothan was watching her. She caught the twitching of his lips as he rolled onto his side and propped his elbow against the ground before laying his head in his hand.

"I suppose we could find something else to do other than sleep, lass," he suggested in a tone edged with wicked suggestion.

Only wicked because ye are thinking the same thing…

Brenda snapped her eyes shut. She heard him chuckle, the sound dark and somewhat suggestive. Without her sight, though, she became more aware of him so close to her. Inside her chest, her heart was pounding, sending her blood speeding through her veins. Her breathing accelerated as it kept pace with her heart, drawing in the scent of Bothan's skin.

She'd never realized she might like the way a man smelled.

Something deep inside her was warming up, stretching, and awakening.

"Aye, ye're likely wise in choosing to sleep," Bothan teased her. He was so close his breath brushed her ear.

She shuddered, and her eyes popped open. It was just a reaction to him being so very near. Controlling it was impossible. Their gazes locked, and she felt herself battling the urge to look at his mouth.

Ye want his kiss…

The craving was hard and strong, rising up through the choices and decisions she'd so carefully made about how her life was going to be once she'd woken up in Grant Tower and heard she'd been granted the freedom to be her own woman.

"I want to kiss ye." Bothan appeared to read her thoughts.

Brenda jerked her attention back to his face to find him grinning at her.

"But I fear we'll both end up frustrated if I do," he finished.

Bothan reached out and pressed his fingers against her lips to still her retort. She might have moved her head away, but the truth was she knew her argument would have been more for her failing composure than for any truth the words represented.

Bothan knew it too.

Brenda closed her eyes, admitting defeat under the cover of darkness. She heard him let out a soft male sound before he was stroking the side of her face. She shivered in response, the contact sending a torrent of sensation through her.

How was it possible to notice a simple touch so very much?

She didn't know. But she could not refute the reality of it either. All she could do was curl her lower lip in and bite it to contain the little gasp that tried to escape and let him know how strongly she was affected.

Bothan pressed his thumb against her chin and pulled her lip free. In the darkness, Brenda felt her cheeks flooding with color.

At least he couldn't see it.

Small comfort, yet she would take it. For now it would be enough, and when sleep finally claimed her, she went happily with the idea of rest restoring her resolve.

⌖

Bothan watched Brenda relax into slumber.

He'd waited a long time to have the chance to

watch her sleep. His men were bone-weary and their horses were being run hard, but it all seemed worth it to be close enough to the woman who had been appearing in his dreams since he'd met her.

More than one man might accuse him of being obsessed. Bothan doubted he would have argued the point. The truth was he wouldn't have bothered to discuss the matter if there was another alternative. Brenda was a topic he found very personal.

His life wasn't one that afforded him many opportunities to indulge in his personal desires. In fact, he'd spent a great deal of his self-discipline on making sure he didn't give in to weaknesses that stemmed from what he personally wanted from life.

A chief put the needs of his people first. The Gunns needed a mistress. That was true enough, but Bothan had to be honest with himself when it came to Brenda. He was chasing her for his own personal reasons.

A match with a Grant was a good one for the Gunns.

The land Brenda came with was going to be a fine addition to the holdings of the clan as well.

But he'd have sought her out without any of it.

Without the beauty that made men compete for her or the things listed on her dowry. He'd craved her from the moment he met her, and even a winter in the Highlands hadn't cooled his need for her.

Yer weakness.

Bothan watched the way she curled toward him. Drawn to him just as clearly as he was to her. He shifted, making space for her against his body. He felt the connection between them as she settled against his side. He smiled, the idea of what she'd say if she realized she'd come to him in her sleep making him grin.

Perhaps he would tell her later. When he had the privacy to kiss her. Brenda might be his weakness, but he was hers as well.

And it was going to be his pleasure to help her admit it.

Three

BOTHAN'S HOME WAS AS HARD AS HE AND HIS MEN WERE.

The twin towers of the Gunn chiefdom rose up against the sky looking like a fortress that was impossible to breach. The stone was dark, almost black in places from the growth of moss. Set on the high ground, around its base a village was thriving. She could see the waterwheel where the mill was grinding grain into flour up at the top of the village. There were chickens and goats and cows in the pastures and stone buildings to prove the Gunns weren't living in hovels made only of sticks and dried mud.

After so many days traveling, she found the sights and sounds of civilization a feast for her senses. The Gunn retainers were happy to be home. Men called out from their workbenches as they rode closer, greeting their friends and relatives. Children rushed to the edge of the road to enjoy the sight of the chief returning. Women appeared in doorways of houses, many of them holding babes. Children peeked around the edges of the doorways, their smiles showing off missing teeth.

The sound of the blacksmith working on his anvil came through the air along with a steady tapping from the carpenter's workshop. Even the clucking of the chickens seemed welcoming after so many days in the wilds. Her mare quickened its pace as the animal recognized its home and the opportunity to be done with traveling for a time.

Brenda felt her belly rumble as the scent of bread filled the air. Bothan hadn't stopped for anything more than to rest the horses. His men had hunted to keep them fed, but her mouth watered at the thought of something more than game animals.

Right after greeting their kin, the Gunn people directed their attention toward her. Men stroked their beards as they contemplated her, while younger women smiled shyly at her.

Bothan rode up to the base of his tower, swinging down and off his horse with a happy grunt.

"We're home, lads," he declared to his men. "I've never rode with a finer lot. Ye've proven yerselves well and against harsh circumstances. I'm proud to have been among yer number."

His men enjoyed the public praise. There were smiles and slaps on backs as they allowed younger boys to lead their horses away. Bothan shook each man's hand, offering private words of praise.

He was a good chief.

Even if Brenda didn't care for the sight of him being so completely in command of the Gunn stronghold, for it tightened the hold he had over her.

She wasn't going to fear him. In fact, she forbade herself to think about just how completely she was under his power now. Doing so would only feed the despair she'd spent the better part of the last week attempting to fend off.

There was a whoop and then several more joining in. The men were throwing off their sword belts and over-jerkins.

"Here now, miss," someone said beside her.

Brenda turned and looked into the face of a Gunn retainer. He had a single feather sticking up on the side of his knitted bonnet.

"Best to look away now," he advised her. "The men are heading down to bathe in the river. Ye'll be seeing more of them than ye care to if ye do nae direct yer attention elsewhere."

Whoever he was, there was a sense of authority in him. He reached up and helped her down, but once her feet were on the ground, she caught him staring at the strip of tartan Bothan had used to secure her wrists.

"I will deal with me wife, Leif."

Bothan appeared from behind his stallion. A man was leading the animal away, clearing the space between them.

"Pleased with yerself, I see," Brenda remarked as Bothan came closer.

Leif tugged on the corner of his knitted cap before withdrawing. In fact, a clearing had formed around them, but the Gunn people were still straining their necks in order to get a glimpse of what they were doing.

Bothan's lips twitched, rising just a bit at the corners, but the sparkle in his eyes betrayed his enjoyment the most.

"Aye," Bothan confirmed in a husky voice. He caught

her wrists, pulling her close to him so that his breath brushed her ear. "I am very pleased to have ye here."

He pulled a knife from his belt and slid the smooth blade through the fabric around her wrists. Brenda looked at him as he jerked the weapon up and through the fabric. A rope would have left bruises on her as it tore into her skin and left her with wounds. The fabric would give her only bruises, and then only because she'd tugged on the fabric in an attempt to free herself.

"Now that we're home, we'll have the privacy to deal with each other without interruptions," Bothan informed her softly.

Something twisted in her belly, a sense of anticipation she would just as soon banish.

Yet her flesh seemed to have other ideas, and her mind was all too willing to offer up a memory of how much she'd fought herself the night he'd laid down next to her.

She pushed away from him, needing space between them so she might think. Bothan was grinning at her as she tugged the remains of the fabric binding from her wrists and tossed them to the ground.

"Such a waste of fabric," she informed him. "Better to have left me on Grant land. Me mind is set. I am too old to accept being chosen as a bride."

Bothan had replaced the knife. He'd crossed his arms over his wide chest, making himself look larger and more formidable than ever. Another sensation snaked through her belly, and this time she knew without a doubt that it was arousal.

"Here ye can run if ye like," Bothan informed her. His statement confused her. Brenda blinked as she tried to decide just what he meant. Bothan closed the distance between them again, clamping his arm around her body to secure her in place.

"Run and I promise I will track ye down, Brenda," he spoke against her ear. "I know me land well. I'll find ye, and I will come alone, so we'll have some privacy when I catch up with ye."

She tried to push away from him, flattening her hands on his chest. She felt the rumble of his amusement, looking up to lock gazes with him.

"I like ye when ye're feeling wild, so run if ye've a mind to," Bothan said before releasing her. "It will give me leave to dispense with courting ye." Something crossed his face that made her breath catch. "The choice is yers."

Brenda stumbled back a few paces before stopping herself because of how hard she'd been straining to escape him.

The truth was she was battling herself. The look of raw desire that had flickered in his eyes touched off the embers still smoldering in her from their encounter. Time didn't appear to have dampened them.

Temptation was wicked and yet oh so very tantalizing.

"I do suggest ye go inside and eat a fine meal first, wife," Bothan said as he backed away from her. "I promise ye ye'll be needing the strength to deal with me."

Brenda propped her hand on her hip. "Perhaps I will stay right here and watch ye stumble through wooing me."

She sent him a look full of warning. Bothan didn't miss it, either. A flash of surprise crossed his face before he was grinning wide enough to show off his teeth. The brute enjoyed her attempt to put him in his place, which only made Brenda more determined to set him on his ear.

"Ye'll be begging yer men to take me home before the end of the month, Chief Gunn. Mark me word on it. I will no' call another man husband. No' in this lifetime," Brenda told him clearly.

Half his men were already on their way to the river to bathe. Stripped down to their boots and kilts, they turned when they heard her proclamation. They looked between Bothan and her, careful to hold back their reaction. Bothan reached up and tugged on the corner of his cap. He stepped back and offered her a low reverence.

"I accept yer challenge, Brenda Grant!" Bothan declared loudly.

His men were delighted, whooping and laughing as Bothan threw off his doublet and charged toward the river with them. Brenda turned as more than one backside flashed at her.

Which left her facing the women of the Gunn clan.

They stood contemplating her with mild amusement on their faces. Younger children watched through wide eyes, likely biting back their inquiries as to why Brenda had been allowed to be so tart to their chief.

Her belly rumbled, though, proving Bothan was correct about her needing a good meal. Walking into his tower wasn't the wisest first step in a campaign designed to free her from his hold, but that was exactly what she turned and did.

He was correct; she was hungry.

But she'd be using the strength to leave him far behind, and that was a promise.

❧

"Ye must be Brenda Grant."

The woman speaking was formidable, to say the least. Like all children, Brenda had heard her share of warnings about how she should listen to those who had experience in life. The woman Brenda faced had time etched into her face with wrinkles, but her eyes still glittered with a sharp mind. For certain, this woman was someone who knew a thing or two about life.

"I am called Alba." The woman offered her a nod of respect.

The woman wore a wool dress that was more serviceable than fashionable. There were patches carefully sewn under the arms where the wool had been worn and along the hem too.

"Are ye the Head of House?" Brenda asked politely.

Alba tilted her head to one side. She wore a cap with a strap that went beneath her chin and buttoned on the side. Only a little tuft of her hair was visible at the front. But there were faint soot stains on the cap, telling Brenda the woman had been working the ovens.

"We're no' much on titles here on Gunn land," Alba replied. "As to the kitchens, I run them, as me mother did before me. Isla is me daughter."

There was another woman behind Alba who lowered herself once her mother introduced her. Isla looked straight at Brenda as well. The lack of formality was refreshing after too many days at court where simpering was expected by nobles who had done so very little to earn it.

"Ye look as though ye've been on the road a good long while," Alba said after sweeping Brenda from head to toe. "Best come into the tower, and we'll get ye a bath while the men are cleaning up."

It was such a simple idea. Yet Brenda struggled to accept it.

What are ye going to do? Stand in the yard?

Symon had agreed with Bothan.

In the end, it was that single idea that prompted Brenda to follow Alba into the first tower. Symon was one of the few men she'd trusted. Knowing he'd watched as Bothan had carried her off had kept Brenda silent for most of the journey north. It wasn't the first time she'd felt alone in the world, but it still seemed to sting just as badly.

The lower floor was where the great hall was located. It was the entire length and width of the tower. There was a wide opening on one side that led to a passageway. Alba kept going through the hall, past the long tables that served as a place for the Gunn retainers to enjoy their meals. At night, the tables would be stacked so the men could roll themselves in their kilts and sleep. Many of the women serving in the kitchens were likely wed to some of the men, and they would lie down in the hall as well. Heating and maintaining a separate residence was a great deal of work, which made making use of the tower far more appealing.

There wasn't a high ground.

Brenda stared at the end of the hall where a raised

platform should have been placed for the chief's table. Bothan and his captains would have eaten there, their status reinforced by the elevation of the seating.

But it wasn't Bothan's style to set himself above his men.

Refreshing…

Brenda passed through the opening and into the passageway with her lips still curved into a smile. What she hadn't seen from the front was the long outer building where the kitchens and storerooms were. They stretched out behind the first tower, set back far enough to keep the tower safe in the event of fire.

The bathhouse was simple as well, but the thought of being clean was far more enticing than the location. There was a sizzle as Isla pushed a newly filled kettle into a huge hearth.

Someone cleared his throat from behind them.

"I brought the mistress's things," Leif said, his tone betraying his desire to be anywhere but there in the women's bathhouse.

"Aye, I can see ye did," Alba replied as she crossed the room to take the bag he offered. "Ye should have sent one of the younger lads. Men do nae belong near the women's bathroom, and ye know it well."

Alba's tone carried the sort of authority only age could grant a person. There was a scuffle on the floor as Leif took off in a hurry like any lad of eight who had thought to snatch a tart before Alba decided to serve them.

Isla slowly smiled, enjoying her mother's ability to command the full-grown captain. She caught Brenda watching her and lifted one shoulder in a shrug.

Brenda laughed. She realized it had been a long time since she'd done so too. The knowledge made her more tired than she'd realized she was.

"Here now." Alba turned her attention toward Brenda and the task at hand. "Let's get ye out of yer dress. It's trailing mud."

"I'm not surprised," Brenda agreed. They'd ridden hard and long. The tub was inviting, even filled with only cold water. She wrinkled her nose as she peeled off her layers of clothing. At best she might describe herself as smelling stale.

"Honestly," Brenda remarked as her bodice was lifted away and her corset unlaced, "I do nae mind that Leif came here, only that he was kind enough to bring me a clean smock."

"The chief rides hard," Alba responded as she pulled Brenda's smock free. "It's a good thing ye have something clean to wear. The weather is turning gray now. This dress will no' be clean until the rain passes."

Isla added hot water to the tub. Brenda was climbing into it before the girl finished. The ability to be clean far surpassed her concern over being chilled.

Ye also do not want to be stared at...

Well, that was also true. Brenda began to pull the pins out of her hair because Isla and her mother were taking the time to look her over. It was a common enough thing, and yet Brenda discovered she had no courage when it came to having her bare body inspected.

She was so tired of being measured against everyone else's standards.

Bothan's people wouldn't care much for her sentiments, though. As his wife, she'd be expected to measure up to whatever expectations they had for her. There would be those who resented her and those who tried to befriend her in an effort to gain favors. Somewhere in it all, she'd have to sort out who was sincere. At the moment, she had no strength for the task.

Alba voiced her opinion. "Stop worrying so much."

Brenda lifted her head and looked over the foot of the tub at her.

Alba shot her a steady look back. She lifted a ladle and pointed at Brenda. "Ye do nae need to worry so much about impressing the Gunns. Even if I think ye are of good character to want to make a fine impression. I've learned folks will think what they will for their own purpose most of the time. Best to enjoy the comforts ye might and leave worrying be, for it will change naught in the end."

Brenda nodded. Alba made a little noise in the back of her throat before she dipped the ladle into the water and lifted it above Brenda's head so she could begin washing her hair.

Yes, people would think what they would. And most of them were motivated by personal gain.

Bothan didn't come seeking yer dowry...

He hadn't. Which left her pondering how she felt about the Gunn chief. He'd come for her.

But would he like who she truly was if she shared it with him?

She picked up a lump of soap and rubbed it across a piece of linen as she contemplated the idea. No one knew her.

Well, no one besides God.

She'd once been foolish enough to think her marriage would include an intimacy of souls where she might be herself behind the closed doors of the bedchamber.

She had been so very dreadfully wrong.

Brenda drew in a deep breath and set to washing her legs and feet. She'd been naive and young. Two things she'd made certain Bothan knew she was not any longer.

So what are ye going to do?

Brenda closed her eyes as Alba began to rinse her hair. She discovered herself slowly smiling.

Well, she was going to do precisely what Bothan had offered her the opportunity to do.

Make him woo her.

❦

Maddox was stroking his beard. Bothan was used to the way his captain watched him. Today, though, Bothan turned away from his stallion and shot Maddox a hard look.

Maddox slowly grinned, proving Bothan's attempt at warning him away had failed.

Bothan let out a word of profanity. He gave his horse a final pat before allowing the animal to settle into the stable stall to enjoy the first night indoors in many weeks.

"Ye're hiding," Maddox accused him.

Bothan grunted, but his captain wasn't deterred.

"Hiding," Maddox repeated louder. "Like an untried lad."

"I'm giving the lass time to bathe," Bothan said, defending himself.

"Brenda is no' some fancy noble lady," Maddox answered. "She'll be finished now. Seems to me a wise man would have timed his arrival before she managed to get her clothing back on."

Bothan pointed at his man. "There is where ye are mistaken. Brenda is no' going to be bent by me arriving and claiming me rights. I do that, and she will never trust me."

Maddox returned to stroking his beard. Bothan might have walked away, but he had a healthy respect for Maddox's insight. His captain took his sweet time before nodding.

"Aye, ye've set yer mind on a woman," Maddox said. "A lass wed young, well, she's easier to lead to the place ye want her, coming as she does at her father's direction. Brenda has tasted free will. That's a dangerous thing for men and women alike. Makes it hard to accept authority."

"I am more concerned over the fact that she tasted what a bad marriage is," Bothan declared as he cast a look across the space between the stables and the towers. "As for free will, I do nae want to rule her."

"Aye, ye do," Maddox argued from behind him. "It's no' a pleasing thing to say, but ye want to run her to ground, and the battle between ye is as much of a draw as the surrender. Ye set yer mind on her because she refuses ye when ye know she craves ye."

Having said his piece, Maddox went through the doorway and headed up to the towers, no doubt ready for a warm meal.

After weeks on the road, Bothan should have followed Maddox.

Instead, Bothan went in search of the thing he'd been unable to forget for the last year. She was there, in his home now.

And he was going to make her his.

~✂~

"This way." Isla took over the duty of showing Brenda abovestairs.

Three stories above the hall, Isla stopped and opened a door. Inside was a chamber that took up the entire floor. Brenda went inside, feeling a ripple of awareness go through her.

This was Bothan's chamber. It was an idea as much as a fact. Her insides tightened as she caught the faint scent of his skin.

Brenda heard Isla leave the room and close the door. *Was this home, then?*

Brenda discovered her mind contemplating the idea. She looked around the room, standing because she couldn't seem to remain still. Sitting down felt like waiting in place for a beast to arrive and eat her.

Ye are being dramatic…

She was. But she smiled as she moved around the chamber. There was no curtain to section off the front of it for a receiving chamber. No, the Gunns didn't waste something such as cloth on the newest notion of how a chamber should be divided up.

Instead, Brenda found the chamber clean and serviceable. There was a large bed off to one side. As sunset approached, that side of the chamber was the darkest, proving the bed was placed where the windows would brighten with the first light of the day.

Serviceable.

Practical.

She decided it suited Bothan. The man was strong and hardened by his environment. The village around the two towers was full of people who were thriving. They were strong, with many of the older ones displaying weathered skin from the elements, but they were not gaunt. The land must be fertile.

She stopped by one of the windows. There were thick shutters to close if the weather was foul, but they were open now, allowing her to see the yard behind the kitchens. Men were gathering as they anticipated the final meal of the day and the chance to sit and take their ease with one another.

"It's a solid tower," Bothan remarked from behind her. "If less fine than what ye find at court."

Brenda turned her head, looking behind her. The light was fading, the sun glowing on the edge of the horizon now. Still, there were rays of light coming through the window to illuminate Bothan.

"I suppose it is a matter of what one considers fine," she answered. "Tapestries on the walls do not cover the stench of too many people living together or ease the pain of being shackled for the sake of some royal personage's desire for gain. If I never see another palace in me life, I shall be most grateful."

His black hair still had droplets of water glistening in it. But he'd combed it and tied back a section of it so it didn't hang in his eyes. His shirt was clean as well, along with the wool that made up his kilt. But he hadn't put on a doublet or chosen a shirt with ruffles at the cuffs. She doubted he owned anything so frivolous.

Ye notice details about him…

Such as how deep a blue his eyes were. More like the color of the sea than a summer sky. She was trans-fixed by the way he focused on her, as though there was nothing else in the room except her.

"I am glad to hear ye say such, Brenda," Bothan said as he drew closer to her. "I would have ye be happy in yer home."

Awareness of him prickled across her skin. She shifted, moving to the side as he watched her.

"Do nae argue against it," he said as he reached out and caught her upper arm. "Ye found me to yer liking very well, so have done with arguing against this union. I'll no' take it as a sign of unconditional surrender. We have a fine summer ahead of us to get to know one another."

Ye are tempted…

And yet still so very resolved.

Brenda pulled against his hold on her arm, gain-ing her freedom only because he let out a grunt and released her.

"I do nae know ye," Brenda responded. "And ye know little of me beyond the fact that ye want to bed me. So do nae think I find any comfort in that."

Bothan tilted his head to one side and grinned at her. "I know a few details about yer tastes, lass, and that's a fact."

Brenda felt her eyes narrowing in response. But she had only herself to blame. Weakness was something she'd learned long ago to seal herself against because the price she'd pay for such lapses in judgment would be very high indeed.

"Ye are far too cocky, Bothan Gunn," she informed him tartly.

He moved across the room and sat on the end of the bed. She felt her cheeks heating because her mind was offering up ideas of just how much she might enjoy sharing the bed with him.

"I want to bed ye," Bothan declared boldly. "Ye were of the same mind after we crawled out of that river."

Same mind? She'd been frantic to have him.

The memory singed her. Reminding her in vivid color of just how intensely she'd wanted to have him inside her. Her clit began to throb softly.

"But I want far more than what we had in that moment," Bothan continued. "Come here, lass. Let me strip ye bare and show ye I have more intent than just fucking ye."

His eyes glittered with promise. The look on his face froze her breath in her chest for a moment.

Dare ye?

Bothan pushed off the bed as she stood contemplating him. Her eyes widened as he crossed to her. He seemed to hold some strange power of fascination over her because even though she was undecided, she couldn't seem to make her feet move. It was only at the last moment that she broke and turned aside.

But it was too late. Bothan clasped her to him, closing his arms around her to bind her to his body.

She heard him let out a sound of frustration. Felt his breath against her neck as his heart beat behind her.

"I suppose it's a matter of trust," he said.

She let out a little scoff. "Ye kept me tied for the

past week. How dare ye ask me for trust when ye have none for me?"

"Aye, that's true enough," Bothan agreed. "I could see in yer eyes ye intended to run if I allowed ye the opportunity."

"Can a woman not long for her home?" Brenda demanded. "Men never seem to think about how often they demand women leave everything they know."

"There is naught for ye at Grant Tower but fear and a slow death where ye watch yer cousin have a family and try to convince yerself ye do nae long for children of yer own," Bothan informed her.

"It is the only place I have ever been free of fear." And Brenda didn't care for how pitiful her words sounded.

Bothan turned her around. Behind her, he'd hidden how truly determined he was. She gasped as she took in his expression and the way his eyes glittered with hard intent. He clasped her to his length as he caught the back of her head to hold her in place.

"No one will hurt ye here," he informed her tightly.

"No one except ye," she argued. "I will be yer chattel."

His eyes narrowed, showing how displeased he was with her words.

"Ye will be me wife," he stated firmly.

She tried to push away from him, but he held her.

"But I will no' force ye, Brenda," he insisted. "Ye are drawn to me. So I will wait for ye to come to me."

He tilted his head to one side and pressed his mouth against hers. The kiss was hard, and she resisted. But Bothan proved himself true to his word. He didn't force her mouth open. He kissed her firmly, tempting her to return the pressure, to dispense with what she thought she wanted in favor of what her body felt. Pleasure was awakening inside her, in too many places to control. Her senses were full of him, the way he smelled, the hardness of his body, and how much she wanted to stroke his chest.

How much she wanted to have him fill her again.

But he released her a moment later.

"The only thing being yer own woman denies ye is an outlet for yer passion," he informed her bluntly. "Returning to Grant land will mean ye cannae shame yer cousin and his new wife by taking lovers in their home. If ye seek out a lover and go to him, what will they tell their children? If they have a daughter, shall Symon demand she remain virtuous while turning a blind eye to yer behavior? Nae, I think not. Ye'll not place yer cousin in such a position."

Bothan shot her a hard look before he headed for the door and left.

She watched him go. Stared at the sight of his kilt swaying with his stride. He left her with the cravings he'd awakened. Left her fighting the urge to call him back.

Left her?

When had the thing she'd decided she wanted above all else, to be her own woman, become something that tormented her?

⁂

Brenda slept past daybreak.

Even with the window shutters open to let the

sunlight in, she awoke to discover she'd buried her head against the soft bedding and shut the light out completely.

She sat up, startled by how bright it was. Her cheeks heated as she fought her way to the edge of the large bed and climbed out. She turned and straightened the bedding, attempting to make amends for being lazy. Alba's words from the day before rose from her memory.

"I've learned folks will think what they will for their own purpose most of the time."

The older woman might be correct, and still, sleeping so late in the day would earn Brenda a label of being lazy.

One she couldn't in good conscience refute.

At least she'd thought to lay her second traveling dress out the night before. Most of the wrinkles had eased from the wool. She had little in clothing since she'd been kidnapped before being rescued and taken to the Scottish court. But Brenda didn't mind. Her traveling clothing was serviceable and easy for her to get into on her own.

Calling a maid up to help her dress would only add to her worry that the Gunns would see her as a nuisance.

She pulled the underdress on and worked the lace through the eyelets that ran up the front. There was boning quilted into the top for support, and once she tugged the lace tight, her breasts were secure. The overdress was nearly the same and had sleeves already tied in place. A few shrugs and it came up over her shoulders. Weeks on the trail had taken a few pounds off her, leaving the garment loose. Brenda tugged on the lace to tighten it up before knotting it and tucking the ends.

She looked around, but her boots were nowhere in sight. Alba had taken them away in the bathhouse because they were caked in mud and needed to be waxed again to make them waterproof. The door was still shut, and she'd fallen asleep soon after Bothan had left her.

"Well…no time for regrets," she muttered as she walked toward the door and opened it. Sitting on the floor just beyond the door were her boots. Someone had cleaned them and left them there to avoid disturbing her.

Brenda sat on the top step to put them on. Below her, she could hear the rest of the inhabitants of the tower. Just muffled sounds as the Gunns worked. A faint scent of fresh bread in the air made her belly rumble.

Once she'd knotted her second boot, Brenda rose and descended. Her hunger wasn't the most pressing need, though. She discovered she was nervous.

The hall was empty, the large doors wide open to let in the fresh air. Brenda followed the scent of bread to the kitchens where five women worked at the long tables. A large side of beef was already fitted to one of the huge bars in the hearth. A boy was slowly turning it as another boy sat on a stool nearby watching an hourglass marked with quarters that would tell him when to change places with the other boy.

"Morning, Mistress," Alba called out in her age-weathered voice.

Brenda turned and lowered herself. "My apologies for sleeping so late."

Alba's lips twitched and curved into a smile. She reached for a wooden plate sitting on the table near her and pulled the linen cover from it before setting it in front of a stool.

"Travel can drain the body of strength," Alba remarked as she turned and filled a mug with water. "Sit."

Brenda sank onto the stool and pulled the linen square across her lap before digging into the food on the plate. On the road, there had been no opportunity for them to enjoy bread. Brenda took her time eating the chunk Alba had provided for her, even drizzling some honey on it.

But her belly had tightened up during her travels as well, and she found herself full before the plate was clean. Alba sent her a raised eyebrow.

"The fare is most excellent," Brenda assured Alba. "Ye have been too generous."

"Yer belly will loosen with time," Alba answered before she turned back to the table and the bread she'd been turning.

Brenda stood as well and tucked the square of linen into her sleeve. There was always work aplenty in spring. The women in the kitchens appeared to have the food preparation in good order, so Brenda left. The first thing to do was to get an idea of how the towers were constructed so she wouldn't have to ask where things were.

She made her way across the great hall. The benches had been placed on top of the tables now that the meal was finished, and two women were sweeping the large expanse of the floor. Brenda continued around to a side doorway and found herself on the other side of the tower. Behind her was the second tower, and the sound of the river was louder. In the distance, she could see a mill with a waterwheel turning. The sunlight glittered off the wet wood of the wheel as it turned.

As she got closer to the mill, Brenda could see the large stones that would grind grain. Right now, though, the stones were apart as two men looked at the wheel. They allowed only a little water to turn it as they inspected it. They caught sight of her, one of them telling the other who she was, but the sound of the river carried their voices away from her hearing. They both reached up and tugged on their caps before returning their attention to the wheel.

"Morning, Mistress." Brenda turned to discover Maddox emerging from one of the exits from the tower. He reached up and tugged on the corner of his cap, but his eyes held a far more determined look. He stopped just a few paces shy of her and planted his feet wide. "There are important matters for ye to attend to inside the tower, Mistress."

Maddox wasn't planning on being ignored. Brenda took in the man's stance and expression. Around them, some of the Gunn retainers had stopped what they were doing to watch. So newly out of bonds, she felt the scrutiny keenly.

"I understand ye very well, Captain," Brenda replied.

Forcing herself to turn around was another matter, though. Brenda sealed herself against the desire to rebel. She'd learned long ago to choose the battles she engaged in wisely, doing so with an eye to whether she could win. Here in the courtyard, with the

Gunn retainers all around her, well, it was a fight she wouldn't get the upper side of.

But once she was facing the entrance to the tower, she caught sight of Leif. The man gave a nod, and Brenda knew without a doubt it was for Maddox. Leif shifted his attention to her and stepped back out of the doorway so she might pass through it.

Caged.

She should have expected as much.

But the truth was she was more disappointed than ever.

❧

"Are ye truly hiding, Brenda?"

Looking up from the account books she'd been working on all day was something Brenda longed to do. She'd been tempted when she heard Alba ring the bells to call everyone into the hall for supper.

Bothan wasn't going to let her ignore him, though. He blew out his breath and moved into the small chamber she'd sat in all day. Looking up became a necessity because she was so intensely aware of him. Somehow, he managed to make the chamber seem smaller just by being inside it with her.

"I am precisely where yer men put me," Brenda informed Bothan. She took a moment to place the quill she'd been working with into a small pottery jar to keep the tip from being ruined and the wood of the desk from stains.

Bothan flattened his hands on either side of the open account book. She'd miscalculated gravely by remaining behind the desk. There was a solid wall to her back, and the only doorway was behind Bothan now.

"I told ye plainly," Bothan stated firmly, "if ye want to run, do so. I will enjoy tracking ye down."

"Yer men seem to have a different opinion on the matter," she replied as she stood. Brenda kept her expression serene as she circled around the desk, intent on slipping past him. "For the moment I stepped outside the tower this morning, Maddox made it clear I was not allowed to."

Brenda went to pass him, but he reached out and caught her wrist. The connection was like a thunderclap right above her head, so jarring every sense she had was jolted.

"I did not order him to do so." Bothan's tone was low.

She searched his face and found only sincerity in his eyes. Brenda drew in a breath and felt the tension that had knotted between her shoulders loosen.

A moment later Bothan tugged her forward. She gasped but collided with his hard body. He released her wrist and encircled her waist with his arm, binding her securely to his frame while he captured the back of her head with his opposite hand.

"I would rather deal with ye meself," he informed her in a husky tone. "This is a matter between us."

He was going to kiss her.

Brenda knew his intent by the flash of fire in his eyes. She flattened her hands on his mouth, surprising him. It gave her a moment to twist free.

But he was moving with her, intercepting her and placing his body in her path once more. She put her hands against his chest, intending to push him back, but he was moving forward, tilting his head to the side to place his mouth against hers. The contact destroyed every thought in her mind.

There was only him and the rush of pleasure his kiss unleashed in her. The hand on the back of her head held her in place so he could command the moment. He kissed her hard but not brutally, giving her a taste of his strength while refraining from bruising her mouth.

The effect was catastrophic to her senses. She felt a response gathering inside her, one she was powerless to keep from him. Kissing him back became a necessity. She rose onto her toes so she might prove to him just how much she wanted to be his equal. His chest rumbled with a male sound of approval.

It was like setting fire to dry straw.

The bright flash of light drew her closer. Placing her hands on him was the only thought in her mind, feeling him more necessary than taking her next breath. She slid her hands up his chest, smoothing over his shoulders.

A moment later, Bothan set her back from him.

It felt like they'd been ripped apart. Brenda heard her own raspy breath and the little click her teeth made when she snapped her jaw shut. He'd cupped her shoulders and straightened his arms. She caught a flash of frustration in his eyes as he held her at arms' length.

"If Maddox frightens ye, lass, I suppose ye'll just have to mind him," Bothan said.

Brenda's jaw dropped open. Bothan winked at her as he flashed one of his cocky grins at her.

"As I explained to ye when ye asked if I had a

mistress," Bothan continued, "here on Gunn land, we do nae have time to squander on niceties. I assure ye, if ye want to test me, I will handle ye very personally, no' set me men to minding ye because I fear ye'll take yer dowry back to yer family. I came for ye, and I will have ye, Brenda."

He released her shoulders and took a step back, the promise in his eyes just as solid as his hold had been. "Yet the matter is between us."

He turned and gave her a view of the longer pleats that made up the back of his kilt as he left. It was a stupid thing to notice, and yet she stood there, unable to form a decent thought while he left.

His ultimatum hung in the air, though.

Ye mean his challenge…

Was it possible Bothan understood her better than anyone else? She found herself contemplating that possibility long after he'd left. Hamell Campbell would have set his men to guarding her, of that she was certain.

Bothan had just thrown open the doors. It wasn't that he'd dared her to go through them, no, he'd made her a solid promise to deal with her himself.

Brenda narrowed her eyes. She just might take him up on the offer.

She'd be a liar if she didn't admit she was curious as to just what the outcome might be.

Aye, and ye'd be lying if ye did no' admit how much a part of ye wants to lose the battle…

Brenda let out a groan born from pure frustration. The sound bounced around the room before coming right back at her.

She was cursed.

❧

"Yet the matter is between us."

Brenda heard Bothan's words rise from her memory the next night when Alba rang the supper bell.

Another day with the books had her back aching and her neck knotted. But she was pleased with the way the desk was looking. When she'd arrived, there had been stacks of letters and papers that needed to be entered into the account books. Well into spring, it had all been left in favor of getting the crops into the ground. The large window in one side of the room allowed the scent of newly turned soil in to freshen the air.

"Yet the matter is between us."

Brenda shook off her thoughts and stood. She pushed the piece of rope covered in wax into the top of the small pottery inkwell before moving out from behind the desk.

She didn't need Bothan to come looking for her again. If the man wanted to deal with her personally, she'd be wise to make sure they had plenty of witnesses.

And she was hungry, too.

The moment she stepped into the passageway, the scent of bread filled her senses. Going without something for weeks on end certainly made it more enticing. Brenda felt her lips curve into a smile as she followed the scent toward the hall. As she got closer, the crowd of men and women talking filtered out from where the Gunn clan was gathering for their meal. There was laughter and excitement in the voices.

The sound of life.

She paused in the archway into the hall. Retainers

were hurrying to take the remaining seats on the benches. Younger boys were sent back to wash if they made the mistake of arriving at the table with dirty hands and faces. They took off, sprinting for the open doors for fear of missing the beginning of the meal and having to make do with whatever was left.

The women were standing along the side of the hall, their hands already full of platters. It seemed an unruly mass of conversation, but someone cleared their throat and the noise died away almost in the same instant, proving everyone was paying attention.

A man rose at the back of the hall. His clothing didn't set him apart, and the only notable difference was a strip of silk hung around his neck. It was placed carefully, though, displaying the embroidered symbols of faith on it. The Gunn retainers pulled their caps off as the hall became silent and still.

"Heavenly Father…" the priest began the evening blessing.

Brenda bowed her head, listening to the prayer. It wasn't very long, just enough to get the important points covered. The priest finished, and there was a shuffling as everyone made the sign of the cross over themselves. Brenda opened her eyes to see the man pulling a round of bread in half. He handed one section to Bothan.

Bothan ripped the section of bread apart, but he looked across the hall to where she was still lingering in the archway, proving he was very much aware of her arrival. Maddox was waiting for part of the bread, but Bothan lifted one hunk up toward her.

She was instantly the center of attention. Brenda

clenched her fingers into fists to keep from raising her hand to her face to smooth her hair back. She did not look her best, and it had been a long time since she'd been so conscious of the fact.

"Yer place is beside me…wife," Bothan said.

The stillness in the hall ensured his voice carried to every corner of the room. The Gunn retainers began to nod in agreement, slapping the top of the table. Bothan remained holding the bread out. Alba had been standing beside him, ready to take the bread to be passed down the line of senior women in the hall. A symbolic representation of unity being the true strength of the clan.

Alba stepped back a pace, clearing a spot for Brenda.

It was a challenge.

Or perhaps a promise.

She might leave, but Bothan would follow her. Brenda didn't doubt him for a moment. But what had her moving forward wasn't fear of what he'd do; no, she picked her feet up because he'd earned the respect of his clan. Unlike many of the other clans in the Highlands, the Gunns elected their chiefs.

Brenda heard her own steps for the first few steps, and then the Gunn retainers were drowning out the sound with hard blows to the top of the tables they sat at. It rose as she closed the distance until the dishes on the tables were rattling because they were bouncing up with every strike, like a drum line announcing her arrive to the clan.

A cheer went up as she took the bread. Without a doubt, it was one of the most honest moments in her life. No fanfare or elaborate dress could have matched the sincerity of the Gunn retainers welcoming her just as she was.

❧

"Ye understand." Bothan announced his arrival with his words.

Brenda looked up from the knot in her hair she'd been intent on combing out. She was sitting on a simple stool, her hairpins lying on the surface of a small table set against the wall of the bedchamber for her to use as a vanity. A small addition to the sparseness of the furnishings of the bedchamber but a sure sign of the welcome Alba and her staff meant to give Brenda.

"Understand what?" Brenda asked for clarification. She lifted the comb and set the teeth into her unbound hair, drawing it down toward the ends.

Bothan's lips twitched. "Ye understand the nature of the Gunns. There is no high ground or laird's table. No ceremony for the sake of having people give attention to anyone who takes it into their mind to think they are above others."

"But there is sincerity, which is far more valuable," Brenda finished for him. "Yer home is a fine one, Bothan."

The comb caught the snarl in her hair. Brenda eased it from the strands as Bothan's attention shifted to her hair.

"I am trying to make it so," Bothan told her as he came closer. "The last chief was a disgrace to the Gunn name. Sided with Bothwell and Mary Stuart in an attempt to take the King off the throne."

Sitting on the stool became impossible. Brenda set

the comb down and stood. Bothan went still, watching her to see where she'd go.

"Dougal MacPherson killed him, as I recall," Brenda replied. "At Sutherland Castle."

Bothan nodded. "Me men elected me because Robert had no son."

"I doubt they would have voted for his offspring," Brenda replied.

Bothan inclined his head. "Aye, life here is no' about who is wearing a crown down in Edinburgh."

"But Sutherland is yer overlord," Brenda said as she realized she didn't care to recall the details Hamell Campbell had presented. "Ye were elected because anyone the earl associated with yer predecessor would be someone who might bring difficulties to the Gunns."

Brenda had pushed the topic to the back of her mind while they traveled, but Hamell Campbell was a large problem. She felt like the walls were suddenly pressing in on her.

"Hamell may have gone to Sutherland and woven a tale the earl thought sounded fair enough," Bothan answered as he stepped closer. "Opposed to seeing ye wed to an Englishman, that is. Now that ye are me wife, Sutherland will rethink the matter."

Brenda locked gazes with Bothan. Something shifted inside her. A new sensation. The need to shield him from the repercussions was strong. "Yer people are fine, Bothan, and ye do nae need the trouble that might come with me staying here. Hamell has buried another wife to have what comes with me. Do not be foolish. A wedding conducted in England will hardly satisfy him if his newly wed wife wasn't an obstacle. Hamell is not an honorable man."

She expected him to be frustrated by her comment. For she certainly was. Instead his lips curved up into a grin. He pointed at her.

"Ye are trying to protect me," he declared softly. "The Gunns are a good people, and ye will be a worthy mistress for them."

She shifted to the side, taking a step away from him as she lifted her shoulder in a shrug. "Ye think I am heartless? That I would receive kindness from yer people and yet stand idle in the face of knowing me presence here might bring harm to them?"

Bothan was watching her in that way he had that made her ultra-aware of him. With him so focused on her, she found it impossible to stand still. He watched her, following her with a slow pace that gave her time to notice how her heart had accelerated.

"Ye are no' unmoved by me, Brenda." He stepped after her.

Maintaining eye contact was difficult. Brenda looked away as she moved, and then she felt like she'd made a grave error in not keeping him in her sights, so she looked back to find him closer than she'd realized. She gasped, feeling her muscles tense as she prepared to jump away from him.

Bothan folded his arms around her, binding her against his body as the warm scent of his skin filled her senses.

"Invite me into yer bed," he whispered.

Brenda didn't lift her chin. He'd kiss her if she did. Time decided to crawl by so slowly she felt trapped in each moment because they lasted so long. Bubbles of time where she was keenly aware of the way Bothan felt.

She liked it too much.

Somehow, she'd never realized how good it felt to be pressed against the hard body of a man. The sensation flooding her was pure pleasure.

"Sutherland will no' be dissolving our union if ye are with child, lass," Bothan said.

Brenda lifted her chin, locking gazes with him. The need to protest died on her lips. She really wasn't certain why, only that her feelings were a tangled mess she had no ability to straighten out.

A child…

Bothan smoothed his hand up her spine, sending little tremors of delight through her. It was a soft, sure motion of his hand that ended when he threaded his fingers through her unbound hair. He lifted a section of it up, combing through it to the ends.

"Ye are stunning," he praised her.

She'd been coveted before for her beauty.

But the way Bothan looked at her was different. For the first time, she felt beautiful instead of like a prized possession.

Bothan returned his hand to her nape, his fingers gently working at the knots he discovered there.

"I told ye, if it was in me mind to force the matter between us, I'd have consummated the wedding at court," Bothan said. "Ye will call me husband by yer own choice."

He let out a harsh breath before releasing her.

Brenda caught a flash of frustration in his eyes before he moved back across the chamber. He paused at the door and turned to look at her.

"I'll be waiting, Brenda."

Brenda ended up dropping onto the stool again, looking between the closed door and the bed. So many days traveling should have seen her hurrying to enjoy the comfort of the bed. But now, all she noticed was how empty it would be without Bothan in it with her.

❧

Some of his men snored.

Bothan found himself staring at the ceiling of the great hall and grinding his teeth. Most of his retainers were rolled in their plaids and sleeping around him. He'd spent plenty of time with them on the road, but tonight was the first time he'd contemplated smothering some of them.

"Chief." Maddox sat up beside him with a disgruntled look on his face. "We've spent our share of sleepless nights together, but tonight I swear I'm close to murdering ye."

There were a couple of chuckles around them, proving more than one man was still awake.

"I am no' snoring," Bothan said to defend himself.

"No." Maddox reached out and hit him on the shoulder. "Ye're just shifting about like a bear trying to get comfortable for the winter."

"I'll be happy to help carry ye back to yer cave where ye and yer wife can settle matters while the rest of us sleep," another man added.

Bothan started to sit up. Maddox punched him on the shoulder and sent him back down to the floor. Or at least to where Bothan caught himself on his elbows, which sent a jolt of pain up his arms from the hard impact.

"Do nae waste yer breath arguing," Maddox said. "Every man here knows what is keeping ye awake."

There were several grumbles around him as his men proved they were very much awake. Bothan grunted but kept his jaw shut. There were few lights still burning in the hall, but even the expense of using candles through the night wouldn't keep the men of his clan from allowing themselves to be taken by surprise.

Bothan sat up, looking across the rows of plaid-wrapped bodies. Near the passageway that led to the kitchens, he could make out the shapes of couples. For the unwed or newly married members of his clan, sleeping in the hall was a means of being frugal. It was far from private, but he suddenly understood that just lying next to the woman of his choice was something to long for.

"What are ye waiting for?" Maddox asked.

His captain used a low tone. Bothan took a moment to decide if Maddox had truly spoken or if Bothan's own thoughts were getting the better of him. Maddox opened his eyes, proving he'd spoken.

"Ye knew full well Brenda was no' going to be a simple woman to bridle. Keep giving her so much rein, and yer beard will be gray by the time ye claim her," Maddox said before closing his eyes and rolling over to sleep.

There were a couple of chuckles at Bothan's

expense before the hall went silent again. He settled back down. Not to sleep, though. No, his mind was full, but he wasn't frustrated by the thoughts.

Maddox was correct.

It was time to craft the next steps in his campaign.

⋐∼⋑

Spring brought challenges along with new life.

Brenda heard the women shouting at first light. The window beside the bed was open, allowing the ruckus into the chamber. She flung off the bedding and went to the window. Below was the yard. Something was happening at the far side of it.

Brenda hurried to dress and ran down the steps while still braiding her hair. The day was yet only half lit, but a good number of the Gunn retainers were up in response. By the time Brenda made it to the source of the shouting, sweat was trickling down her back in spite of the mild temperature of early morning. The mist was just starting to burn off. All around them were wispy traces of it, and the mountaintops were still shrouded.

"That's eight hens and both the cocks," a woman declared.

At the far end of the yard was an area for the chickens. Placed inside the stone fence that enclosed the yard, it should have been a safe place for the birds to roost. The scene being illuminated by morning light proved otherwise. The four dozen nesting boxes showed signs of attack. Several of them were torn clean open, feathers sticking to the half-dried blood smeared on the sides of the wood. Half of the nest boxes were made of stone, and the hens were poking their heads out as they shrieked.

"Wolves," Leif offered in explanation.

"Aye," Bothan agreed from beyond the fence line.

Brenda moved through the opening to find her husband kneeling down and looking at fresh tracks.

"They'll be back, too," Leif said. "Now that they know where to find an easy meal."

Isla was gathering the dead hens in her apron. "Terrible waste of eggs." She turned to carry them back toward the kitchens for cooking.

The women joined Isla while the men clustered around Bothan. Maddox was pointing into the distance where the edge of the forest began, explaining where to search for the wolves. Bothan looked back, sensing her attention on him. Brenda felt her cheeks heating as his men turned to see what had distracted their chief.

She whirled around, hearing their chuckles follow her back toward the tower.

Her cheeks were stinging. Brenda hurried back up to the chamber she'd slept in to hide. But once the doors were closed, she was alone with the heat turning her cheeks scarlet.

"Running, Brenda?"

Brenda gasped, spinning around to face the door so fast her skirts flared up. Bothan offered her a cocky grin as he pointed at her.

"Blushing too," he remarked in a tone rich with enjoyment. "Dare I think ye are worried about me going out to hunt the wolves?"

The hunt was a far safer topic than her blushing. Brenda nodded and looked away. "Wolves are dangerous. I'd be hard-hearted if I did not spare a thought for yer health while ye pit yerself against them."

She'd made a tactical error in looking away from him. Bothan took full advantage of it by closing the distance between them. As she finished talking, he'd made it to her side, grasping a handful of her skirts to secure her in place while he cupped her chin and raised her face so their gazes met.

"I thought ye wanted me to believe ye hardhearted, Brenda," he whispered.

"I do—"

He sealed her response beneath his lips, controlling her attempt to shift away by the grip he had on her skirts. The hand beneath her chin slid back along her jawline and into her hair. All the running had caused her hasty braid to unweave itself so only a few inches of loose braid remained. Bothan combed his fingers through the strands, pulling it all free. He lifted his mouth from hers and watched as her hair fell down in a curtain of crimson tresses that matched the color of her cheeks.

"Since ye want me to think ye hard-hearted, lass," he said as he returned his gaze to hers, "I shall have to make certain I leave ye with a reason to rethink yer position."

She gasped as a promise flashed through his eyes. An insane twist of anticipation went through her belly. Brenda was still sucking in her breath when Bothan scooped her off her feet. He turned and took her toward the bed.

"Bothan...ye must—"

"Me thoughts as well," he said as the bed ropes creaked beneath their weight. He followed her down onto the bed, capturing her wrists and pinning them to the surface of the comforter. "I must no' allow ye to rebuild yer walls while I am away." His eyes glittered with promise. "So I'll knock them down now."

He pressed his mouth to hers, kissing her hard. She writhed, but the truth was pleasure made her shift beneath him. There was a flood of sensation hitting her. Remaining still was impossible. She needed to move, to release it all somehow.

And Bothan's hard body offered her plenty of places to release her impulses.

He was only in his shirt, his doublet no doubt left behind when he heard the raised voices that morning. The ties at the neck were open too, affording her a chance to slip her hands beneath the fabric. She shivered as she came into contact with his bare skin and moaned in anticipation.

"I want to hear ye, Brenda." Bothan lifted his head from hers. But there was only a fraction of space between them. She felt his breath on the surface of her wet lips. "Christ...I want to carry the memory of the sounds I wring from ye with me."

His jaw tightened with some decision. Brenda felt her breath catch in response. A moment later he was shifting, moving down her body and off the edge of the bed.

She gasped and sat up. Bothan flipped her skirts up, proving he wasn't leaving her.

"I'm going to make ye cry out, Brenda," he

promised her. "And I'm going to keep me head while ye lose yers."

Bothan would never be satisfied with claiming her body. No, he wanted her unconditional surrender.

That's why ye fear him…

The knowledge hit her as Bothan cupped her knees and pushed her thighs open. She tried to twist away, but he moved forward, giving her no time to escape. She felt the brush of his lips against her slit, and then there was nothing but an explosion of need.

She was helpless against it, unable to do anything but lift her hips to his mouth. Bothan didn't leave her wanting, either. He pulled her slit wide open as he sucked on the center of her pleasure. The pressure sent a shaft of hot need through her. The sensation was so intense she gasped and clawed at the bedding beneath her.

"Aye," he rasped out. "That's what I want…to hear ye gasp…"

There was naught to do except comply with his demands. He returned to her slit, licking her from the opening to her passage to her little pearl once more. She was twisting with the need to climax, the need to be filled. He seemed to sense it too, fingering her opening with one digit before thrusting it deep inside her passage.

She let out a moan.

And heard him release a little sound of male satisfaction.

"As much as I enjoyed riding ye," Bothan declared gruffly, "there is much to be said for no' being distracted by me own desire."

He withdrew his finger and pushed it back up into her again.

"I want to see ye lifting yer hips for me." He repeated his motions as he spoke. "Like that, lass…ride me fingers…let me see ye seeking pleasure from me…"

Brenda wasn't thinking about what he said, only reacting to his words. She wasn't even sure who was speaking because what he said mirrored the cravings filling her.

It was happening too fast. Her heart was racing as she gasped for enough breath to sustain the frantic pace. The need for release was building up, increasing in intensity before Bothan leaned down and sucked her clitoris once more. Brenda cried out, feeling the moment of climax hit her. It was blinding and searing hot, ripping her into pieces as pleasure twisted in her belly for endless moments.

When it passed, she opened her eyes and looked up at the ceiling. Her body was lax on the surface of the bed as Bothan smoothed his hand along the top of her bare thigh.

"Look at me, Brenda," he ordered her.

He kept his voice low, and she realized that the window shutters were wide open, allowing conversation from the yard below to filter in.

Her eyes rounded as she looked at the window and heard the unmistakable sound of Bothan chuckling.

But it wasn't a happy sort of sound; no, he was pleased with himself and enjoying the moment of victory. He stroked her thigh once more, driving home once again how much she liked his touch.

"Look at me," he repeated.

She turned her head, catching a glimpse of the victory in his eyes.

"Aye," Bothan said. "I am pleased." He leaned down over her body so his face was hovering above her own again. "But no' because I crave making ye my conquest," he informed her.

"Then what do ye want?" she asked.

His lips curved up as he gently stroked the back of her cheek with his fingers.

"I want yer passion," he answered her softly. "Ye've locked it away because the only men ye've known were intent on ignoring yer needs so they might use ye to sate their own."

He kissed her again. A long, slow motion of his lips against hers. He pressed her mouth open, demanding everything she had to give. And there wasn't any way to resist. No, pleasure was glowing softly in her belly, and yet there was something deeper to be gained by the kiss. A different sort of need, to be wanted once passion had been satisfied.

Bothan seemed to know she needed it, kissing her long and hard before pushing back from her.

He caught her skirt and pulled it down to cover her legs as he stood.

"I'll remember ye like this, and I will be back to finish what we've started," he declared before he turned and left the chamber.

Brenda curled up on the bed. Tears eased from the corners of her eyes as she tried to make her mind reason out her feelings. But she was doomed to failure because her walls were precisely where Bothan had said he intended them to be.

Crushed and lying on the ground. Leaving her open to everything she'd tried so hard to deny herself.

❦

Leif and Maddox were waiting for him in the stable. Bothan inclined his head as they both reached up to tug on the corner of their bonnets when he approached.

"We can handle tracking the wolves," Maddox said slowly.

Bothan grabbed the saddle lying over the rail between the stalls and eyed his captain as he carried it to his stallion. "I can see to me own courtship without the pair of ye deciding I need to stop taking care of me duties in order to accomplish the matter."

Maddox wasn't deterred. He stroked his beard as he watched Bothan secure the saddle. "Brenda Grant is no' an ordinary sort of bride."

Bothan tugged a strap and made sure it wasn't too tight across the belly of his horse. "Aye, she is no'."

His captains were expecting more of an explanation. Bothan ignored them as he finished preparing for the hunt. But their stares wore on his patience. With his own desire still raging, he found his temper short.

"A woman such as Brenda," Bothan exclaimed gruffly, "needs to run a bit between rides."

Leif and Maddox stared at him for a long moment before both of them grinned, which earned them a scowl from Bothan. They weren't intimidated in the least. Both of them whistled as they followed him from the stables.

"Ye're both unwed," Bothan informed them

once they'd stopped to mount. "A fact I will be remembering."

His threat didn't make his men less inclined to grin at his expense. Not that Bothan had much attention to give to them once he mounted. His cock was still rock-hard with need, and sitting in the saddle sent pain through the engorged flesh. He tightened his jaw and set out, not waiting for his men.

The sooner he left, the faster he'd be back.

Four

"Tracking wolves takes time," Alba said.

Brenda looked at the Head of House and nodded. "I understand it is more complicated than just finding them."

Alba clucked her tongue as she glanced across the kitchen, taking notice of what the boys roasting meat were doing. She was competent in her duties and vigilant as well. Alba never left her attention on one thing for too long.

"Wolves do as much good as bad," Brenda said, proving she understood why Bothan and his men hadn't returned after nearly a week.

"Kill them and ye weaken the spirit of the land," Isla added from where she was working on a pastry shell.

Brenda knew the stories. What child of the Highlands didn't? Winter nights had been filled with tales of spirits, ones the Church frowned on, and yet there seemed no way to kill the traditions of firelight tales when the snow had them all trapped inside.

Superstitions?

Aye, and yet no one was fool enough to forget to

share a little of their first mug of spring ale with the grandfather oak tree. The Lord above might be in charge of all their fates, but Brenda knew for certain that luck was something to covet.

Besides, she knew Alba was just attempting to reassure her Bothan would return soon. Brenda looked up and found the veteran member of the Gunn clan watching her.

"I am not concerned," Brenda assured Alba.

Isla made a little sound under her breath. Two of the maids working at the large kitchen table giggled in response.

"Perhaps it was a poor choice of words to describe how ye feel about the chief being gone," Alba replied.

Anyone else Brenda might have argued with. The Head of House knew it too. Alba offered her a smile that Brenda could have labeled smug if it wasn't coupled with the wisdom glittering in the older woman's eyes.

Which left Brenda with cheeks that stung with another blush.

Ye do miss Bothan…

The man knew too much about stirring her passion. Brenda left the kitchen, intent on cooling her emotions or at least in search of enough work to keep her busy until she was tired enough to fall into bed and sleep through the night.

Ye'll still notice how much ye want Bothan there beside ye…

Another truth. Brenda didn't have to argue with herself when she was alone. Spring was starting to give way to summer, which meant there was work aplenty.

As soon as dawn broke, it was time to rise and fight to bring in the best harvest possible. From the doorway of the tower, she could see the fields. New plants were rising from the recently planted fields. The longer days of sunlight nurtured the young plants.

She moved down the steps and out of the fenced yard. She'd finally caught the books up enough to indulge in some exploring.

Getting to know yer new home?

So what if she was? Brenda scoffed at herself. The Gunns were a good clan. She found the lack of pomp and ceremony refreshing. Even now, there were no retainers trailing her. On Grant land, the moment she stepped beyond the castle, someone would have taken after her and stuck to her until she returned.

But Gunn land was remote enough that the retainers could simply look up and note her motions. The men were busy building a section of the fence to keep the hens and goats safe. If Bothan drove the wolves far enough away, by the time the pack made it back, they wouldn't find it so easy to claim a meal.

Some might call it a simple life, but Brenda would have used the word *wholesome* to describe Bothan's land.

Brenda climbed onto the riverbank to see what was beyond the river. It served as a natural defense for the towers, having cut a deep bank. The Gunns had built up a section of it where the wheel was operating. A faint sound came from upriver. Brenda looked up, but a bend in the course of the waterway prevented her from seeing what was making the sound.

Brenda followed the sound, turning the bend and leaving the mill behind. The sound was louder now, a sniffling and then more weeping. The river became wider here, spreading out to be only a couple of feet deep. A young girl stood on the far side of the bank, looking beyond where Brenda could see as she wept.

"Here now." Brenda made certain her voice was soft. "What has ye crying on such a fine morning?"

The child rubbed some of the tears with a grubby fist and lifted her face. Her eyes were still filled with water, but she looked to Brenda with hope in her gaze. She must have been about ten winters, but Brenda doubted she was any older. Her limbs were thin and long, while her eyes were large in her face. When she opened her mouth to speak, two large adult-sized front teeth were there, but the two on either side were missing.

"I failed," she said pitifully. "And now…me brother and I will starve next winter for I fell asleep and forgot to mind me duty."

More tears spilled from her little eyes. Brenda crossed to where the girl stood, pulled the linen square from her belt where she'd tucked it, and used the fabric to clean the tears from the girl's face.

"Why don't ye explain the situation to me?" Brenda suggested with a smile. "And let us see if we can't find a solution. What was yer duty?"

The girl hesitated in that way children often tried to avoid voicing what they'd done when they knew it was wrong. Brenda nodded at her encouragingly.

"I can't see as how one little nap on such a fine spring day could mean starvation for two people," Brenda offered hopefully.

"I was told to mind the new calf," the child explained.

"To take her out to graze because me father was going to milk her mother for the first time."

"I see." Brenda understood very well. When a calf was old enough, a family would begin to harvest a portion of the milk for their use while teaching the calf to graze on the abundant new spring grass. The snow had given way to land that was lush and green as the days became longer.

"She was doing very well on her own," the child continued. "So well, I fell asleep, and when I woke up…I heard her crying…and she is lost…"

Fresh tears fell from the child's eyes.

"Here now," Brenda softly admonished the child. "Crying solves naught. Dry yer eyes, and let us attempt to find the calf."

"I know where she is," the child declared before she wiped her nose and eyes across her sleeve. She pointed across what appeared to be an expanse of green meadow.

At least that was what a young girl might think. Brenda had learned through experience that the land was never to be trusted. When the sun shone bright and hot as it was now, the ice in the mountains above them melted. The water would cascade down on its way to the ocean, cutting into the land like a hot knife. Just because there had never been a river in one place didn't mean there might not be one there when the water came down in torrents and went where it wanted.

"Show me." Brenda took the child by the hand.

The girl drew in a deep breath and hiccupped once before gathering her composure. A look of determination replaced the forlorn expression before she took off across the meadow. The ground was wet and squishy beneath Brenda's feet, making her wary.

They heard the calf long before they came upon it, desperate calls from the creature for its mother. The high-pitched sound only a baby made as she hoped to be rescued by the parent who had seen to all of its needs so far in life.

"Just up here." The girl encouraged Brenda to move faster.

Brenda pulled the child to a stop. Her boot had sunk three inches into the ground, the wet earth sucking on her foot. Ahead, she spotted the calf. It was struggling to pull its front hooves from the mire. Dark mud coated its forelegs all the way past its knobby knees.

"It's stuck in a bog," Brenda warned the child. "If we go any farther, we'll be caught as well."

The girl looked up at Brenda, her eyes filling with fresh tears. "Me brother and I will starve without the calf."

"No more tears," Brenda told her firmly. "If ye are old enough to be charged with minding the calf, well, ye need to be thinking yer way through this, no' weeping in despair."

The girl snapped her mouth shut and drew her arm across her face once again. When she lowered her arm, there was a fresh look of determination on her young face.

"Good," Brenda praised her. "Now let us see what there is about for us to use."

The area was green with grass, but when Brenda tested around where the calf was, the land gave way.

"Rocks," Brenda said after a time of searching for

a different direction to approach where the calf was stuck. "Let's go back to the river and bring back some rocks to fill in this bog."

The girl's lips split in a smile before she turned and ran back the way they'd come. She reached the riverbank first and knelt down to fill her hands with gravel.

Brenda stopped her from rushing back to the bog. "If we take only handfuls, it will take all day and night." Brenda handed the girl the linen square. "Fill that."

"A very fine idea! We shall have her free in no time," the girl declared. She bent her young knees and spread the cloth wide before digging into the gravel and scooping it by handfuls onto the fabric.

Brenda gave a little sigh before she unlaced the top of her overdress and shrugged out of it. She forbade herself to worry about getting it dirty. The sun was bright, and she hoped her other dress was washed and drying. She began to scoop up gravel and pile it in the center of her spread-out dress.

"Oh yes!" the child exclaimed with a clap of her dirty hands. "We'll have the calf free before me brother comes in from the field."

The child's enthusiasm kept Brenda working through the afternoon. The calf seemed to sense rescue was at hand, for it stopped calling for its mother as Brenda and the girl carried load after load of gravel and dirt to the bog. The wet ground sucked it up, sending them back to the river's edge for more. But at last, as the sun was setting, the calf managed to find solid ground.

Brenda tested the edge of the bog and found it firm enough. She ventured closer to the stranded animal as the calf struggled to climb out. But it was weak from the hours of fighting to escape. Its hind legs were still a foot into the dark mud. The calf looked at Brenda, its large eyes pitiful. Brenda took another step, felt the mud grip her up past her ankle.

Just a little bit farther…

Another step, and Brenda was able to throw her dress over the calf. Stretching out, Brenda reached beneath the animal and caught a handful of the wool. Yanking hard, Brenda pulled it beneath the calf and gripped both ends of her dress.

"Well done!" The girl clapped her filthy hands together as she jumped up and down. "Pull her out!"

"Stay there," Brenda warned her sternly. She was knee-deep in mud that felt like it had a grip on her. It was well over the tops of her boots now, the cold muck filling them.

Brenda focused on the task at hand as she reminded herself there was a fine bathhouse waiting back at the tower for her.

"Come on now," Brenda ordered the calf. "Together…"

Brenda pulled, straining with every last bit of strength she had. The animal felt like a dead weight for seconds that felt like hours. Pain snaked through Brenda's belly and shoulders as she forced herself to pull harder. She was gritting her teeth as the animal suddenly seemed to catch on to what it needed to do in order to free itself. The calf snorted and tried to lift one leg from the mud.

It felt like a battle that couldn't be won. The calf was struggling as Brenda strained to pull her free. The bog held her, refusing to give up its prize.

And then, suddenly, the mud gave way with a sucking sound. Brenda went tumbling backward as the calf came forward a whole foot. The animal let out a cry before it was desperately trying to get its legs unfolded. This time, the creature found stable ground and stood before leaping forward in a frantic escape.

Brenda threw her arms up to shield her face as the calf ran right over her, trampling her in its panic to be free. When Brenda lowered her arms, she watched as the girl ran after the calf. Up in the distance, a boy was waving his arms as a large cow bellowed long and low.

"That's gratitude for ye."

Brenda jerked her head around. Bothan was approaching where she lay in the mud. He looked up to where the calf was just reaching its mother, going beneath the belly of the creature in search of her udders and a warm meal.

"No' even a lick for ye," Bothan declared as he looked down to where Brenda lay in the mud.

She suddenly felt filthy. He contemplated her for a long moment before he took a couple of steps and braced his feet wide. Reaching down, he caught her by her upper arms and pulled her to her feet.

"I could have managed," Brenda said as she dragged her hands down her arms and flung glops of dark, wet mud to the ground.

"I did promise ye I would track ye down if ye wandered," Bothan said as he grabbed her overdress from where it lay in the mud. It was a dark mess of dirt and smelly water now.

Brenda propped her hands on her hips. "Do nae

make it sound like I've been doing something I should no' have been."

Bothan tilted his head to one side and swept her from head to toe with his blue eyes. "Ye appear to have been doing something completely…filthy…sure enough, lass!"

Brenda made a sound under her breath. She scooped up some more mud from where it clung to her arm and flicked it at him. The mud stuck to him, making a dark spot on the front of his shirt.

Bothan looked at it before his grin became wider. "Just like the day I met ye, Brenda, as the good wives told me if I venture too close to ye, I'll be dragged into yer debauchery and lust!"

"As if ye'd be so fortunate!" she snapped at him before reaching down to scoop up a handful of muck.

Bothan didn't give her time to lift her hand and launch it at him. He reached for her, intending to trap her against him with a hard embrace.

But he'd failed to realize how strong a grip the bog had on his feet. He stumbled when it took longer for him to pull his feet from the bog than he'd anticipated. He still caught her, but he was falling forward. She gasped and clutched at him. He managed to turn as they plummeted to the ground, the mud splattering all along their bodies and gripping them.

Brenda felt them sinking into the mud. Cold and slimy, it went right through the fibers of her remaining clothing.

And then she laughed. Brenda had no idea why, but she started chuckling, and it turned into full-body amusement. Bothan joined her as they fought against the bog and managed to stand. Bothan used his greater strength to pull her away from the center of the bog. Her underdress was sagging; even though it was made of lightweight linen, it felt like it was constructed of the thickest wool. She struggled to walk under the weight.

"Come on, lass," Bothan encouraged her. "There's a good deep spot in the river up ahead. We can clean this muck away and leave ye being praised for rescuing a calf without the details of nearly drowning in a bog to ruin yer heroic deeds."

"The good wives have already said plenty about me darker deeds," Brenda agreed as she grabbed two handfuls of the front of her dress and lifted it high so she might walk. Mud felt like it was everywhere, between her toes and breasts and other places she'd rather not contemplate.

The sound of the river drew her toward the promise of rinsing some of the muck from her. Now that the calf was no longer looking to her for rescue, she felt unbearably grimy. While working to free the animal, she'd been distracted from just how foul the bog smelled. Now, the stench was almost too much to bear.

So much so Brenda waded right into the water. She felt it chill her skin, but being cold was an improvement over being coated in thick, foul-smelling mud. Bothan stopped at the shore to pull his sword belt up and over his head. He looked around before setting the weapon against a large rock near the water's edge.

Brenda heard him splashing into the water as she

held her breath and dunked her whole head beneath the surface of the water. When she stood, Brenda felt the water running down her back, carrying dirt with it.

She went under again and again until her teeth were chattering.

"Here." Bothan offered her a lump of something.

In the fading light, she ventured closer to see what he held. The lump of soap was scented with rosemary.

"Ye have soap?" she asked him before taking it with a smile.

"Aye," he answered before pulling his shirt up and over his shoulders. "I'd just come up from bathing when Alba said she'd no' seen ye for hours."

"And ye came looking—" Brenda shut her mouth as she felt tension returning. The calf had consumed her attention for the afternoon.

Bothan sent her a hard look. "Of course I went looking for ye," he admonished her gruffly. "Ye might have been the one stuck in a bog instead of that calf."

Brenda tossed her head and lifted her chin. "I know better than to get stuck in a bog."

Bothan flashed her a grin. "But ye got trampled by a calf, now didn't ye?"

He was enjoying the situation hugely. Brenda narrowed her eyes at him before giving him her back and washing her hair.

"It was funny, and ye know it," he said after a bit.

She turned, the tension relieved by the scent of rosemary stripping the stench from her skin. "No matter how well we clean up here, the tale will still make its way once those children are finished with their evening chores."

"No doubt," Bothan agreed as he extended his hand for the lump of soap.

Brenda handed it over before she realized he'd stripped his kilt off. The wet wool was lying up on the shore as he stood just deep enough to cover his cock.

He snorted at her. "Do nae look so shocked…wife. Ye've seen a man before."

"Not really…" Brenda turned around, ready to cut her own tongue out. It was one thing to know in her own head but quite another to allow her words to slip so easily past her tongue to incriminate her. The truth was she'd fanned the flames of the gossips and let them make her into something far bolder than she was.

The words left unspoken were far stronger than the ones she might hurl in anger.

She heard Bothan splashing in the water as he washed. The evening breeze was blowing now, chilling her to the bone. But she still craved being clean over warming up. So she sat down and pulled her boots off, stripping her stockings from her legs so the mud between her toes might be washed away.

There was a pop and crackle from the shore. Orange light flashed at her from where Bothan had struck a flint stone and dropped sparks into a pile of tinder. A flame caught and licked up the sides of a piece of wood he'd found along the shoreline. Staying in the water was impossible with the promise of warming herself.

She stood and carried her boots with her to the shore.

"Yer husband bedded ye in full view of the court, and yet he did nae strip down for the event?" Bothan asked her as he tended the fire without a care for the fact that he was bare skinned. She was fascinated by the way he worked to build up the fire and spread out his clothing without a single shiver to betray that he felt the evening chill.

Her teeth chattered, proving she wasn't as hearty as he was.

"Sit down behind the rocks," he said, proving he was very much aware of her feeling the cold. "They will cut the breeze. Strip yer clothing off, and ye will warm up very quickly, I promise ye."

The hair on his chest had been a dark mat of wet fur. Now it was curling up and away from his skin.

"If I was going to demand me rights as yer husband, I would have done it with witnesses, Brenda," he said gruffly. "There is no need for ye to stand there and clutch yer clothing to ye like a shield."

She drew in a stiff breath. "I know ye have treated me kindly."

Far more so than she'd ever thought possible in a world where wives were chattel to their husbands.

Bothan locked gazes with her. "Then get out of that wet dress before ye catch a chill. When I dreamed of having ye in bed for hours on end, there was no fever."

"We can return to the tower." She looked toward the Gunn stronghold.

"We're farther from it than ye seem to realize, lass," Bothan advised her.

Darkness was rapidly falling. Brenda expected to see the lights of the village in the distance, but even after she blinked, there was nothing there to welcome her with the promise of shelter.

"I came after ye because ye do nae know me land," he explained further. "The bog the calf was stuck in is nae the only one here. If we go trying to return to the towers now, we're just as likely to end up needing to be rescued ourselves. The night will be long and chilly, though, before the sun rises to illuminate our plight."

While she'd been worried about the muck between her toes, he'd realized they needed to find shelter for the night. He'd chosen a space between tall rocks, where the sand promised a soft spot to rest. The fire was blazing now, and he'd shaken his clothing out and laid the garments over the rocks facing the fire. Steam was rising from the fabric as the heat dried it. He picked something else up, and she realized it was her cloak. He gave it a shake before laying it down on the sand between the rocks.

"Get out of yer dress, Brenda," Bothan repeated. "The night is about to turn very cold."

He'd left his boots on, showing he was thinking while she'd been busy reacting.

Of course.

From the moment she'd met him, Bothan had struck her as hardened. It was a compliment. One she didn't bestow lightly. The Highlands were a place where strength meant the difference between life and death. Just as the calf had needed to find the strength to escape the bog, men who lived in the northern parts of the country had to employ their wills against the elements if they planned on surviving.

Bothan thrived in his home.

It was etched into the hard muscles covering his

body. From his head to his arms to his thighs, there were solid, corded muscles on display.

She felt a different heat as she blinked and looked away from his cock. This warmth was spreading up from inside her as she pulled the knot free from where it was nestled between her breasts. A little tug and it opened, allowing her to work the lace loose. She looked at Bothan, but he wasn't watching her.

See? He's focused on doing what he must to make certain we do nae freeze…

She needed to prioritize as well.

And stop acting like such a frightened rabbit. He'd already had her. Well, in truth, they'd had each other, for she'd demanded him just as much as he'd taken her. The memory of the way he'd left her surfaced, kindling a new desire to have him please her again.

So why deny yerself tonight? Do ye nae keep saying ye will be yer own woman? Why are ye allowing others to force ye into submission?

Brenda let the idea rub her temper until she was pulling the lace free from her bodice without a care for her modesty. He was bare and he knew what a woman looked like, so there was no reason for her to be skittish.

Patience wasn't his strongest trait.

Bothan gritted his teeth and adjusted the length of wool that made up his kilt.

All he wanted to do was watch Brenda disrobe.

The need was fierce, clawing at his insides. She'd always pushed him to the edge of control, and the truth was he craved more of the feeling.

But he also longed for her trust.

She was pulling the lace loose that held the front of her bodice closed. He moved around the fire, picking at the drying wool while she snuck little glances at him.

Christ, ye want to kill her first husband.

Along with every one of the man's family members, who had made her endure a marriage where she'd been beaten down and taught to distrust men. Fine, he was no fool, and he understood marriage was a business. But there seemed too many who forgot it was also a Christian union.

She rose from it, though. Became strong. It was what drew ye to her.

Bothan recalled the first time he'd seen her, at a market harvest time fair where she'd boldly debated what the gossips were saying about her.

❧

Brenda made to step around him.

"*Ye did no' allow me to introduce meself,*" *he insisted.*

He stepped into her path. She spotted other men wearing his colors hanging back, making sure no one interrupted them.

"*Ye are a Gunn.*"

"*And you.*" *His expression became serious.* "*Ye are Brenda Grant, widow of a Campbell, who took Bhaic MacPherson as yer lover before ye landed in the keeping of the Earl of Morton.*"

"*I'm no' flattered by how much ye know.*"

He contemplated her for a moment. "*Ye should be. I do nae waste me time, Mistress Grant.*"

"*If that is so, why is it that ye listen to so much gossip?*" *she asked pointedly.*

"Clearly ye do nae know what a sensation ye cause when ye pass by." He offered her a soft chuckle. "There I was this morning, set to enjoy a mug of fine cider, no' even looking at the lasses."

"Ye strike me as the sort of innocent to be doing such a thing on harvest festival morning." Her voice was dripping sarcasm, but it was also husky, betraying how much she was enjoying the encounter.

His lips thinned in a purely sensual fashion. One that sent a touch of heat into her cheeks.

"Aye, as I said, ye passed by." He made a walking motion with his fingers. "And the good wives began to chatter about ye."

"And of course their word is so very reliable," Brenda said and then bit her lip.

"Which is why I doubt ye truly intend to dance naked under the moon tonight." He sounded pitifully disappointed, even pushing his lower lip out. "Truth be told, I was holding out hope for that one to be true. I do nae suppose ye might consider being generous toward me opinion of ye?"

Brenda snorted at him and propped her hands on her hips but couldn't help but admit to being amused by his humor. Not that she intended to allow him to know it.

"Bothan Gunn." He opened his arms and offered her a low courtesy, but he winked at her as he rose back to his full height.

❦

The memory had replayed so often in his mind. Nights when he should have been focused on matters of the Gunn chiefdom or selecting a suitable wife, he'd been reliving that moment when he'd spied her auburn hair and determined stance. She'd boldly kept her chin high as good wives sent her disapproving looks.

Christ, ye want her to dance naked beneath the moon with ye tonight.

His mouth nearly watered, and he made sure to keep his back to her as he felt his cock harden and stand straight out from his body.

His senses were heightened by his passion. He clearly heard the soft sound her dress made as it slumped to the ground. He caught the crunching sound her feet made as she stepped out of the garment and heard it hit the face of the rock to spread it out.

"Ye can turn around, Bothan…"

Brenda's voice was husky and soft, like the first time he'd met her. He felt it ripple through him as his cock jerked with need.

"Are ye finished being timid?" he asked her as he turned and let her see his rigid length.

Brenda was staring straight at him, the fire dancing in her eyes. The orange light bathed her body, but what made him suck his breath in through gritted teeth was the way she stared at him.

Straight at him.

This was the woman who had so boldly taken a lover among the ranking lairds of Scotland. She was unashamed of her passion, intent on having a full measure of pleasure just as any man experienced.

She'd accept nothing less from him.

And he wanted to measure up to her challenge more than anything he'd ever done.

"I am ready to see ye," she said boldly.

He spread his arms wide, enjoying the way the

darkness surrounded them and the firelight flicked across his skin. In that moment, he was hard and needy.

"Then look yer fill and tell me what ye crave," he advised her.

※

Brenda knew what she craved from him.

The Church really did have a point about nakedness being sinful.

Because for every eyelet she pulled her lace free of, a ripple of need shot through her. It built as steadily as the fire Bothan added more wood to, until she was full of anticipation. Her nipples had contracted into tight points, and it wasn't due to the chill in the air.

No. There was a fire in her belly, one which was burning fiercely.

Taking her clothing off was a relief. Almost as if she'd freed herself from shackles. She might have left her smock on, but she knew it would be a cowardly action.

She was suddenly finished with fear.

So she tugged the garment up and over her head, baring herself completely. Bothan made a soft sound in the back of his throat. She watched the way he swept her from head to toe, and then his gaze returned to her breasts.

"I made a mistake when I took ye before," he informed her gruffly.

"Is that so?" she asked. He was closing the distance between them, causing her insides to clench. Her heart was already racing, making her breath come in short pants.

"Aye." He reached her and cupped one of her breasts. "I failed to strip ye bare…and enjoy these."

He encircled her waist with one hard arm, bringing her to him as he leaned over and sucked one of her nipples. She gasped, arching back as pleasure jolted through her. Somehow, she'd never realized her breasts could be so sensitive. Bothan's mouth was nearly too hot, and yet she bent back, offering her breast to him.

"I want to spend hours with ye with naught but skin between us." He'd lifted his head to speak to her. Brenda opened her eyes, locking gazes with him. The look in his eyes made her shudder. The hard promise there was both exciting and intimidating.

He swept her off her feet and lowered her to the surface of the cloak. He'd chosen the spot well, for once they were down on the ground, the wind was cut by the rocks.

And his body was warm.

And hard.

She reached for him, needing to pull him closer.

"No' so quickly, lass." He was cupping her breast once more, kneading it as he teased the tight nipple with his thumb. "I'm going to demonstrate me merit as a lover."

"Perhaps I do nae care to have ye in command of me," Brenda argued. She had no idea why she was intent on needling him, only that the urge came from deep inside her where impulses ruled.

She reached down and wrapped her fingers around his cock. His teeth appeared as his lips curled back and his jaw tightened. His cock was covered in soft, smooth skin. Beneath it, though, he was rock hard.

She drew her hand up to the head, teasing the slit on the top with her forefinger.

"I will do me best to change yer thinking, Brenda," he muttered before he pressed a hard kiss against her mouth.

Brenda kissed him back. She reached up and threaded her fingers through his hair as she met him with all the passion boiling inside her. She didn't want to be taken; she wanted to be his equal.

"No." He pulled his head away and clasped her wrist, pushing her arm above her head and holding her still. "I will no' be hurried this time," he warned her.

She strained against his hold. Bothan kept her in place, watching her try to dislodge him. She should have detested the feeling, and yet there was something primal about it. Somewhere deep inside her, she enjoyed knowing how strong he was.

"Fine," she whispered with a smile. "I thought ye came for me because ye wanted something more than a submissive wife."

He snorted at her. But his fingers loosened around her wrist as his eyes narrowed.

"Ye test me, woman."

"Good," she declared as she curled up and pushed him over.

He rolled onto his back as she came up on top of him. A gleam of male satisfaction in his eyes betrayed how much he liked what she was doing.

"There is merit in listening to yer ideas, wife," he informed her as he lifted his hands and cupped her breasts. "Are ye going to dance by the moonlight for me, then?"

She laughed softly at the reference to their first meeting. His cock was pressed to her slit, the hard length of it driving her nearly insane. Fluid was seeping from her body, coating his length. She moved her hips, thrusting forward so that she slid along his member.

"Do ye want me to stand and dance?" she asked.

He slid his hands down to her hips, gripping them and holding her in place. Raw need glittered in his eyes. She curled her hands and raked her nails down his chest, drawing them along his skin with just enough force to make him growl at her. He started to rise, but she pushed him back down.

"Stay," she ordered. "Be mine."

His expression darkened, but he remained on his back. But he wasn't as submissive as he appeared. Bothan reached forward into the front of her slit where he teased the little pearl hidden there.

She gasped, rising up in surprise. He sat up, clasping her body with one arm while he continued to finger her clit.

"As ye will belong to me, Brenda," he promised her.

She was twisting as he held her steady and drove her closer to the edge of reason with his finger. His cock had straightened up beneath her, and the way he held her turned the situation to his favor because she was helpless there as he continued to rub her clit. The head of his cock had slipped into the opening of her passage, the fluid from her body coating it and making her quiver with anticipation.

"I want…more…" she rasped out, unwilling to allow her pride to keep her from the deep satisfaction she craved.

"As do I."

Brenda locked gazes with him. His eyes were full of the need to claim her. She struggled to send him just as fierce a look, but her body was too needy. He seemed to know her too well, as though he was in tune with her passion. He pressed harder, bending her back so he could sit up all the way.

"I want to make ye see I am the only one who will ever satisfy ye."

Her knees were still on either side of him, but he bent her back, and his hips kept her thighs spread for him. She might have been on top, but she was very much his captive in that moment. He thrust his fingers into her passage, sending her closer to climax. She heard her own little sounds of desperation and was powerless to contain them.

"Ye will call me husband," he rasped out before he pressed his fingers against her clit and rubbed it again.

This time there was no stopping the moment. Her body wanted satisfaction too much, and she jerked as pleasure tore through her. It was sharp and quick.

Too quick.

Her breath caught on a sob as she came back down, her body throbbing but still yearning for something more.

"That…wasn't…what I wanted!" she said.

"I know."

Brenda opened her eyes, caught in the grip of frustration. But his face was a mask of determination. He caught the side of her face, holding her prisoner as their gazes fused.

"I can satisfy ye," he promised her in a hard tone. "But there is a price."

He suddenly turned them over, pressing her down onto her back as he rolled over and settled between her thighs. He lowered his weight onto her, stopping just shy of hurting her.

"Ye will…call me…*husband*."

His breath teased her lips, awakening the delicate surface and leaving her rolling them in to moisten them. His eyes flashed with hard intent before he was tilting his head and pressing his mouth against hers.

It was a hard kiss. But she shivered and tried to raise her arms so she might pull him even closer.

Bothan denied her, pinning her wrists to the surface of the cloak while he opened her mouth with his and swept his tongue across the sensitive skin of her lips.

He is going to make ye mindless…

Brenda realized his intent, but the truth was she wasn't interested in thinking about it.

Only in experiencing it.

She was still at war with herself. Thinking one thing while craving another. At that moment, they were combining to produce a passion so hot it was melting everything, leaving her twisting in the heat of the moment.

He lifted his head, looking down at her. Satisfaction appeared on his face a moment before he released her wrists and placed his hands beneath her knees.

"Ye belong to me," he said as he pressed her legs up past her waist to bare her slit to him. "And I am going to enjoy showing ye just how much ye will like being mine."

His cock was poised over her open slit. She watched him rub it against her folds before he thrust into her. Not in one hard push. No, Bothan controlled the motion, savoring it, with a discipline that made her want to scream.

"I want ye!" she cried out. "Get on with it."

He growled at her, sank deep inside her. "I know me land…do ye wonder why I did no' take ye back to the tower?"

She opened her eyes wide, only to find him watching her with an expression that sent a shiver down her spine.

He was planning on being ruthless.

She'd sensed it in him, and now it was directed at her. She'd denied him openly, and he was going to make her claim him just as publicly.

His lips twitched as her eyes widened.

"I want to hear ye scream," he confessed.

"I will not be yer toy!" she declared.

His lips split into a grin that was far more menacing than anything else. He pulled his cock free and pressed it back into her with a hard motion of his hips, sending a shaft of pleasure straight through her.

"Ye will be…*mine!*" he declared.

His grin melted as his lips thinned. The time for talking was over. She felt something shift between them before he began to ride her, slowly at first. Each thrust was controlled. She wanted to lift up to meet him, but he had his arms beneath her knees and had folded her legs back so her knees were nearly at her shoulders. The position allowed him complete control.

Bothan made full use of it, too.

She wanted to care.

Brenda felt the thought move through her mind, but it dissipated as passion rose inside her once more. This time the pleasure was deeper, his cock filling her and stroking all the places the first release had denied her. It was too encompassing, too complete to allow for anything such as thinking.

No, there was only feeling.

Her eyes closed as her head fell back. Her back arched as he increased his pace, thrusting hard and deep into her body as she tried to drag in enough breath to support her racing heart. She was straining toward him, fighting to get closer because there was nothing except their union left. She could no more deny it than her next breath.

"Open yer eyes!" Bothan ordered her. "I want to see yer pleasure, lass."

Brenda forced her eyelids up, denying him unthinkable. It was the last straw, though. The glittering determination in his eyes sent her over the edge into a vortex of sensation. Was it pleasure or pain? The edges were so blurred she couldn't tell the difference.

But she cried out, lifting herself up as the climax ripped through her. It wrung her, refusing to release her until she felt her passage gripping Bothan's cock. He growled and buried himself inside her. His seed hit her in a thick stream that set off a second ripple of satisfaction deep inside her belly.

Every muscle she had felt strained when she could think again. Bothan rolled to the side, releasing her legs and stroking her sides before he landed heavily on his back, his chest heaving. The night air was a balm for how hot they both were, soothing them as Brenda surrendered to the blackness.

Nothing really mattered, not in that moment. She didn't have a thought to spare.

Bothan fell into a deep sleep. Weeks of tracking had taken their toll. Now that every breath he drew pulled her scent into his lungs, the need he'd ignored for sleep took its due. He spared only one last thought and opened his eyes to see that the fire was burning down. Soon, it would be only coals covered in ashes. The moon was only a sliver in the night sky, so no one would know where they were.

Five

BRENDA STIRRED WHILE IT WAS STILL DARK.

Fatigue was weighing her down, and Bothan's warmth made it hard to wake up. Still, something refused to be ignored. She blinked and opened her eyes. The fire had burned down, leaving only a bed of glowing coals. A tiny amount of wind made it to them, blowing across them and making them bright for a moment.

It was enough for her to see the shape of a man. She gasped, sitting up as Bothan opened his eyes and moved. He was on his feet before he saw what she did. Reaching out for his sword, he shoved her to the side, drawing the weapon from the sheath and swinging it in a high arc above his head.

Brenda landed on her backside. She wasn't wearing a stitch, but she was far more concerned with identifying the danger they were in. Horror gripped her as she saw more than one shape in the dark. Bothan thrust his blade through one, only to be struck from behind as he was withdrawing his weapon.

She heard the sound of his skull being hit with a

heavy club. His body jerked, and then he slumped to the side in a boneless heap.

"No!" she screamed as she launched herself toward him. She reached him, frantically searching for signs of life.

"I believe I'd enjoy taking ye home in naught but yer skin, Brenda," Hamell Campbell declared gleefully.

Icy dread gripped her as she recognized him. There was dirt smeared on his legs and arms to mask his scent. So close to the river, Bothan hadn't heard him or his men approaching.

They were both so very stupid.

But she took the larger share of the guilt on herself because she knew the Campbells. Their greed made them pressure her father to wed her against her mother's concerns over how young she'd been. Her sire had loved her, but he'd been a man who had a clan to worry about, and with neighbors like the Campbells, he'd had to placate them or risk a feud.

She'd been the price, and it seemed Bothan was now paying as well.

Hamell tossed her smock to her with a wink. "I'm no' of a mind to share ye with me men…yet."

Brenda bit back the argument she wanted to make. She'd learned early that life often offered her two choices: She might be right, or happy. Today, she'd take being clothed over blistering Hamell with words he deserved.

"Chief Gunn isn't dead," one of the Campbells observed after watching Bothan's chest rise and fall.

Hamell shifted his attention to Bothan. Brenda pulled her smock over her head and got her arms through the sleeves. Her breath caught in her throat as she waited to see what Hamell would decide.

Hamell looked at her. "I could kill him."

Brenda felt her heart stop.

Hamell read the horror on her face. "But I think it will serve me better to have ye fear for his life. Come away with me now, or I'll put a sword through yer lover while ye watch."

She bit back the correction she wanted to voice.

Husband…he's yer husband…

Fate was feeling especially cruel in making her long to say the words Bothan had wished for when she was about to agree to leaving with another man.

She had to.

There was no resistance in her when it came to nodding agreement. She had to give Bothan a chance at life.

Hamell grunted at her. He reached out to lock one hand around her wrist before he tugged her away from where Bothan lay. She turned her head, desperate for a last look at him. Just one final memory to sustain her.

She very much feared it would be the only balm her soul would have for the rest of her life.

He'd been a fool.

Bothan's mind was offering up the thought as he started to wake. It was harder than it should have been. His mind was stirring, and yet breaking through to consciousness was proving difficult.

He needed to wake.

He felt those words hit him like a bucket of icy

water. As he came closer to the edge of consciousness, a wave of pain tried to warn him against waking
completely.

No, there was something he had to do.

Brenda…

Bothan came awake with a roar. He rolled over and
up onto his feet. His vision swam in dizzy waves, but
he pushed up to his full height.

Christ, ye are an idiot!

The makeshift camp only accentuated how great
a fool he'd been. So close to the river's edge, he'd
placed them in a vulnerable position because the water
masked the sound of any intruders.

Maddox would never let him hear the end of it.

Not that Bothan cared too much about having his
captain tear a strip off his back. He'd let the man bring
it up for decades if it meant Brenda was there to laugh
over it.

What mattered was tracking down Hamell Campbell.

And killing the man.

Bothan took the time to dress because he wasn't
planning on staying at the tower long. Hamell was
hardened enough to ride at night, which meant
Bothan would have to strive harder.

And perhaps smarter.

Maddox was on his feet the moment Bothan gave
the bell outside the kitchen a ring. Men gained their
feet in an instant as torches were lit and the clan came
together to see what was wrong.

"Christ," Maddox exclaimed as he caught a glimpse
of the blood running down the side of Bothan's face.

"Hamell Campbell has stolen me wife," Bothan

declared. "I'm riding after him, and it will be bloody. I'm looking for volunteers."

His men formed up, their faces betraying their anticipation of the coming fight. Even the women watching sent Bothan firm glances. Hamell and his men had made a grave error in trespassing so close to their home. It wasn't the blood sport they all craved but the peace of mind to lay their heads down at night and sleep.

Men were pulling the horses into the yard. Alba was directing her staff to pack every bit of bread and cheese into bundles for them. Maddox caught Bothan watching it all.

"Do no' look so surprised, Chief," Maddox informed him. "Ye're a fine chief, and the lass is the right fit for the Gunns."

Bothan finished securing his saddle and looked at Maddox. "I'm proud to call meself yer chief."

Maddox slowly grinned. "Ye should be." He mounted his horse and clung to the back of the beast as it shifted. "Unlike the thieving Campbells...we Gunns fight our battles straight on!"

The retainers making ready to ride out with them roared with approval. Bothan swung up onto the back of his stallion and dug his heels into the sides of his horse.

Unlike Hamell Campbell, Bothan would be the victor.

Brenda was his.

⤸⤹

"Get yer tits under control." Hamell followed his crude comment by tossing Brenda's underdress at her.

Brenda caught it.

Hamell's men were watering the horses. He'd taken them down near the water's edge, where there was abundant cover from trees and rocks alike.

"I enjoy watching ye bite back that temper of yers," Hamell taunted her as she struggled to get into her underdress.

At least the tie was still dangling from the last eyelet. Brenda started threading it through the rest of the eyelets while Hamell smirked at her plight, denying her privacy simply because he might.

He was such a petty creature.

"Ye were always such a proud little bitch," he continued without a care for how lewd it was to watch her dressing. "Truth is"—he lowered his voice so his men wouldn't hear—"I wouldn't have been interested in wedding ye if ye'd given me a taste of yer honey."

Brenda knotted the lace and sent him a hard look. "Ye dare to admonish me for no' turning adulterous?"

Hamell shrugged. "Ye were a good little wife to me cousin. Faithful, obedient enough. But what has that gained ye?" He leaned closer, sharing his sour breath with her. "Me cousin was a bastard to ye. Used to seat his mistress right there at the high table next to you."

Brenda raised one of her eyebrows. "A few of the reasons why I refuse to wed…ever again."

"Ye married Chief Gunn," Hamell was quick to point out.

Brenda lifted her hands into the air. "An action that benefited both of us. I needed out of the arrangement made by the King, and Chief Gunn wanted me cousin Symon to owe him. It will end in annulment."

"So why were ye fucking him?" Hamell demanded.

"Why shouldn't I?" Brenda steeled herself against the crudeness of the comment. When fighting with a dog, she had to get into the gutter. "My maidenhead was taken long ago. No one will know if I enjoy meself or no'. Besides, I even have the Church's blessing."

Hamell held one finger up in her face. "No' the true Church."

"Ye have buried four wives," Brenda said softly. "I do nae think ye are any authority at all when it comes to God."

His eyes narrowed. A moment later his hand collided with her face. It was a hard blow, one his men heard clearly. Two of the younger ones turned to look their way, but what frightened her the most was how the rest of them ignored what their leader was doing.

Ye shouldn't be surprised.

Brenda realized the feeling filling her wasn't surprise. No, it was longing for the way Bothan had treated her.

"I like yer spirit, Brenda." Hamell reached out and grabbed a handful of her hair. He pulled closer as he sniffed at the auburn strands in his grip. "It goes well with yer fiery hair."

He shifted his attention to the side of her face that was throbbing. Satisfaction filled his eyes before he released her hair.

"Bringing ye to heel will be amusing."

He turned his back on her after giving her cleavage a long look. Brenda reached down and caught the edge of her smock. She gave it a good tug, pulling the fabric up higher.

Not that it would matter much. Hamell knew she was at his mercy.

He wants to toy with ye…

Brenda latched onto the idea. However flimsy a thought it was, the alternative was despair.

So she'd gather her courage and face her fate. As for lament, she'd dispense with it. Perhaps she'd failed to savor her time with Bothan while she was in it, but at least she had the memories.

It was better than naught.

And likely better than what the future would afford her.

⚬⚬⚬

Bothan found Hamell's tracks easily enough.

"The bastard is heading to Sutherland." Maddox voiced what Bothan thought.

Bothan nodded and stood. "It's his only haven, and he knows it. If he takes Brenda back to Campbell land, I can argue against the dowry on grounds that I wed her before the English Queen."

Bothan mounted as Maddox nodded.

"Hamell would think ye are only interested in the dowry," Maddox added.

Bothan turned his horse in the direction of the Sutherland stronghold. "Someday soon, I am going to sit down with Symon Grant and enjoy drinking to the end of this matter."

"I hope that part will happen after we kill some Campbells," Maddox said without a hint of remorse.

Bothan heard his men adding their approval.

It wasn't bloodlust.

It was justice.

❧

Hamell took her to Sutherland Castle.

Brenda felt her belly tighten into a knot at the first sight of the Sutherland stronghold.

Gunn Towers had impressed her with their strength, and Sutherland Castle was everything she might have expected of Bothan's overlord.

Hamell's as well.

Her belly twisted tighter as she absorbed the reality she faced. Hamell was riding fast. A couple of the horses had been abandoned along the trail as they failed to have the stamina to keep up.

And Brenda understood the reason.

Out on the road, Bothan would take Hamell man to man. The Campbell retainers riding with Hamell might guard their laird's nephew, but they were still Highlanders. Sneaking up on Bothan allowed Hamell to steal her without anyone raising a complaint. But if Bothan caught them and issued a challenge, Hamell would have to face it or risk having his own men turn on him.

Cowards didn't last very long in the Highlands.

But Hamell was no stranger to fighting. Brenda looked at the scars crisscrossing the man's arms and neck. He was just as hardened as Bothan. She didn't want to think about the pair of them fighting over her.

Because ye fear to lose Bothan…

It was the truth, one she didn't shy away from. Instead she tried to gather it close to her heart as Hamell took them down the road toward Sutherland

Castle. It rose up taller than she'd thought it was as they drew near. The huge towers had thick walls between them. The entrance was watched by two archer positions. As they rode through it, arrows might have been unleashed on them from above.

Once inside, the Sutherland retainers closed in behind them, making it clear they wouldn't be leaving until the earl said they might.

As far as the Highlands went, Sutherland was the only earldom. The King might hold higher rank over the earl, but the King was very far away.

"Hamell Campbell." The man who spoke was also hardened. He stood on the steps of one of the largest towers, watching them as they entered his yard.

Brenda slid from the back of her horse but had to hold onto the saddle for a moment because her knees were weak.

"I did no' expect to see ye back, Hamell," the man addressing them stated firmly. The tone in his voice made it clear that whoever he was, he wasn't feeling very welcoming toward the Campbells.

"I'm here to see yer father's words made law," Hamell informed their host.

Cormac Sutherland.

Brenda knew the name of the eldest son of the Earl of Sutherland. This man was backed by rough men who looked ready and almost eager to deal with the men Cormac was making clear he didn't want to welcome into the castle.

Cormac looked at her. His eyes narrowed. "Bring her inside."

If Brenda had doubted how much authority Cormac

had, she was left with no further illusions when the retainers behind her moved forward and caught her by her upper arms.

"I can walk," she assured them.

They must have heard, her but they didn't give her any indication they had. She was walked across the yard and up the steps that led to the tower. She gained a glimpse of a massive great hall before she was being escorted through a passageway. Window shutters were open, affording her a glimpse of expensive glass. When the weather was wet or snowy, there would still be light in the stone hallway.

Cormac was ahead of them, the longer pleats that made up the back of his kilt swaying with his determined stride. The heir to the Sutherland earldom had blond hair, and when his men finally followed him into one of the smaller towers where the bottom floor was used as a weapons room, she gained a glimpse of blue eyes.

Hamell had been left to follow them on his own. Cormac gestured to the men escorting her forward, which meant she was delivered right in front of him. A childhood full of training meant she was lowering herself out of habit. Cormac watched her perform the polite courtesy, but he didn't return it.

"Brenda Grant," Cormac stated firmly. "Yer hair is as red as I've heard."

Brenda quelled the urge to shift. "I do nae understand the fascination with red hair," she replied with her chin held steady.

Cormac's lips twitched. It was a little cocky motion, one that momentarily transformed his face into something very handsome. But his expression hardened as Hamell grunted.

"I'm here to wed her," Hamell insisted. "As yer father promised me I might."

"My father is nae here," Cormac informed him softly.

Brenda felt the tension in the room rising. Cormac's expression might not give anything away, but a glitter in his eyes made her suspect he didn't agree with his father.

Ye're seeing what ye want to see…

Maybe. Brenda held onto the flicker of hope as Cormac stared at Hamell.

"Where did ye get her?" Cormac demanded.

Hamell crossed his arms over his chest. "What does it matter? Yer father granted me the right to wed her."

Cormac gestured with his fingers. His men understood instantly, gripping her upper arms and pulling her back so he could move closer to Hamell.

"It matters," Cormac declared in a low tone. "The only reason my father agreed with yer suit was to keep peace between the Campbells and Sutherlands. Feuds are no good for any of us."

"She's here," Hamell said. "Ye needn't look like ye've got a bug up your arse, man."

"Where did ye get her?" Cormac repeated. "Do ye think I'm blind, man? Ye've ridden yer horses half to death and she"—Cormac pointed at Brenda—"appears to have most of the road on her from the pace ye've been pushing yer men. I am no' still on the breast, man. Ye stole her and brought her to Sutherland."

"So what if I stole her?" Hamell said, defending

himself. "I had yer father's permission to wed her. So it stands to reason I'd need to have her in me possession to do so. She's hardly the first bride taken for her dowry."

"I would know who ye stole her from," Cormac demanded. "My father wasn't giving ye free rein to start a feud."

"She's a woman," Hamell hedged. "No' even a maiden. The matter will be forgotten soon enough."

"He stole me from Chief Bothan Gunn," Brenda interrupted. "Me husband."

Hamell growled and raised his hand to strike her. The retainers at her sides moved in a flash, putting themselves between Hamell and herself. Hamell froze, realizing he was beat, but there was a flash of promise in his eyes.

"Aye, Chief Bothan Gunn." Hamell shrugged and looked back at Cormac. "If a man can no' keep a prize, he does nae have the right to it."

Cormac's lips rose in a mocking grin. "If that is yer thinking, perhaps I should put ye outside the gates and see if ye can best the man when he arrives."

"He is no' coming for her," Hamell stated. His tone might have been firm, but he shifted, betraying how much he didn't like what Cormac had said.

"So ye do think I'm newly weaned," Cormac growled. "Ye would no' be riding so hard if ye did nae have a reason."

"My laird ordered me to wed her," Hamell reiterated. He stepped closer to Cormac. "Ye jump when yer father tells ye to. I do nae have the blessing of being a firstborn son and heir. Me laird sent me out to wed Brenda Grant, and I dare not fail."

Brenda didn't care for Hamell's reasoning.

But she could not refute it either. Her own father had bent beneath the demands of Laird Campbell.

Cormac Sutherland might not have cared for the circumstances, but he wasn't ignorant of the realities of life either. The castle they stood in hadn't been built from good deeds. No, there had been marriages arranged for gain and power struggles. Blood had flowed, she didn't dare doubt it.

"My father," Cormac said, "isn't here."

Hamell wasn't intimidated by the statement. "His word is still law. The earl gave Brenda Grant to me in marriage. I'm here with her, and I expect ye to abide by yer father's decree."

"She claims she is married," Cormac argued. "If she has a living husband, even the Earl of Sutherland cannot give her to ye in marriage."

Hamell smiled. The expression chilled Brenda's blood. "They wed in England, so under the bastard Queen Elizabeth's church. All we need is a priest."

"And a stronghold to protect ye from the wrath of Bothan Gunn while ye conduct yer wedding and consummation." Cormac wasn't going to yield so easily.

"Ye think to deny me what yer father promised?" Hamell asked. "My laird will no' be happy to hear about it."

The threat hung in the air. Every man in the room heard it. Brenda curled her fingers into fists as she watched Cormac. He was playing a dangerous game. One that might spell disaster for Sutherland if a clan the size of the Campbells decided to take offense. He might personally wish to do something different, but defying his father would have consequences.

Dire ones.

Cormac suddenly looked up. A retainer was standing in the doorway.

"Chief Bothan Gunn is arriving," the Sutherland retainer declared.

"She is mine!" Hamell declared loudly. "Yer father said it was so! Lock yer gates, or I swear the Campbells will hear of yer interference in this matter."

The retainers in the room didn't care for Hamell's tone.

Or perhaps it was his threats.

It didn't matter which offended them; they shifted closer to Hamell, seeking any excuse to deal with him.

"As ye are so very quick to point out," Cormac informed Hamell, "my father is the earl. I would no more deny one clan under him entrance to Sutherland than another."

The heir to the earldom of Sutherland stepped up until he was only a step away from Hamell.

"Such a thing," Cormac continued, "would be for me father to decide."

Cormac looked at Brenda. He was a serious young man. It was clear he'd been raised to be the Earl of Sutherland's successor. His expression gave nothing away. Not even a single shred of hope for her to latch onto. In his world, decisions would be made with the political situation firmly in mind.

Oh, she understood the reasoning.

And it was hardly the first time she'd lamented that hard facts would dictate the direction of her life.

Today, though, she felt the sting more deeply. As though her heart was being torn from her chest.

"I will receive Chief Gunn," Cormac declared. His tone left no room for argument.

But Hamell wasn't wise enough to heed the warning.

"Ye will nae!" Hamell insisted.

Hamell made the mistake of stepping toward Cormac. The Sutherland retainers reacted in a flash. They surged forward, grabbing Hamell and his men. Brenda was tugged back by a hard pull on her skirts as the two Sutherland retainers behind her came around her and placed themselves in front of her.

The fight didn't last long, and there wasn't any doubt who the victor would be. At least Brenda saw the reality of how badly the Campbells were outnumbered. Any levelheaded person would have recognized the folly of trying to win against the Sutherlands inside their own castle. Hamell, though, didn't seem to acknowledge any of those facts. He fought hard but was dragged out of the room by the Sutherland retainers.

Cormac wiped his mouth on his sleeve, a vicious smile of enjoyment on his face. It vanished just as quickly as the fabric of his shirt soaked up the trickle of blood from his split lip. He caught her watching him. Something flashed in his eyes. It looked a lot like pleasure, but he covered the lapse in composure without admitting anything to her.

"Ye seem to bring out an interesting trait in the men who attempt to claim ye, Mistress Grant," Cormac told her.

Brenda offered him a slight scoffing sound. It earned her a twitch from one side of his mouth, which might have been called a grin if it hadn't melted away by the time she took her next breath. He looked at the Sutherland retainers still in the room.

"Keep her here," Cormac ordered.

It wasn't that Brenda had believed she had any freedom before, but once Cormac spoke, the retainers nearby moved closer. They were rigid and immovable.

And she was very much their prisoner.

❧

Cormac Sutherland met Bothan in the yard. Bothan reached up and tugged on the corner of his knitted bonnet. The single gesture was as formal as Bothan planned to be.

Bothan climbed the steps until he was eye to eye with the man. "Expecting me, are ye, Cormac?"

"I would be disappointed if ye were no' following close behind Brenda Grant," Cormac replied.

Cormac turned and walked into the tower. Sutherland retainers were guarding the doorway.

On the other side, Brenda stood behind the crossed pikes of another set of Sutherland retainers. Bothan took a moment to look her over. His temper had been kept in check as he rode and made sure he was using his wits to solve the matter instead of charging headfirst into a fight. He knew the value of keeping a cool head, but the sight of the dirt smeared down his wife's clothing threatened to break his hold.

Bothan looked at Cormac. "What game are ye playing, Cormac? Brenda is me wife."

Cormac stood up to Bothan's direct gaze. Unlike Hamell, Bothan wasn't using the names of his relatives to sway the next in line to the earldom.

"This is no' a matter of politics, Cormac," Bothan stated firmly. "Perhaps before I wed her it might have been, but the deed is done now. Blessed and consummated. Stealing a bride is one thing. Brenda is me wife and might well be carrying me child. The matter is done."

Cormac let out a grunt.

"My father is more than my sire," Cormac informed Bothan. "He's the Earl of Sutherland and overlord to both of us." He held up a thick finger when Bothan started to speak. "And he is no' here."

"So?" Bothan questioned the man. "Me wife is, and I'll thank ye to tell yer men to get out of the way between what is mine by law of the Church."

"But ye wed her in the English church," Cormac stated firmly. "Hamell Campbell is using the lack of Catholic blessing on yer union as a reason to declare it null and void. Since it is Brenda's second marriage, ye cannae hold her by physical relations alone."

Bothan let out a grunt. "I've had a belly full of kings and politics! I've served Sutherland well, and I never thought getting a bridle on Brenda would prove to be a simpler task than dealing with everyone's ideas of what constitutes a wedding."

Bothan was close to losing his temper, but he remained facing Cormac. "I pledged meself before God and witness to this woman."

"Ye should have consummated the vows with witnesses," Cormac answered. "When land is concerned, ye know well men will fight dirty to gain the upper hand."

Bothan grunted. "When the bride is a redhead, a man is wise to let her think she's got a choice."

He looked across the room at Brenda and the way her cheeks were turning red with temper.

"The truth is I was giving her slack before pulling her in. An English wedding meant Brenda rode into Scotland with me and gave me time to ease me way into her bed."

Brenda let out a sound that was very close to a growl.

Cormac made a choking sound. "Take Mistress Grant abovestairs."

The retainers didn't hesitate to act. Brenda let out a huff as she was turned and taken out the doorway behind her.

"Stay," Cormac ordered Bothan when he went to follow her.

Bothan turned to face Cormac slowly. "I'm dangerously low on patience, man."

"I understand," Cormac replied, stepping half in front of Bothan. "For I feel the same."

Bothan grunted. "Explain, Cormac, and I warn ye, I'm in need of killing someone. So do nae press yer luck."

Cormac grinned. It wasn't a friendly sort of curving of his lips. No, it was more of the sort of expression Bothan wanted to see on the face of a man who was going into a fight next to him. There was a flash of comradeship in Cormac's eyes.

"Ye have reason to think yer wife might be carrying yer child?" Cormac asked.

Bothan felt his own lips curving. "It is a definite possibility."

Cormac's lips split into a wide smile. "As I told ye, my father is no' here. Perhaps he'll arrive by tomorrow. I cannae make any choice between ye or the Campbells concerning this matter. Mind ye, if there is a question of there being issue from yer union, I believe my father would see the matter as a handfasting in need of the sacrament."

Bothan nodded. "More than one man would agree with ye."

Cormac reached out and slapped Bothan on the shoulder. "Hamell Campbell will be spending the night in the Sutherland dungeons for attacking me. I cannae have a man with such a lack of control over his temper loose in my father's castle while me sister is here."

"And me?" Bothan asked pointedly.

"Ye have stated yer position," Cormac replied. "And I've told ye I cannae decide the matter because it was me father who gave permission to Hamell to go after Mistress Grant. It seems ye will have to wait upon me father's return."

The heir to the earldom of Sutherland drew in a deep breath and let it out, still grinning like a boy intent on sneaking tarts from the kitchen under the eye of the cook. Not just for the joy of enjoying a treat but for the thrill of knowing he'd pulled something over on those around him who thought themselves so much more experienced.

"Chief Gunn, ye've given me no reason to lock ye away. I cannae allow Mistress Grant to leave Sutherland, but since ye claim to have wed her—"

"I did marry her," Bothan insisted.

Cormac shrugged. "Who am I to decide which church is the rightful one? It's a matter for my father. He is the Earl of Sutherland."

There were both permission and warning in Cormac's voice. Bothan reached up and tugged on the corner of his bonnet.

Cormac's grin twisted into a smirk, his eyes glittering with mischief. "Mind ye, I heard ye say ye intended to get a bridle on yer wife." Cormac closed his fingers into a fist and hit Bothan on the upper arm. "If she throws yer body out the window of the chamber I had her placed in, I give ye fair warning...I am going to have a good laugh over yer plight. Do nae ye know better than to tangle with a redhead?"

Bothan returned his friend's grin, but he pointed at Cormac. "I'm sorry to see ye have no' found the courage to try one."

It wasn't a jest though.

Bothan turned and left the room. Stairs rose up along the side of the tower. He took to them with a determined stride, the separation between him and Brenda becoming too much to bear now that he knew she was his to reclaim.

The chamber to which Brenda was taken was quite nice.

But she found she had no appreciation for the fine furnishings. The doors were closed tightly behind her, the two retainers shooting her hard looks before they were blocked out by the solid wood. She crossed the area of the receiving chamber to look out of the window.

It was more than three stories to the ground. A death sentence if she tried to jump.

Not that she'd get too far without a horse. The Sutherlands would only run her to ground.

But the doors opened again, and this time Bothan was there. He stood for a moment at the entrance as the retainers closed the doors again.

Brenda found herself staring at him.

The days of frantic travel suddenly dissolved as she took in the way he was looking her over. The fear that had gripped her heart during that time of never seeing him again and perhaps hearing he'd died there between those rocks finally dissipated.

And his words rushed back through her mind as he came forward.

"Need to get a bridle on me?" Brenda demanded. "Letting out some slack on the rope so ye can make me think I'm free?"

She'd propped her hands on her hips as she confronted Bothan. He was watching her, letting her vent at him. The surge of emotion didn't make any sense. But she was swamped by it, tumbled in the wave of relief and renewed worry over just what the Earl of Sutherland would say when he arrived.

"Insufferable man," she declared when he remained silent. Brenda went to turn her back on him.

Bothan caught her, closing his arms around her as he came up behind her. She gasped, trying to free herself, only to suffer the knowledge that he was far stronger than she.

Oh, but he is so wonderfully alive…

"Have ye no' learned yet, me lovely lass," he cooed against her ear, "not to turn yer back on me when ye decide to take issue with me? I will take every challenge ye cast down, Brenda…count on it."

"Let go," Brenda hissed.

She stumbled when he complied, opening his arms so she ended up pitching forward because she'd been straining away from him. She caught herself, stopping with a little skidding sound from her boots. Her skirts swayed forward with her movement. Bothan scooped her up before the fabric settled back down.

"I do let the rope out on ye," he explained on his way toward the bed. He dropped her onto it in a tangle of skirts and limbs. "I let ye run because I love the sight of ye tossing yer head and daring me to try to ride ye," he finished.

"Why am I no' surprised to hear ye say something such as that?"

Bothan grinned at her. It was the most menacing curving of lips she'd ever seen. He tossed his doublet aside and opened his belt. Her eyes widened as she realized precisely what he had on his mind.

"Do nae be thinking we're going to—" Her tongue suddenly refused to perform as she started to push her way across the large bed.

The length of wool that formed his kilt puddled around his ankles before he lunged after her in only his shirt.

"What I think I am going to do," Bothan declared as he landed on top of her, "is help ye use yer passion for something much more enjoyable."

She started to sputter, but he rolled over until she was sitting on top of him. The change in position took her by surprise, shocking her into silence. Bothan cupped her hips, pressing her down onto his body. The position had her straddling his cock between the folds of her slit as her dress spread out around them.

Christ, he feels good…

And the grip on her hips sent a shudder of excitement through her core.

He chuckled and rubbed her hips. "Ye like it…me touch."

Brenda set her teeth into her lower lip. "There is more to a marriage than passion, Bothan."

"Aye," he agreed more solemnly than she'd expected. "And like anything in life, there is a time… and place for it."

He reached up and pulled the lace holding her bodice closed. The knot popped instantly, and he tugged the lace from the eyelets. Her breasts sagged down, feeling heavy and needy. No matter what her mind wanted, her body craved his. Desire was flowing through her veins like rich French wine. No matter how much she wanted to argue, she knew it would intoxicate her even as she tried to maintain her protest.

So she might as well take his advice.

"A time and a place?" Brenda inquired. Bothan raised his gaze to hers in response. "Well then, husband, I believe it time for ye to be taken…"

He was cupping her breasts, his fingers kneading the soft flesh as her nipples contracted into tight points. Her core was melting as her mind settled on a course of action. She cupped his shoulders and rose up. His cock sprang up, hard and rigid.

"Maybe I think yer place is beneath me," Brenda declared as she lowered herself onto his length.

His eyes narrowed. She watched the way his expression transformed with pleasure. A deep, sexual sort of pleasure.

She felt it too.

Hunger was a living force inside her, and Brenda had no intention of ignoring it. There was a wildness inside her, breathing and pulsing with the need to hold onto him while the opportunity was hers.

Bothan gripped her hips, rising up off the bed to thrust into her as she came down. She lamented not taking time to remove more of her clothing because she was hot, but stopping was out of the question.

And her husband wasn't going to let her keep the dominant position either. He growled at her before rolling her over and onto her back.

"Ye're mine, Brenda," he hissed as he pinned her beneath him, grasping her wrists and pulling them high above her head.

"I am more than just…yers," she declared.

He lowered his head so that their faces were close enough for her to feel his breath on the delicate surface of her lips.

"Ye are the only woman who is mine," he growled. "And I will show ye the merit in enjoying the position."

He wanted to master her. Brenda recognized the flash of male intent in his eyes.

And yet there was something new about it. This

wasn't the cold, calculated look of a man who felt he was superior to her simply because of his gender.

No, what she witnessed flickering in Bothan's eyes was the need to prove himself to her. To pleasure her in a way that would keep her from ever straying from his side because she knew he was the only man who could feed the need raging inside her. He wanted to take her beyond the carnal needs of passion to the place inside her where she'd always felt so very alone.

But her body wasn't going to allow her to linger in the moment. Everything was building, raging out of control. Brenda didn't fight it; no, she flung herself into the fury, letting it rip at her and twist her insides until everything burst in one fiery explosion.

Was it pleasure?

Or torment?

She didn't care. The only thing of any importance was that Bothan was there with her. His scent filling her senses, his hard body slamming into hers as his growls mixed with her cries.

Nothing else mattered.

Nothing at all.

෫ఌ

Brenda fell asleep beside him.

Bothan felt the moment that her breathing slowed and her body relaxed. He was weary, but fatigue was no match for the memory of what had happened the last time he allowed himself to sleep while she was depending on him for protection.

He stroked her face, enjoying the moment of freedom to touch her as he pleased. It was surreal in a way because she'd appeared in his dreams so often since he'd met her.

Now she was real.

But for how long?

He eased away from her, covering her so she'd stay warm. She snuggled down into the bedding, a contented little curve on her lips.

Bothan dressed and went to the doors. The Sutherland retainers had orders to keep Brenda in the chamber. They eyed him, a pair of smirks on their lips. Brenda likely wouldn't thank him for making sure there were witnesses, but she also knew the world was full of unpleasant necessities.

He'd do what needed doing to keep her.

Or at least to keep her away from Hamell.

"I know my father." Cormac Sutherland was sitting in the weapons room at the base of the tower. He looked at Bothan, gesturing him forward to share the food in front of him.

Bothan sat and broke off a piece of bread from a large round. He had a feeling he'd better eat while he might. The look on Cormac's face wasn't very promising.

"My father will weigh the strength of the Campbells against the Gunns," Cormac continued.

"Brenda is a Grant," Bothan added.

Cormac nodded in agreement. "The Grants are a long way from Sutherland."

"And the Campbells are closer?" Bothan asked the unnecessary question.

"Better to think of another way to deal with Hamell," Cormac suggested. "Once my father returns, I fear you will lose the chance to keep yer wife."

"That is something I have already thought of," Bothan said. "Do you really think I came here without thinking the matter through?"

Cormac tilted his head to one side. He was chewing on a piece of cheese. Once he swallowed, he washed it down with a sip of ale. "I've always liked ye, Bothan. Mostly because you are an honorable man. My father sees endless appeals for judgment from men who would rather wheedle their way to what they want instead of earning it themselves."

"Such as Hamell Campbell," Bothan suggested.

Cormac shrugged. "He is simply an instrument of Laird Campbell."

"And yet," Bothan continued, "not so innocent."

Cormac lifted an eyebrow and waited for Bothan to continue.

Bothan held up four fingers. "Four wives in their graves. No issue to inherit. He's guilty of looking the other way at best."

"And murder at worst," Cormac agreed. "But my father will always choose the path that is best for Sutherland."

"Aye." Bothan picked up the round of bread and stood. "I suspected ye might tell me so. But I thank ye for giving me time to keep yer father from giving Brenda to Hamell."

Cormac nodded. "He'll have to wait until she is proven to not be carrying yer child. My father will not cross that line of tradition. If there is a babe, my father will consider it a handfasting."

"Or risk angering a large number of his men," Bothan confirmed.

"I've no liking for the need for witnesses either," Cormac stated grimly. "Yet it seems a necessary evil."

"I need fresh horses," Bothan declared, "and yer word that ye will safeguard me wife."

"Where are ye heading?" Cormac asked.

"Better that ye do nae know," Bothan replied. "Yer father might ask ye."

Cormac took a moment to consider Bothan's words before he nodded. "Take what ye need, and I bid ye good luck."

Cormac offered Bothan his hand. They clasped wrists before Cormac swept the remains of their meal into the cloth laid out on the table and tied it into a bundle. Bothan took it with him as he disappeared into the dark passageway. The castle wasn't completely black, and the windows allowed enough moonlight in for him to see by. Hamell might prefer to gain his prizes by wheedling, but Bothan had always fought his fights straight out.

But this time, Bothan realized the stakes were the highest they'd ever been.

For he was fighting for his wife.

Six

THE BELLS RANG ON THE WALLS OF SUTHERLAND Castle just before sunset the next day.

The tolling began with the two atop the gate towers but spread until every bell was ringing loudly and clearly. Brenda crossed to the window and watched as riders entered the yard to the delight of the Sutherlands. From the height of her chamber room, there was no way to make out features, but she knew the earl from the way his people clamored for his attention.

He was helped from his horse before making his way into the great hall in the center of the castle yard.

Bothan has left ye.

Brenda walked back across the room. Her feet were sore from her pacing, and her belly rumbled with hunger because a single meal had arrived at dawn and the day was waning now.

Would ye care to see him made a prisoner along with ye?

The answer was no. Brenda nursed her injured feelings on her way across the floor. She'd just felt so... intimate with him the night before. Waking up alone had her fighting off tears of loneliness. Not that anyone would ever know about those little drops that had covered her hands in the darkest hours of the night.

She sniffed and blinked her eyes, refusing to cry again. If naught else, she didn't need to be any thirstier.

It was a pathetic little thing to be in control of.

Helpless…

Brenda didn't care for how the word came to mind and how impossible it seemed to be to uproot it. A rap finally sounded on the doors. Brenda turned and watched as the retainers opened them.

"Stay in there, Mistress," one of them warned her sternly, "or ye'll go without yer supper."

Brenda forced herself to stand still as a neat row of maids entered. The younger ones were curious, looking at her as they carried in a variety of plates. Everything was set down, and the maids turned around in answer to the snapping of the retainer's fingers.

The man wasn't planning on dealing with his laird being upset over losing her. He watched Brenda as the maids left, his expression softening a small amount as she remained in place.

"Thank ye," he muttered before closing the doors.

Brenda let out a snarl. Oh, it wasn't a fitting sound for a lady to make, but no one was there to hear her frustration. She moved toward the plates, seeing what had been sent to her. There was more than enough food for a meal and two buckets of water for washing.

But what Brenda noted was the fact that the Sutherlands weren't planning on there being many opportunities for the doors to be opened.

Helplessness…

Brenda felt her temper rise, and she allowed it to rage. At least the flames burnt away the feeling of being trapped. Where did that leave her? She honestly didn't know. But it wasn't helpless, so she'd take what she could get.

✎

"Yer son had me locked in yer dungeon!" Hamell raged at the Earl of Sutherland. "My uncle is no' going to like hearing of it."

The earl had gray hair. He wore a flat cap to conceal the spot on top of his head where his hair had thinned. But his eyes were still sharp.

"I understand you tried to start a fight inside my home," the earl began. "You're lucky to still be standing inside Sutherland."

Hamell wasn't fool enough to continue with his tirade. He drew up short and bit back his next outburst.

The earl didn't miss it either. The older man nodded firmly. "Now, what is this matter of you arriving with a stolen woman?"

"Ye granted me the right to wed Brenda Grant," Hamell exclaimed.

"I did no' give ye permission to attack Chief Gunn," the earl interrupted, "or to bring him to my castle with a valid reason to appeal to me for justice."

Hamell wasn't deterred. He opened his arms wide. "The woman has a dowry that had the King taking notice of how valuable it is."

The earl grunted. "Well, as to that point, I agree."

Hamell smiled with victory.

"Which is no' me saying I will turn a deaf ear to

Chief Gunn," the earl was quick to add. "He's a loyal man to Sutherland and claims he wed the Grant lass. If the deed is accomplished, I cannot undo it."

"It was an English wedding," Hamell argued. "The Grants are Catholic. So are you."

The earl slowly smiled. "Yet it was the King of Scotland who sent Brenda Grant to England to be wed. The King might be young, but he knows the English Queen is head of her English church."

Hamell's complexion was darkening. "The King is a long way from here. He meddled enough in this matter. Brenda Grant is from the Highlands. Better the dowry stay within the clans than be given to England."

"A fine idea," the earl agreed.

Hamell was back to grinning. The earl contemplated him for a moment before shifting his gaze toward his son Cormac.

"Chief Gunn has appealed to me for the lass on the grounds of consummation and possible issue from the union," the earl said.

"Chief Gunn left England without consummating the union," Hamell insisted. "There are no witnesses."

"There are Sutherland witnesses," Cormac declared. "There was no reason to deny Chief Gunn the company of his wife." Cormac flashed Hamell a grin. "Bothan didn't attack me."

Hamell's eyes bulged. "Ye bastard!" he raged as he lunged toward Cormac.

The retainers in the room moved to protect their laird's son, but Cormac didn't need help. He lowered his head and rammed into Hamell, twisting him around and locking his arm around the man's neck.

Straightening up, Cormac choked Hamell while the man frantically tried to break the hold.

"Cormac," the earl called out to his son. "Ye've made yer point."

Cormac let out a disgusted sound before releasing Hamell. The chamber was filled with the sound of Hamell staggering away from the heir to the earldom. The retainers watching made it plain they enjoyed seeing the display of their future laird's ability.

"Yer son," Hamell declared, "knew full well of yer blessing on me wedding Brenda Grant!"

"True," the earl conceded.

"Laird Campbell is going to hear of this," Hamell threatened.

"No one is going anywhere just yet," the earl declared. "Chief Gunn is not here, and it seems we'll all be waiting to see if the lass is with child or not. If there is issue, ye've lost her."

"There are ways to deal with unwanted issue," Hamell suggested.

The earl slowly smiled. "It seems I find meself in agreement with me son on the matter of keeping ye in the dungeon."

"Laird Campbell will hear—" Hamell protested as the retainers behind him grabbed him by the upper arms.

"Ye can be certain of it!" The earl raised his voice. "Laird Campbell will hear of how I watched ye try to kill me only son...right before me eyes! And that ye tried to have me agree with killing an unborn child, which is a mortal sin in the Church ye claim to be a member of!"

The earl looked at his men. "Toss him back in the dungeon."

The Sutherland retainers didn't hesitate to carry out the earl's orders. They hauled Hamell and his men out the door, leaving the chamber quiet.

"Ye know I must consider the Campbells' strength." The earl spoke softly to his son.

Cormac had been waiting for his father to speak. Now that they were alone, his sire would make it clear that he expected Cormac to think of Sutherland first and foremost.

"As we should keep in mind the Gunns and Grants," Cormac replied.

The earl tilted his head to one side. "Ye know the Campbells pose a far more immediate threat to us."

Cormac didn't falter. He stared straight at his father.

The earl grunted, but his lips rose into a grin that was full of pride. "I was a young man like ye once, Cormac. I see the need for justice in yer eyes, and in me heart, I agree. Hamell is a sniveling, whining excuse of a man. It turns me stomach to think of watching him carry off a prize."

"Which is why I made certain there would be witnesses to Bothan bedding his wife," Cormac told his father.

"Where is Chief Gunn?" the earl asked.

"I do not know," Cormac answered. "But he will be back, of that I'm certain."

The earl grunted. "Ye made it so he has time."

Cormac nodded.

"Even with time," the earl warned his son, "I doubt

Chief Gunn can find the means to making me rule in his favor."

Cormac flashed a look at his father. "If any man could beat the odds, I'd bet me money on Chief Gunn."

⁂

"Ye'll not tell me no."

Brenda heard a woman outside her doors a few days later. She crossed the floor to listen.

"Yer father has given strict instructions to keep the doors shut tight," one of the retainers on guard duty told whoever it was.

"Ye may close them tight…behind me," the girl insisted. "Now get out of my way."

Brenda backed up a few paces. The retainers were obviously debating the issue, but the doors creaked and opened wide. The woman standing there locked gazes with her.

"I am Annella." She introduced herself and came straight into the chamber.

"Lady Annella," one of the retainers informed Brenda with a stern look. "The earl's daughter."

Brenda offered the girl a quick courtesy. The retainer grunted with approval.

"Enough of that." Annella waved her hand through the air. "We're abovestairs, after all. No need for formalities."

The retainers who had so diligently been standing in the open doorway had to make way for a line of younger boys. They were carrying a tub, and following close behind them were a dozen bearing buckets of water.

"Since ye cannot come below," Annella declared sweetly, "I have brought a bath to ye."

Annella had blond hair and blue eyes. She looked like a fairy, delicate and petite. Her dress might have been made of wool, but it was some of the finest fabric Brenda had ever seen. It fit her perfectly too, with shoulder details someone had spent endless hours sewing for nothing more than decoration.

The boys left without a single one of them forgetting to tug on the corner of his bonnet toward the lady. Annella had a sweet smile on her lips, but after the doors were closed, Brenda looked at her.

"Found an excuse to see the woman all the castle is gossiping about?" Brenda asked pointedly.

Annella fluttered her eyelashes, but Brenda propped her hand on her hip in response. Annella let out a peal of delicate laughter.

"I suppose," Annella said. "Being the daughter of a laird, ye know how to appear innocent."

"Cousin of the laird," Brenda replied. "But ye are correct."

Annella came toward her. "Let me help ye disrobe before the water grows cold."

Brenda felt a little chill go down her back. Annella held her expression perfectly. The look on the girl's face was serene and sweet, as though the girl didn't have a single wit in her head.

Brenda wasn't deceived.

So much attention to her clothing meant Annella had likely been given a very good education.

Including instruction on how to appear the perfect model of obedience and submission while keeping her mind sharp.

Whatever the girl wanted, Brenda decided it wasn't

worth her giving up the opportunity to bathe. Annella could have had the Sutherland retainers enforce her will on Brenda.

Better to take the offering of something she wanted. Brenda wasn't fool enough to think the earl's daughter wouldn't get her way. But Brenda was so tired of playing games.

"Ye could just ask me what is on yer mind," Brenda said. "Yer father's men will make certain ye get whatever information ye are here for."

Annella froze. Her hands had been reaching for the tie on Brenda's bodice. Brenda watched something flicker in the girl's eyes.

"Cormac sees through me as well," Annella admitted at last. "It's quite vexing."

Brenda was opening the front of her underdress. "Me cousin Symon was always able to unmask me as well. What do ye want to know?"

"Are ye breeding?" Annella asked bluntly.

Brenda froze.

Annella offered her a delicate shrug. "Me brother made sure yer husband might visit ye, and the retainers outside the door stood as witness…"

Brenda shouldn't have been shocked. She turned away to hide her reaction because she just couldn't help feeling exposed.

Would she never learn?

The world was full of those who saw her as a possession.

Bothan wanted ye for yerself…

He had, and now she'd become his curse.

"Chief Gunn, at last." The Earl of Sutherland said his name as Bothan was shown into the man's private rooms a week later.

Bothan reached up and tugged on the corner of his bonnet, but that was as far as his manners went.

The earl let out a little sound of approval. "Aye, ye're no' one for formalities, Chief Gunn. I imagine ye found the court near impossible to tolerate. Those nobles have an affection for frivolous pastimes."

"And plots," Bothan answered. "It's true I've had a belly full of schemes."

"Hmm." The earl nodded. "Fair enough."

"I'd appreciate it greatly if ye'd get on with the matter of returning me wife to me," Bothan said.

"Hamell Campbell has made a claim for the Grant lass," the earl responded. "One I agreed with and gave me word on."

Bothan tilted his head to one side. "That was before ye knew the King had sent her to England and another match."

"True."

"So there is no difficulty." Bothan pressed his case. "There is new information to be considered by yer lordship."

"When dealing with the matter of land, there is always difficulty," the earl cut back. "Ye'd be a fool to think otherwise."

"Brenda is no' a bride to be stolen." Bothan refused to back down. "The vows have been made and consummated."

"Aye." The earl sat forward. "Me son made sure to make this a difficult situation for me. If I'd been home, ye'd have never gotten abovestairs to yer wife."

"Because ye prefer the Campbells to the Gunns?" Bothan demanded.

"I'd be a fool to no' see the strength in the Campbells," the earl insisted.

"And a bigger fool to not see they will keep taking more and more if ye spoil them," Bothan said.

The room was quiet for a long moment. The earl tried to stare Bothan down but failed.

"I understand yer point, lad," the earl said in a tired voice. "But the lass is no' with child."

"I do nae care," Bothan answered. "She is me wife."

"She will be married tomorrow morning to Hamell Campbell," the earl said firmly. "Yer choice is to be in me dungeon or no'."

Biting back his retort was the hardest thing Bothan had ever done. He stood for a long moment before turning and leaving the room. He strode down the passageway until he was away from the Sutherland retainers.

"Maddox?" Bothan asked softly for his man.

"Aye. I know what to do," his captain answered.

Bothan stood still on the steps that lead up to the great hall of the Sutherland stronghold. For all its grandeur, he noticed only the stench of evil clinging to the castle. Strangled dreams and the blood of innocents had given rise to the huge fortification.

He wanted nothing more than to return to his towers.

With Brenda...

She might not have ye...

Bothan couldn't hide from his own doubts. He'd

failed to protect her. It was something he could not forgive. But he'd free her from Sutherland and the Campbells because it was his duty. If she rejected him afterward, he had no one to blame but himself.

And he'd have the rest of his life to mourn her loss.

&

Someone rapped on the outer doors of the chamber. Brenda turned around, but the two men who had positioned themselves outside were already opening the doors.

The Earl of Sutherland was there, and his men were reaching up to tug on the corners of their caps as the man passed through the doorway. A maid brought in a tray with two goblets on it.

"Close the doors, lads," the earl said. "I'm no' so old yet that I do nae welcome any lass who looks like she might be trying her hand at smothering me in the bedding! If ye hear the bed ropes groaning, do an old man a favor and leave me to me fate!"

The Sutherland retainers chuckled before they both looked toward her. One of them boldly winked at her before pulling one side of the door shut as his companion closed the other side. The earl was looking at her, both his hands on the top of his walking cane.

"Have some wine, lass." The earl took up one of the goblets. "'Tis time to be done with the business between us."

Brenda picked up the goblet out of habit. Years of being instructed in hospitality left her raising it to her lips and drinking down some of the fine French wine without hesitation because the earl was doing the same.

"To die in the bed of a redhead," the earl spoke firmly. "Now there is a fitting end for a Highlander."

Brenda propped her hand on her hip. "I had no more control over the color of me hair than ye did, sir."

The earl let out a bark of amusement. There was a scuff against the floor as he began to tap at the floor with his walking stick. Age had taken his speed, but there was still an air of authority about him even if it did take him time to compose his thoughts. Brenda took a few more sips of the wine as she waited.

"Come and sit here beside me, lass," the earl said after he sat down and put his own goblet aside.

Brenda offered him a courtesy before she took the seat facing him. His eyes were just as blue as his son's. Behind the wrinkled skin and gray eyelashes, she caught sight of a twinkle still alive and well in his eyes. She put her half-empty goblet down.

And his gaze was still keen. Brenda sat still as the man took her measure.

"Ye are no lass," the earl said after contemplating her. "And yet ye're still young. Yer years have been hard ones. I see the evidence in yer eyes. Ye're no stranger to bitterness."

"They've taught me a great deal," Brenda answered.

The earl nodded, but it wasn't really praise. No, Brenda detected a hint of commiseration in his gaze.

Which chilled her blood.

"Ye're woman enough to understand I cannae give ye to Chief Gunn now that I know ye do nae carry his babe."

Brenda felt her heart stop. The sense of unease that had hit her when she'd started to bleed at the beginning of the week blossomed into full dread. Fate was once again proving to be her enemy.

"He is me husband," she informed the earl. "Issue is not a requirement of marriage."

"Aye," Sutherland agreed. "But this is no' a matter of one couple, and ye know it well. Being the daughter of a son of a laird, ye know well yer marriage bed would no' be made to suit yer heart."

She did.

Christ in heaven, why is fate so determined to cut ye with sharp edges?

The chair became unbearable. She stood, pacing away from the earl, but the chamber's window offered her a view of how high up they were.

Ye mean how impossible escape is…

"If I give ye to the Gunns, the Campbells will ride against them." The earl voiced what Brenda knew too well. "The King will not concern himself with Highland feuds, and even if he did, the blood spilled would be long dried by the time any royal decree was handed down."

Brenda stared out the window, willing her mind to offer up some solution.

"The Gunns are fearless, but they are outnumbered," the earl continued.

"Because Campbells are allowed to accumulate wealth no matter if they do so through criminal means." Brenda turned and voiced her frustration. "Are ye offering to say naught over me plight because ye hope they will be sated and no' notice yer own daughter is ripe for harvesting?"

The earl grunted. "Ye're a daring lass. More than

one would say too much so, to be threatening me own family."

"Perhaps," Brenda agreed. "Behaving and minding me place gained me naught but grief. I'll take me chances with courage now. At least I might like meself, even if no one else does."

The earl smiled at her. There was genuine approval in his expression. But he stamped his walking cane against the floor. "Discretion is the greater part of valor, lass. Do ye really care to end up like some hero in a tale where the man fought for what was right and yet ended up dead in the last battle? Do ye wish to remember him for the rest of yer days?"

"I do nae care to see Bothan dead, no," she agreed.

The earl nodded. "Nor do I, and before ye ask, I've no love for the Campbells' greed either, but ye are what I called ye, a woman." His expression tightened. "Annella is me only daughter. I too need to consider long and hard before angering the Campbells."

"Feed a wolf once, and it will be back for more," Brenda argued. "I would be Hamell's fifth wife."

The earl nodded. "Aye, and he'll have to let ye live or risk having the Church look into his dealings."

Brenda's chest was tight. Men were calculating beasts through and through. "And ye take comfort in that idea? Forgive me if I do not."

The earl lifted his walking stick and pointed it at her. "As I noted, ye have bitterness in yer eyes." He pressed his lips into a hard line. "Hamell will keep ye alive, and ye're wise enough to know such a thing will no' be a blessing."

Brenda faced him straight on. "And yet ye will give

yer blessing to the union, even keep Bothan from riding after me?"

The earl took a long moment to consider her words before he nodded a single time.

She felt like thunder had cracked the sky open above her. The moment was so final. So very inescapable.

There was a scuffing sound as the earl moved toward her. He cupped her shoulder, pushing gently on it.

"Sit before ye fall," the earl encouraged her softly.

Allowing her knees to fold was more of a relief than a concession. Brenda dropped onto one of the huge chairs in the receiving chamber. Her strength felt like it was flowing from her, draining away in the face of reality.

She jerked as she realized the truth and fought to keep her drooping eyelids open. The earl only watched her with sympathy in his eyes.

"Better to drug ye," he said without a hint of remorse in his tone. "Otherwise, I would have had to post me men in here tonight to ensure ye did no' decide to escape by killing yerself."

He stood and contemplated her. "Ye'll be wed to Hamell Campbell in the morning."

She wanted to protest, felt like a scream was lodged in her chest but the ability to push it into the world was beyond her. Instead, Brenda watched as the Earl of Sutherland turned and left her to the fate he'd pronounced.

Cursed…

Aye, she was cursed.

Cormac Sutherland was waiting for Bothan in the stables. The heir to the earldom of Sutherland seemed very much at ease in the humble surroundings.

"Yer wife is no' carrying yer babe," Cormac stated bluntly.

Bothan gave the horse he'd ridden for the better part of two days a firm pat. The animal tossed its head, making it clear it wanted to rest.

"There are a great many people in the Highlands who covet yer position as the earl's son," Bothan replied. "It's the truth I am no' one of them."

Cormac let out a bark of amusement. "If ye are speaking of the fact that I can hardly take a piss without someone knowing the color of it…aye, there are parts of being the earl's son that are no' very pleasant."

"Such as being sent here to talk sense into me?" Bothan boldly addressed the topic he knew Cormac was trying to ease into.

Cormac nodded, just a single, curt motion of his head. "My father values ye, Bothan, or he would no' care if ye ended up dragged away to the dungeon for raging at him."

"Brenda is me wife," Bothan stated clearly. "If yer father is so aware of the worth I have, go tell him to let me take her away now."

"If it were me, I'd let ye," Cormac said. "But allowing ye into her chamber while my father was gone was the best I might do for ye. He is the earl and me father. There was a time ye were bound to follow a Gunn chief ye did no' agree with."

"But me word had been given." Bothan acknowledged the point.

"Fealty is no' a matter of the moment," Cormac added. "Once ye kneel and pledge yerself to a laird, no man can pick and choose what orders to heed."

Cormac patted Bothan on the shoulder as he passed him on the way back to the castle. Torches were lit to illuminate the yard, but it was quiet as the inhabitants settled in for the night. Somewhere, there was a breathless whisper as a pair of lovers found a dark shadow to steal away to.

"Chief?" Maddox asked softly beside him.

Bothan turned his head. His men were bone-weary. He'd pushed them hard, but they were still on their feet, not a single one seeking out a spot to sleep in while they waited on his word.

Aye, fealty wasn't something a man could choose the timing of.

And Bothan couldn't blame the Sutherland retainers who would do their duty in the morning.

"Rest," Bothan told his men. "Ye've earned it and more. I'm proud to be called yer chief."

They enjoyed his praise, all of them reaching up to tug on the corners of their caps before they headed toward a few vacant stalls and began unbuckling their plaids. Somewhere, in one of the towers of the castle, Cormac had a bed waiting for him. The staff would have made sure it was turned down and the fire in his chambers lit.

Bothan was proud to ride with men who were simple and strong enough to face the trials of the Highlands.

"Ye're no good to Brenda half dead from lack of sleep," Maddox said when Bothan didn't join his men.

Bothan nodded. "I'm going to see the priest before I sleep."

Bothan knew Maddox watched him go. Sutherland Castle had its own chapel. One with a priest. Bothan headed across the yard toward it. Maddox likely shook his head, but Bothan didn't care. Nothing mattered but freeing Brenda.

If she rejected him afterward, well, he'd still consider his duty toward her fulfilled.

❦

"I am no' wearing that dress," Brenda declared.

The maids in the room looked between her and the Head of House, who was attempting to oversee dressing Brenda for her wedding.

Annella sighed from where she was watching in the corner. Brenda snapped her head around to send the girl a glare, only to find the earl's daughter smiling at her.

"Good," Annella said. "I was hoping ye'd maintain yer dignity."

"If ye mean I refuse to be dressed like a dessert for Hamell Campbell, then aye," Brenda declared.

She sat down and pulled on her stockings. The ones she'd arrived in were clean and serviceable.

"Perhaps ye might consider accepting an overdress?" Annella gestured to one of the maids. "Since ye arrived without one, I had another brought up."

Brenda was working the lace through the eyelets on the front of her underdress. The maid held up a sturdy-looking wool overdress. It was cranberry in color and likely something she'd enjoy having on the road.

She refused to say the word *home*.

Campbell Castle had never been her home.

Gunn Towers had, though...

Hush, do not torment yerself with such thoughts.

"Thank ye." Brenda forced her mind to the tasks at hand.

Dressing didn't take very long. She took a moment to look at her reflection in the mirror. One of the maids braided her hair while Brenda tried to decide just why fate was so vindictive toward her.

Understanding will bring ye little comfort...

That was a solid truth. She'd understood her father's reasons for wedding her the first time so very well. She'd understood why the young King had sent her to England. The only thing she had never truly understood was Bothan's determination to have her.

Ye'll be glad of it, though...

Aye. She'd hold the memories close to her heart. The Sutherland retainers formed an escort around her the moment she emerged from the chamber, two of them in front of her and another two behind. Three flights of stairs had never taken so long to descend, and then she was being taken through the passageways toward the huge double doors that opened to the yard.

Staff members peeked at her through doorways, whispering as she passed. The entire castle seemed quite aware of her circumstances.

Of course they would be—politics always drew attention.

She was sure to have been a source of conversation for the past week. Married to one man and stolen by another.

It made her ill to think of it.

The sunlight was bright, offering her no hope that the heavens might decide to unleash some fury on the Earl of Sutherland for his part in the day's planned activities.

When have ye ever been so fortunate?

Brenda held her chin steady as the earl appeared in front of her. But she looked past him to where Bothan was standing.

Pain tore through her in response. Her step faltered, and one of the men behind her reached forward to steady her. Bothan's eyes narrowed. He started toward her.

"Chief Gunn," the earl called out. "I expect ye to mind me in this matter."

Brenda watched the flash of anger in Bothan's eyes. He controlled his expression though and reached up to tug on the corner of his bonnet.

The earl grunted approval before he turned back to the party of Campbells surrounding Hamell.

"Let's get on with it," the earl snapped. "Get up to the church doors and wed her. Ye've wasted enough of me time with this matter, Hamell Campbell. Yer laird will be in debt to me for a favor, and I will make certain to collect on it."

Hamell snorted, but he turned and went toward the small chapel. It was built onto the side of one of the towers and no bigger than a private chamber. The people of Sutherland would stand outside to receive the mass and blessings while the priest maintained the small space as the house of the Lord. Only a devoted member of the clergy could actually enter the chapel.

Hamell braced his hands on either side of the open doors and leaned in. "There is no priest here."

The earl looked surprised. "The man is likely down in the village giving last rites. Ride out and retrieve him."

Hamell grunted and tugged on the corner of his cap. "Chief Gunn should go."

The earl let out a frustrated sound. "Ye've heard me tell Chief Gunn to mind my word in this matter. Now get the bloody priest or I swear I will rethink the matter, for I'm growing tired of standing here in the sun for something Laird Campbell isn't here to ask for himself."

The earl grumbled as Hamell turned and gestured to some of his men. They took a moment to mount up and then rode out the gate.

"Why did no one think to warn the priest of the wedding I planned this morning?" the earl demanded.

"Perhaps the man knew," Bothan answered, "and decided he did not want to be part of the matter."

The earl turned on Bothan, but true to his nature, Bothan stood his ground.

Christ, but Brenda enjoyed the sight.

"I believe it might be time for ye to see the Sutherland dungeon, Chief Gunn," the earl began ominously.

"Ye'll miss the moment," Bothan replied.

The earl wasn't happy. Brenda watched the way he had to bite back his anger because years of experience seemed to make him want to question Bothan's confidence.

And her husband was confident. Brenda caught the flash of intent in his eyes as he pointed up to the walls surrounding them.

"Ye'll want to climb up to get a better view," Bothan suggested to the earl.

The earl looked between Bothan and the men on the walls. Several of them were leaning forward, clearly trying to decide what was happening on the stretch of land in front of the castle.

"What have ye managed?" the earl demanded.

He didn't wait for Bothan to answer. For all his years, the Earl of Sutherland made it up the steps to the top of the wall fairly quickly.

Brenda didn't care. Bothan was at her side, pulling her into his embrace as the sound of sword meeting sword came through the open gate.

"What...what did you do?" Brenda demanded in a hushed voice. She struggled to push Bothan away. "Are yer men out there doing murder? The earl will hang ye...go! Quickly before—"

"Hush." Bothan covered her mouth with his hand. She was stuck in his embrace, his strength overwhelming her as it always had. "They are not my men."

Screams came next, drawing Brenda's attention to the open gate.

"Chief Gunn, I will remember this!" the earl declared from the top of the wall.

"As will I." There was a new voice now. Brenda looked through the open gates at a man who rode up. His horse was still dancing from being ridden into battle. He stuck to the agitated creature's back, though, and pointed his bloodied sword at the earl.

"I am Morey Hay," he declared. "I'm grateful to ye for letting me know the whereabouts of the man who wed me sister less than a year ago and then put her in her grave."

The earl had descended from the wall. He faced off with Morey Hay. The clansman was huge. Once he dismounted and sheathed his sword, he still towered over the Earl of Sutherland. But he lowered himself once he came into the castle, tugging on the corner of his bonnet as the earl received the acknowledgment of his higher station.

"I'd have ridden to Campbell land to claim justice," Morey continued. "Ye have my gratitude for not making me risk more men in doing what I needed to do for me sister."

"Of course," the earl stammered.

Morey Hay looked past the earl to where Bothan stood next to her. Her husband was suddenly urging her forward. The Gunn retainers were making their way toward the gate, offering the earl quick tugs on their hats while more Hay retainers lined up on the other side of the gate.

Bothan gave Brenda a push toward Maddox. She stumbled, still in shock at how completely everything had changed. Maddox gripped her wrist and tugged her away from Bothan as he stopped and faced off with the earl.

"I'll bid ye farewell," Bothan informed the earl firmly.

Maddox tossed her onto the back of a horse and slapped the mare on the hindquarters as Bothan spoke. Brenda glimpsed the anger on the earl's face before she was forced to concentrate on staying on the back of the horse.

And then she was on the other side of the gate.
So simple.
So unexpected.
So very amazing.

༄

The Gunn retainers rode hard for the edge of Sutherland land. The Hay retainers had joined them, making them a force to be reckoned with. The few villages they came across cleared their roads as the men rode through. Morey Hay's home was much like Bothan's towers. The stone structures rose up from the high ground as Brenda heard a bell being rung at the top of the guard tower.

She doubted Bothan would have stopped if the horses hadn't needed a good rest. Brenda slid from the back of her mount as Maddox took the animal away for a very well-earned supper. Her own belly was rumbling.

"Plenty of supper inside," Morey Hay declared. He looked toward Brenda.

Morey was covered in dirt from the hard ride, but there had been blood splattered across his face before he took to the saddle. Now, the dirt emphasized the blood.

"Ye did not look away," Morey noted as he caught her looking at the dried blood.

Brenda locked gazes with him. Bothan came up beside her. Morey considered them both.

"I expect no less of any woman Bothan would wed," Morey added. He turned and let out a whistle. An older woman came across the yard in response. "Mary will take ye abovestairs and see ye have what ye need," Morey said before moving over to where his men were beginning to wash up in long troughs of water set out at the end of the yard. The stone structures were built at an angle so the water drained out the low end and back into the river.

"Come with me," Mary instructed. "The yard is no' a fit place for a woman when the men come in from battle."

The maids and other females of the Hay clan who had come out to greet their laird were nowhere in sight now. Mary pointed toward the entrance of the tower. Brenda grabbed a handful of her skirts and climbed the steps.

Once inside, there were plenty of women, but the mood was grim. Tight expressions decorated everyone's faces as they went about getting supper onto the tables for the men who had just returned.

"Justice is no' a cure for the ache in the soul," Mary explained as she led Brenda up a flight of stairs. "The laird's sister was a sweet soul. Yer husband did a fine favor to the Hay in informing us Hamell Campbell was close enough for the justice he deserved."

Mary opened a door and waited for Brenda to cross into the room. A shiver went down her spine as she complied, too many hours in the Sutherland stronghold souring her taste for chambers with doors.

"No one will disturb ye," Mary said. "I must see to supper."

Brenda turned and lowered herself. The older woman nodded before turning and disappearing into the darkening stairwell.

But the door remained open.

Brenda drew in a breath and let her tension dissipate. She walked back toward the door and smiled at the lack of burly retainers standing there to keep her prisoner.

It's over...

She closed the door, fighting the urge to begin worrying. The impossible had happened, and she needed to be grateful.

So very grateful...

A bowl of stew was sitting on a table, steam gently rising from it. Brenda caught the scent, and her mouth started watering. She took too big a mouthful the first time, singeing her tongue. But the taste was amazing, far better than any food she'd eaten in weeks. Brenda took the next few bites slowly, reminding herself to savor the meal.

The chamber itself was simple, with a sturdy, warm-looking bed against one wall and two chairs. The table was near the window. A chest sat beside it, completing the furnishings in the room.

Someone rapped on the door.

"Yes?" Brenda called out.

"The cook thought ye'd like some water," a man said as he pushed the door open. He waited for Brenda to nod.

A few scuffs on the floor and he'd delivered a pair of buckets of water. A maid was on his heels with a kettle of hot water. She placed it carefully on the floor before reaching into her apron pocket and withdrawing a bundle of linen.

"Thank you," Brenda said as they both made their way out.

Of course. Their laird was home, and there was the

matter of their murdered mistress. No doubt the clan was drawing together to comfort one another. Brenda opened the linen bundle to see what there was.

A lump of soap and a comb were there along with a smaller square of linen. Brenda smiled, her skin suddenly itching. She stripped down and added the hot water to the buckets before scrubbing herself from head to toe. It wasn't as relaxing as soaking in a tub, but she enjoyed the feeling of clean skin so much she didn't care how it came about.

She pulled her smock back on and began to pull the pins from her hair. In the first light from the moon, she used the comb to straighten the tangles from it.

"Ye have an unfair advantage, lass."

Brenda froze, turning her face toward the door. Bothan had arrived, his boots in his hands, which accounted for how silent his steps had been.

"I think I should claim ye've caught me at the disadvantage," she muttered as she drew the comb to the ends of her hair and set it aside.

"Ye'd be wrong," Bothan muttered. There was a soft sound as his boots hit the floor. "Ye're a siren, and I am but a mortal man, ensnared by yer charms."

She'd been told she was beautiful. Her red hair and flawless complexion had been used during negotiations by her father and relatives. Even after her wedding, Hamell had been one of the many to covet her for her beauty.

Tonight, though, the look in Bothan's eyes made her feel pretty for the very first time.

"What are ye thinking, lass?" he asked in a whisper. He'd made it to her, was just a breath away from touching her. Brenda realized she was holding her breath, poised on the point of anticipation.

"I think the look in yer eyes makes me feel beautiful," she answered him truthfully.

In that moment, everything had been stripped from her, leaving her bare to him. The reason was simple: nothing really mattered except the way he saw her and how very much she needed him to desire her.

"I've been enchanted since the first time I laid eyes on ye," he confessed.

There was a flash of frustration in his eyes. She felt it like a sharp dagger pushed into her flesh. "I never meant to—"

He laid a fingertip against her lips to still them.

"Yet we are here, Brenda," he rasped out.

He was moving closer, gathering her hair up and burying his face in it. She heard him draw in a deep breath before letting it loose.

He is going to touch ye…

She was so unbearably aware of him, all of her senses keen and ultra-sensitive. Time was flowing so slowly, like honey from a spoon lifted above a plate. She caught the scent of the sweet concoction before it pooled on the surface of the plate and long before she actually got a taste of it.

But the moment was worth waiting for.

Like his kiss…

Brenda watched the way Bothan's expression set as he decided on his next move. He lifted his gaze to her face, locking eyes with her for a moment.

And then he was shifting, moving in front of her as he reached further into the cloud of her hair to cup the back of her neck with his hand. She felt him grip her head, tightening his hold as he took the final step between them and tilted his head to one side so he might fit his mouth against hers.

Time was both enemy and friend.

She was acutely aware of the seconds it took for him to complete the intimacy. Felt his kiss increasing in pressure as he locked her against him.

And he didn't rush the moment.

No, Bothan took the time to kiss her gently, as though he was savoring the moment just as much as she herself was. She shifted toward him, flattening her hand against his chest and sliding her fingers up to his shoulder.

There was a soft vibration beneath her fingers. The sound of his growl surrounded her as he lifted his mouth and returned it to hers in a harder kiss.

She drew in a hard breath, feeling the surge of arousal as it flooded through her. Just like too much wine, the heat was traveling along her limbs, heating her from the inside out. Her lack of clothing suited the moment now, as she shifted and found the edge of her smock. Bothan didn't want to release her. He let her go with a sound of disgruntlement.

"If I'm a siren," Brenda teased him gently, "I should play the part completely."

She stepped back before drawing her garment off. His eyes narrowed, and he stood for a long moment, taking in the sight of her.

"Indeed ye should," Bothan praised her.

He released the wide leather belt holding his kilt around his lean waist, and the wool fabric puddled around his feet. Their gazes were still locked as he reached up and behind his neck to grasp the collar of his shirt and pull it up. The creamy linen rose, baring him for her before he chucked the shirt aside and faced her.

Brenda looked at the hardened body facing her. She knew she was softer, and yet they were crafted to complement each other.

A strange sense of rightness enveloped her, as though she was precisely where she was meant to be for the first time in her life. Logical thinking hadn't brought her to it, no—impulses and needs had.

So she was going to listen to them completely.

Brenda lifted her hand, offering it to him. She smiled at the expression that covered his face.

Male satisfaction.

She thought she'd seen it before. Looking at Bothan as he put his hand into hers made her realize she'd never seen a man as honest as he was. The look on his face lacked pride of ownership. Bothan found the act of her inviting him into her bed far more of a privilege than anything else.

She closed her fingers around his hand, turning and tugging him toward the bed. They made it only a few paces before he was moving faster, sweeping up beside her and taking her off her feet.

He did it so effortlessly.

Cradling her against his body for the few short steps between them and the bed.

"I've dreamt so often of laying ye down in me bed," Bothan muttered as he settled her on the bed.

He came down on top of her, pressing her thighs apart as he framed her face with his hands.

"Putting ye where I could lay me hands on ye," he whispered against her mouth. "Claim ye...taste ye..."

He kissed her hard. Pressing his mouth against hers as the slow pace they'd been using evaporated like a bubble popping. Now there was a hard urgency. His mouth opened hers, determined to claim her.

Brenda surged up to meet him. They seemed to clash, both of their needs colliding and setting off sparks.

Which only made the combination even more unpredictable.

He demanded. Kissing her in an effort to subdue her.

She drew her nails down his back, making sure he felt her strength in return.

He arched up, sucking his breath through his teeth before he looked back down at her, the flash of intent so powerful she shivered. But the truth was she wasn't sure if it was from the separation between them or the anticipation of what was to come.

Bothan didn't allow her time to contemplate the issue, and she didn't want it.

All she craved was him. He settled back down on top of her, destroying everything except for the feeling of being in contact with him. She didn't know where he ended or she began, only that she needed to be closer to him. The end of it all came too soon, leaving her gasping on the surface of the bed without the strength or will to move.

But in the darkness, there was no need to do anything but bask in the moment. Bothan surrounded her, his scent, the warmth of his skin. The night was like a haven created for them before reality might arrive with the light of day to illuminate all of the reasons why happiness wasn't something more than a fleeting moment stolen in the dark hours.

Bothan was gone when she woke.

Brenda curled up, catching the bedding as it slipped down to reveal her bare breasts. The edge of the horizon wasn't even pink yet, and still he was gone.

Siren.

Enchanted.

All the words a man used when he wanted to cut a woman from his life instead of allowing her power over him.

He was finished with her.

He'd followed her all the way to England, but now that the Campbells and the Sutherlands were involved, Bothan was wise enough to recognize the limits of keeping her. Somehow, she'd decided she meant more to him.

What do ye expect? Love?

Not that she truly understood what love was, anyway.

Ye do now…ye love him…

The realization made his rejection of her even more painful.

She crawled out of the bed, staggering under the blow. Pain was ripping her to shreds as she gave up and let hot tears trickle down her cheeks.

She truly was cursed. The beauty and position looked on by so many as advantages in life were weighing her down, dragging her straight into hell.

Except she was still breathing, which meant she could look forward to many, many years of living with the knowledge of just what fate had deprived her of.

Perhaps ye're being emotional…

Brenda looked around the chamber, noting the fact that everything of his was gone.

It wasn't the first time she'd been shown she had no worth after she'd been bedded. So many people thought her a tease for the way she brazenly told men she would not have them, and yet the truth was she knew from bitter experience her worth lay only in the challenge she presented.

And the dowry she might bring.

Bothan is no' so shallow…

No, he was a practical man. One who lived a simple life. And she represented trouble with the Campbells. A clan that would never leave the Gunns in peace if she remained with them.

Perhaps it was a kindness to leave her before she woke next to him.

Brenda wiped her tears and dressed. Bothan was precisely what she had always admired about him.

A good chief.

He is a fine man, as well…

Yet he was gone now as the dawn lit the horizon. Just as she would need to resume her role as the cousin of the Grant laird. The Earl of Sutherland had said it so very well—she had always known her marriage bed would not be crafted to suit her personal choices.

No, there would only be stolen moments in the darkness when she might follow her heart and passion.

She found her composure in the fact that Bothan

was no different. Happy unions were the domain of the simple people. They had no position, no wealth, but they had free choice. The world was such a strange place where everyone coveted what the other had without thinking about how much they themselves were envied.

&

He'd take her home.

Bothan tightened his grip on his emotions. He'd failed to safeguard his own wife.

It was a deficit there was no making excuses for. At least, he would not be offering any. The decision tore at his gut. Yet he wrestled with it, forbidding himself to go to Brenda.

All he wanted to do was linger beside her, watch her wake after sleeping next to him, and see the way she took him in, still there next to him.

Christ, he wanted to watch her recall how she'd invited him into her bed.

But it would be the coward's way.

Bothan gritted his teeth and worked to saddle his mount. He had failed in the most basic duty of a husband, so he wouldn't force Brenda to accept him. Passion was one thing, but there had to be more between them.

He wasn't going to have her settle for less from him.

He might not have a castle, but he'd protect her, and if he couldn't, he'd send her back to her family, where she would never again know the fear of waking up with someone like Hamell Campbell looming over her.

Seven

THE GUNNS WERE HAPPY TO SEE THEIR CHIEF RETURN.

Brenda heard the bells ringing in the towers as they were sighted on the road. By the time they made it to the yard, it was full of women eager to greet their men and children laughing as they spied their fathers.

Joy.

One she'd done a lot to destroy since Bothan had first brought her to the stronghold.

She slid off her mare and did her best to conceal how much she wanted to flinch over the open happiness around her. Guilt was weighing her down.

Ye were hoping things might resolve themselves?

Well, if she had been holding out hope for a way to stay with Bothan, one look at his back as he took his horse to the stable without a single glance toward her was enough to remind her of all the harsh realities between them.

He had to do what was best for his people.

And that wasn't keeping her there when the Campbells weren't going to leave her in peace.

She gave a little grunt of frustration and went to

seek out the tower chamber. In the morning, there would be another week of long, hard riding for her. She should take the comfort there was to be enjoyed while she might.

It was best to forget about the things that could never be.

∽

Brenda didn't wake until well into the night. The towers had quieted down, the fires burning low. Her belly rumbled low and long.

She sat up because there was no going back to sleep as hunger gnawed at her insides. The moon was full, allowing her to make her way down the steps and through the passageways well enough. The two boys who worked in the kitchens were asleep along the edge of the kitchen wall on pallets they kept rolled up during the day.

Brenda stepped carefully, reaching for some bread left on the table. A hunk of cheese was there as well and a bowl of newly harvested berries. She gathered up the food and turned around to retrace her steps.

Bothan stood behind her, just as dark and huge as the first time she'd seen him.

The bowl slipped from her distracted fingers. He moved in a flash, swooping close to catch the pottery before it smashed against the floor.

She let out a little sound of astonishment as he succeeded.

And then she trembled as the scent of his skin filled her head.

How had she thought she could live without him?

When have ye ever been able to tell yerself how to feel about him?

She smiled, enjoying the jest at her own expense. Bothan looked at her, appearing shocked by the smile on her lips. For the first time since they'd left Sutherland Castle, his lips twitched up into the grin she'd come to expect from him.

But he caught her wrist and turned around before she could investigate the reaction further. He pulled her along, retracing her steps up to his chamber.

"I suppose I should have thought to have some food put in yer room for when ye woke," he said once they'd made it back inside the chamber.

"Do nae worry," she assured him. "I can see to me own needs."

He contemplated her for a moment before he nodded and turned to leave.

"Stay with me," she said. The words just crossed her lips. Even her pride had melted away beneath the weight of her need to have him. "I know I'm too much trouble to keep." She dropped the food on a table. "And ye can send me away in the morning, but no one will know if ye stay with me now."

She was begging.

And she didn't care what he thought of it.

Bothan snapped back around to peg her with a hard gaze. She felt it jab into her as surely as she might have a dagger.

"I've caused ye too much trouble," she conceded. "Little wonder ye want me on my way."

His eyes widened. "How could ye want me, Brenda?"

Bothan moved toward her, grasping her forearms as he looked down into her startled face.

"I failed to protect ye on me own land!" he hissed. "Worse still, I knew the way back but chose to seduce ye instead of making certain ye were safe!"

He released her, as though he'd just realized he'd grabbed her. "I am no' worthy of ye, Brenda."

Shock held her silent. Bothan was seething, but she suddenly realized it was with self-loathing. He took her silence as confirmation, turning away in disgust.

"Husband," Brenda called after him.

He froze in the doorway, standing for a moment that felt like an hour before he faced her.

"I'm a lot of trouble," Brenda began as she stepped toward him. "Ye followed me to England when I told ye I would no' have ye."

He'd turned all the way around and stood contemplating her.

"I bedded ye and still demanded to be set free when me cousin Symon arrived," she continued.

"Ye did," Bothan agreed.

She stepped up so she needed to tip her head back to maintain eye contact with him. "So if ye set yer mind to seduce me, it would seem I'm as much to blame as ye are for what happened."

He shook his head. "On my land…" Bothan began to move toward her. She fell back a step and then another. "I am chief…"

"Aye," she agreed, still moving backward.

"I put ye at risk, Brenda," he growled. "And ye have the right to reject me over it."

The bed was close behind her. Bothan had backed

her nearly all the way to it. She reached out and grabbed his shirtfront.

"I am cursed," she said.

He grinned at her, the same arrogant curving of his lips he'd first flashed at her at the harvest festival when they'd met.

"You're interesting, lass," he muttered as he reached out to touch her hair. "I expect nothing less of a redhead. Nature marked ye for all to see, and I did follow ye all the way to England without a care for knowing ye were no' going to ever be boring."

His words soothed the wounds she'd been licking for the past week, filling her with a sensation she'd never expected to encounter in a life filled with harsh realities.

"I love ye, Bothan Gunn." She pulled on his shirt and heard the seams protesting. "And I am no'…no' going anywhere."

He caught her up against him, giving her a taste of his strength as he tilted his head to one side. "Ye're going to bed, lass. My bed."

Bothan scooped her up, but he didn't hurry to the bed. He held her against his chest, allowing her to feel his heart beating while their breaths mingled. She reached up and laid her hand against the side of his face, delighting in the feeling of their flesh meeting.

"I love ye, Brenda," he muttered softly. "Ye've heard me pledge me life to ye, but it's me heart that had me following ye to England."

"And it's my heart that will no' allow ye to be a stubborn fool and send me away," she answered.

He started to speak, but she pressed a fingertip against his lips.

"Take me to bed, husband. We've done enough talking," she implored him.

"Aye, lass, we have indeed."

❧

The window shutters were still open.

Brenda stirred at first light as the summer sun came into the room. For a moment, she felt fear stalking her with doubt that the night before had been only the longing of her heart.

The cock at the far end of the yard started to crow.

"I'm thinking of asking Alba for chicken for supper," Bothan grumbled beside her.

The fowl in the yard continued to greet the morning as Bothan stirred behind her. He reached out and slid his hand along her hip and across her lower belly as he came close.

She shivered. The connection between their bare flesh sent a jolt through her system.

"Hmm," Bothan muttered against her ear as he cupped her bare breast and rolled her nipple between his thumb and forefinger. "Perhaps that bird might become me best friend if it wakes me early enough to enjoy ye before the rest of the men have thought to look for me."

He was hard and ready, his member teasing her backside. Brenda rubbed her bottom against it, earning a husky chuckle from her bed partner.

His hand slid lower, teasing her curls before dipping into her folds to rub her little pearl.

"Say it again," Bothan implored her.

"Confess I am cursed and far too much trouble to keep around?" Brenda teased him.

He bit her neck in reprimand, just a nip that sent a twist of anticipation through her belly.

"Ye know the word I long to hear, Brenda." He rolled her over, coming up to settle between her thighs.

She opened her legs for him, purring with delight as his weight pressed her down, but he held back from giving her the final thing she wanted, capturing her wrists when she slid her hands down his back and tried to press him forward with a hand on each of his hips.

"Say it," he rasped, his tone betraying how much effort it was costing him to hold back.

Brenda lifted her eyelids and locked gazes with him. Demand glittered in his eyes, just as hard and relentless as the day she'd first denied him. She curled her fingers into talons and felt her fingernails sink into his skin. His lips thinned with enjoyment as his eyes narrowed with determination.

"Husband," she muttered huskily.

He thrust forward, filling her.

"Husband…" she said louder as he started to move.

Her body was quick to build toward a peak. The bed ropes groaned as Bothan rode her harder and faster in pursuit of satisfaction. She let her eyes slide shut, surrendering completely to the moment and the man she trusted more than herself.

But at the moment she felt it all breaking loose inside her, Brenda opened her eyes and locked gazes with her partner.

"Husband!" she declared.

Bothan growled his approval as pleasure tore through her. She was clenching him tightly between her thighs, lifting up and off the bed to take him as deep as possible.

And he was thrusting into her, riding her through the moment before spilling his seed.

❧

"I'm famished," Bothan declared as he watched her try to finish dressing. "And yet the thought of telling ye to hurry up and cover those plump tits seems misplaced."

Brenda sent him a glare. "Ye can no' be ready for another round just—"

She bit back her last word as he raised an eyebrow.

"That was no' a challenge." She pulled her lace through an eyelet so fast it snapped.

"An honest mistake." Bothan shrugged into his doublet. "Ye do tend to toss out the barbed comments…wife."

Brenda shrugged and finished dressing. Her own belly was rumbling. The food she'd collected from the kitchen the night before was on the table where they'd both forgotten it. Bothan captured her hand and took her down the steps toward the hall, where the scent of porridge was very welcome.

Alba was ladling out portions of it to a line of men waiting to break their fast.

"Good," Maddox said as he spied Bothan and Brenda. The captain let out a whistle. "Leif! Get the lads up to see what is wrong with the laird's chamber door. For some reason…" Maddox looked at Bothan. "It seems the damned thing will no' close, and let out every noise all through the night. I did no' get a single wink of sleep!"

Brenda lost her grip on her bowl. Once again, Bothan caught the pottery before it ended up smashing onto the floor.

"Yer face is the same color as yer hair," Bothan whispered as he set the bowl down on a table.

He kissed her cheek as his men dissolved into laughter at their expense. Bothan settled beside her as the Gunn retainers joined them.

"Do nay take offense, Brenda." Bothan patted her thigh beneath the tabletop. "Maddox is just having a wee bit of fun."

Brenda turned a smile toward her husband. "Let him."

Bothan offered her a smile before he turned to enjoy his meal. Brenda looked at the men and women of the Gunn clan. They were practical. Pretense and ceremony were minimal, and she loved it more than any castle or palace she'd ever attended.

It would seem she was home at long last.

❦

It would be dark soon.

Brenda drew in a deep breath, savoring the scent of Gunn land. Alba had rung the supper bell some time ago. Brenda had watched the Gunn people moving toward the towers and smiled. Now the light was gone, making the windows in the tower glow in the night.

Home...

Tears burned her eyes, but she smiled as joy felt like it was radiating from inside her.

"What are ye doing out here, wife?" Bothan asked.

Brenda cast a look behind her, watching her husband climb the incline she was standing atop. The evening wind tried to tug on her cloak as she locked gazes with him.

"Do nae ye recall, Bothan?" she asked him sweetly.

He was close now, awakening her senses with his presence. She inclined her head toward the rising moon.

"Did I no' promise to do me best to no' disappoint ye…husband?" Brenda asked him.

His lips curved up as his expression showed her how much he enjoyed hearing her call him husband. He cupped her hips, coming up behind her.

"Aye, I remember," Bothan whispered against her ear.

He pressed a kiss against her throat that sent a shiver down her back. Brenda let the moment engulf her.

"So let us return to our bed…wife." Bothan encouraged her by pulling her tighter against him.

Brenda turned so she was facing him. An eyebrow lifted as he took in her expression.

"I could no' leave ye holding out hope any longer," Brenda informed him huskily. "After all, ye spoke so brazenly to me at that market fair because ye had heard the gossip about me."

"I did," Bothan declared as he crossed his arms over his chest. "So what is yer plan, lass?"

Brenda smiled broadly as she stepped back. "I'm going to dance naked under the full moon, of course!"

She released the hold she had on her cloak and shrugged out of the garment. Bothan's face filled with enjoyment as his lips thinned with hunger.

"No' if I catch ye first!" Bothan declared.

Brenda turned and ran. Her husband was fighting to free himself from his clothing. They left a trail of garments behind them before she squealed as he clamped his arms around her waist and lifted her high, turning around with her as the yellow light from the full moon bathed them both.

Aye, she was home.

And the journey to find it had been worth it.

Note from the Author

This is the last Highland Weddings book: six stories of courtship and bumpy roads that lead to love. Not a single one of them would have been possible without every reader who picked up one of these titles and took a chance on reading the tale. Thank you for giving my characters a chance to entertain you, and thank you for reading my work. As to where the future will take my imagination, well, check my website, MaryWine.com, for updates!

*Read on for an excerpt from the very
first Highland Weddings story*

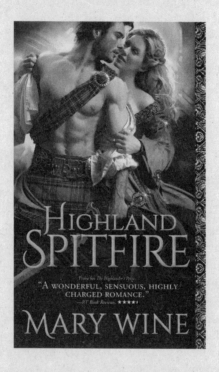

**HIGHLAND
SPITFIRE**

Praise for The Highlander's Prize

"A WONDERFUL, SENSUOUS, HIGHLY
CHARGED ROMANCE."
—RT Book Reviews, ★★★★½

MARY WINE

"YE'RE AS HEADSTRONG AS YER MOTHER WAS."

Ailis stretched up to kiss her father on the cheek
before flashing his captain a smile of victory. Her
father rolled his eyes then offered her a hand to help
her up onto the back of her mare. The horse tossed its
mane as Ailis took the reins in a steady grip.

Laird Liam Robertson's beard was gray and thin,
but he still held himself proudly as two hundred of his

men assembled to ride out with him. Behind them, Robertson Castle basked in the golden light of morning. The hills were green, and the sound of rushing water filled the air—the rivers were full with melting snow. It was too soon for heather or flowers, but Ailis could smell the changing season in the air. She lifted her face and let the sun warm her nose for the first time in weeks. She was tired of having to huddle close to the hearth to chase the cold from her flesh or pull her wrap up to avoid the frigid wind.

"I was invited," Ailis reminded her father.

"So ye were, but I do no' like the man—even if he is the king's regent—telling me how to direct me own daughter. His business should be with me. No' a woman."

Her father puffed out his chest in a display of authority, but she could see the acquiescence in his eyes. He may not have agreed with the new regent, but he did like to grant her requests when there was no solid reason to deny her.

It made it so easy to love him. She smiled, and he groaned, his Highlander pride requiring some form of bluster to make sure everyone knew he'd at least argued against complying completely with the summons.

"Maybe the man will take the tale of how fetching ye are back to court. It's time ye wed," the laird continued.

"Of course it is, Father," Ailis agreed demurely.

Her father pointed at the twinkle in her eyes. "Just like yer mother," he accused, then climbed onto the back of his horse. "I had to court her for two seasons before she agreed to me suit." He held up two time-weathered fingers. "Two! As if I had naught better to do with me time."

The Robertson retainers making ready to ride laughed with their laird.

The men were looking forward to the journey. They wanted to stretch their legs too. Highlanders might enjoy telling stories by the fireside, but their true love was creating those tales. They jested with one another as their kilts swayed with their motions. The horses shook their heads, adjusting to their bridles and stamping impatiently on the cobblestones in the inner yard. Ailis's mother had insisted on the cobblestones, to keep the mud out of the castle. Ailis had heard the Grants were going to lay stone during the summer because it worked so well.

She lifted her chin and inhaled the scent of new greenery. The last thing she had on her mind was a husband. Ailis was almost sure her father agreed with her, but as a daughter of the laird, it was her duty to think of alliances. So her sire would make the expected comments from time to time. The truth was he didn't want her to go anywhere, and the stack of offers sitting in his study remained untouched. No regent needed to carry tales about her back to court. Offers had been arriving since she'd turned fifteen. But in the last two years, her father hadn't opened a single one, only asked her if he should.

That was a blessing—one many girls didn't enjoy. She looked at the men making ready to ride out with her father, searching among their hard bodies for anything that might stir a longing inside her for marriage.

All she felt was a sense of approval for their forms. Ailis smiled.

Well, at least she was not repulsed by men. She just wasn't overly interested in them. So marriage could wait another season.

But going out for a springtime ride to meet the Earl of Morton at the abbey sounded fine. She adored her childhood home, but the winter had been long, and she wanted to walk and feel the sun on her skin.

She would be very happy to return when their meeting was concluded.

Laird Shamus MacPherson wasn't one to admit that his hair was thinning. But he had taken to wearing a thick wool bonnet, even when sitting at his desk in his study while a fire crackled behind him in the hearth. Bhaic MacPherson watched his father read the message in front of him and growl at it.

"I'll go see the new regent meself," Shamus decided.

Bhaic didn't interrupt. Shamus MacPherson was busy poking the Earl of Morton's summons where it lay on the table. "Bloody waste of time. How like a lowlander regent to think everyone has time to squander on foolish ceremonies, such as riding down from the Highlands to reaffirm the peace. As if I do nae know who me king is!"

"I'll be riding with ye, Father," Bhaic told his sire and laird.

Shamus looked at him and frowned. "I refuse to let that man waste yer time as well. It will fall on yer shoulders soon enough, this duty to ignore what truly needs doing in favor of riding off to meet with whatever man has managed to bribe enough fellow councillors to gain the position of regent. It is nae as if we've had a king that lasted any too long."

"At least we have a king, and no' his mother."

"Bhaic MacPherson—"

Bhaic answered his father in a firm tone. "Do nae scold me for saying what everyone is thinking. I'm a Highlander, nae some lowland Scot more concerned with appearances than maintaining his honor."

His father nodded, pride lighting his eyes. "Ye are right there, me lad. Right as rain in the summer." Shamus stood up, tugging his doublet down. "Mary Stuart may have been a queen of Scotland, but it's a king we really need. So we will have to put up with regents until young James is old enough to manage. I'll do me duty and ride out to meet his regent, and judge his mood. Maybe this one will last until the boy is grown."

"I would nae count too much upon that," Bhaic warned his father. "The earl is the fourth regent, and the king is only seven years old." He stood and shook out his shoulders. "So I'll be going along to meet this regent. I want a look at him meself."

"Very well, no doubt that's wise," his father said as he came around the table and walked toward the doors that opened into the great hall. Two MacPherson retainers stood guard, reaching up to pull on their bonnets when their laird appeared. Shamus started down the aisle toward the doors with a determined pace, the maids they passed all lowering themselves before returning to the duty of clearing away the remains of the morning meal. The great hall was still full of long tables and benches that welcomed all the inhabitants of the castle at mealtimes.

"Yes, it's wise of ye to ride along with me to meet this regent," Shamus continued for the benefit of those listening. "Ye are making sure ye are seen, so there will be no question who will become the next laird of the MacPhersons."

"There never was a question of that, Father, and it is nae why I am riding out with ye," Bhaic stated. "It's because ye are me laird, no' just me sire."

His father turned and winked. "But, me boy, I fully enjoyed begetting ye!"

There were a few muffled chuckles from the retainers close enough to hear. Shamus's eyes twinkled with merriment as he finished making his way to the huge double doors of the outer wall.

The yard beyond the open doors of the keep was full of horses already. MacPherson retainers were busy making ready to ride out with their laird. Many of the lowland Scots had taken to wearing britches instead of kilts, but the MacPherson men wore their colors proudly.

Bhaic grinned. The lowland Scots called him a savage, but he enjoyed knowing they feared him. His colors were a constant reminder that he was part of something more than just his own family. No man wore the colors of the MacPherson without earning the right by conducting himself with honor. There was no greater shame to a Highlander than being stripped of his kilt.

The lowland Scots were welcome to their britches. Let their regent see the MacPhersons in their kilts.

He was a MacPherson and a Highlander. Let them worry about his mood.

❧

The Earl of Morton was a rough man.

He'd seen his share of the harder side of life. That fact accounted for the task he was embarking on today. He'd dressed for the occasion, wearing a thick leather over-doublet to protect against smaller blades.

He lifted one gauntlet-clad hand and pointed at the forest surrounding the abbey. "Make sure our men are posted along that line of trees. I want musket and pike there—these Highlanders must know they are surrounded, or we'll have a bloodbath."

"Might have that anyway," his captain remarked. "They *are* Highlanders. Not likely to bend."

"Today, they are going to put being Scotsmen above their clan loyalties."

The captain didn't correct his noble lord, but he surely didn't agree with the man. Highlanders were different. Only a man living inside a palace would be so naive about that.

❧

Ailis leaned low over the neck of her mare when the abbey came into view. The older portion, which had been built a century before, was crumbling. She tucked in her heels and let the horse have its freedom. The animal raced down the hill, across the meadow, and through the remaining arches of the old medieval church.

"Ailis!" her father scolded, still up on the hillside where the forest thinned.

She lifted her arm and waved to him, then slid from the saddle with a happy smile on her lips.

"Ailis!"

The tone of her father's voice had changed. It sent a chill down her spine, and she turned to look back. His retainers were surging down the hillside, their teeth bared and their kilts flapping with the motion of their horses. They were riding hard, but there was no way to reach her before the men waiting behind her made their move.

She jumped back, making a grab for her horse, but one of them had already taken the animal's reins, which left her facing six men. She pulled a small dagger from where she'd tucked it in the top of her sleeve.

They converged on her. She got off only one jab before she was trapped. She struggled against the hold on her arms, straining to break free, but she knew it was hopeless. She'd ridden straight into a trap—and her kin were honor bound to try and rescue her.

Ye are such a fool!

Berating herself didn't change the fact that there were hard fingers digging into her flesh. Or that she could smell the scent of horses and gunpowder on her captors. The sun shone cheerfully, and the grass was growing, but she felt the cold kiss of steel against her throat.

It seemed surreal, like a dream spun in her ear by a fae while she napped on the grass in the afternoon of a long summer day.

But the men holding her were real. Their breeches frightened her the most because it meant they were not Highlanders. She strained against their hold, snarling as she tried to break free.

"Stay back if you do not want her blood spilled!" the one holding her said.

Her heart was pounding, and sweat trickled down the side of her face from her struggle, but the blade against her throat was too terrifying to fight against. She could feel how sharp it was, feel it already slicing into the surface of her tender skin.

"Hold!" her father yelled. The first of his retainers had made it to the arches. They jumped from their saddles and had their swords drawn before her father's voice halted their impulse to rescue her. They froze, pure, raw fury in their eyes.

Guilt fell on her like a stone. It was crushing, burning its way through her as she witnessed the distress she'd caused by being impulsive. There would be blood spilled, and it was her fault for leaving her escort behind.

She'd known the cost of such recklessness since she was eight years old and had made the mistake of wandering during a spring festival. The memory normally chilled her blood; today, it was already near freezing.

"The earl is waiting for you, Laird Robertson," her captor said.

"I will nae be meeting with a man who sends his men to put a blade to me daughter's throat!" her father declared.

"Your daughter is in no danger."

Ailis shifted her gaze to find the newcomer. He stood over to one side, flanked by a dozen men with black-powder guns all aimed at her father and kin.

"I do nae agree with ye, boy," her father retorted. "Tell yer men to get their hands off me child. I thought it was only the bloody MacPhersons we had to worry about."

"How very interesting to hear you say that name." The man gestured to the men holding her, and they marched her toward him. "I am the Earl of Morton, Regent for James VI of Scotland." He studied her for a long moment before looking past her to her father. "Let us go inside to discuss this."

Ailis didn't have any choice. She was muscled through the garden that fed the inhabitants of the abbey and into the kitchens.

The bruising grips on her arms didn't bother her half as much as the knowledge that her kin were being drawn after her. Better her throat had been slit in the garden.

For now, she was the bait.

"Do nae—" She turned her head and screamed, but the man holding her clamped his hand over her mouth, smothering her warning.

Aye, she'd rather be dead than watch her father's men coming after her.

She deserved death for being so foolish.

But she very much feared that she was going to be forced to live through the consequences of her actions.

❧

"Bloody Robertsons," a MacPherson retainer snarled.

"At least we do nae hide behind skirts," a Robertson growled back.

Ailis looked over to see the other side of the church filled with the tartan of her father's enemy, the MacPherson. More men stood guard over them with long muskets. The MacPhersons looked as furious as her kin did. But they were outnumbered by the earl's men, who surrounded the entire abbey, more of them posted in the alcoves above to ensure they had a clear shot at their prisoners.

"Regent or nae, ye're a bloody coward." Her father's voice bounced around the inside the abbey. It was built of dark stone, making it seem like a cave. The stained glass windows served only to darken the sanctuary even further. The earl's men removed the blade from her throat and marched her up the aisle to the front pew.

"What I am is a man set on a course of action," the earl said as he stood at the front of the church. There wasn't a hint of remorse in his expression. Two priests stood at the altar, their fingers moving on the prayer beads hanging from their belts.

"Only a coward uses a man's daughter," her father protested.

"Or a man who is ready to crawl out of the barbaric traditions you Highlanders cling to," the earl answered. "I needed your attention, and now I have it."

"I'll nae leave behind me honor in favor of a man who hides behind a woman," one of the MacPhersons argued. He stood up, boldly offering his chest to the gunners.

"Instead, you would all continue to fight over something that happened more than three generations ago?" the earl asked.

Ailis found herself biting her lower lip. It was the truth, and she was slightly shamed when she was forced to hear it spoken aloud. Three generations was a long time—there was no denying it.

"It's none of yer concern," the MacPherson insisted. He was a large man, with midnight-black hair. Unlike a number of his clansmen, his face was scraped clean. Attached to the side of his bonnet were three feathers, two of them pointing straight up. It was Laird Shamus MacPherson's son, Bhaic, which accounted for his boldness. He would be the next Laird MacPherson. The feathers confirmed that he was the clan Tanis. It was more than blood that put him in line for the lairdship; the rest of the clan's leaders had voted him into the position.

"Join Mistress Ailis in the front pew," the earl ordered.

Bhaic smiled, showing off even white teeth, and crossed his arms over his chest. He had his shirtsleeves pulled up, granting her a view of his muscular arms. A touch of heat stroked her cheeks, and she looked back at the earl.

"Shoot me where I stand," Bhaic taunted. "If ye've got the balls to."

"Mind yer mouth, MacPherson, me daughter is present."

Bhaic shrugged. "I am nae the fool who brought a woman along."

"The Regent is the one who insisted me daughter come along!" her father protested. "For a man who thinks we Highlanders are stuck in the Middle Ages, Lord Morton, ye are the one acting like a savage. I never thought to question the terms of yer message as if ye were some sort of English scum."

"I find myself agreeing with Laird Robertson." Bhaic sat back down in defiance of the earl's demand.

"So now that I am completely disgusted, what do ye want, Regent?"

"An end to this feud," the earl informed them.

A ripple went through the sanctuary, the scuffing of boot heels against the stone floor as the men shifted, the reality of their long feud shaming more of them than would be willing to admit it was so.

The earl didn't miss it either.

"The crown and the king will no longer tolerate unrest in the Highlands," Morton informed them.

"What are ye planning to do?" her father demanded. "Kill us all?" He chuckled ominously. "Ye'll nae be the first nobleman who fails at that task."

The abbey was full of laughter, the sound bouncing between the dark stone walls.

About the Author

Mary Wine is a multi-published author in romantic suspense, fantasy, and Western romance. Her interest in historical reenactment and costuming also inspired her to turn her pen to historical romance with her popular Highlander series. She lives with her husband and sons in Southern California, where the whole family enjoys participating in historical reenactment.

Also by Mary Wine